That Thing You Do

That Thing You Do

Kayti McGee

St. Martin's Paperbacks

This is a work of fiction. All of the characters, organizations, and events portrayed in this novel are either products of the author's imagination or are used fictitiously.

THAT THING YOU DO

Copyright © 2017 Kayti McGee.

For information address St. Martin's Press, 175 Fifth Avenue, New York, NY 10010.

ISBN: 978-1-250-08650-1

Our books may be purchased in bulk for promotional, educational, or business use. Please contact your local bookseller or the Macmillan Corporate and Premium Sales Department at 1-800-221-7945, ext. 5442, or by e-mail at MacmillanSpecialMarkets@macmillan.com.

Printed in the United States of America

St. Martin's Paperbacks edition / September 2017

St. Martin's Paperbacks are published by St. Martin's Press, 175 Fifth Avenue, New York, NY 10010.

10 9 8 7 6 5 4 3 2 1

To Eileen, for everything you do to make books better.

Acknowledgments

The depths of my gratitude know no bounds for everyone who worked to get this book written and polished. Natalie Lakosil brokered the deal. Eileen Rothschild knew she had to have a DJ book. Laurelin Paige, Sierra Simone, and my beloved Melanie Harlow never let me stop working, even in October. Even when there were spiders. Even when the spiders were replaced by bears. Even when the bears became surrealist paintings of the abyss and they had to gently remind me to put the coffeewine down and go to sleep. Angie, Sheri, Jen, and Paula helped with that too. This book was written all over the place—from taverns to hotel balconies, from one coast to the other. If you put me up or put up with me, thank you! Shea Brazill, that means you. I can't say enough nice things about the St. Martin's team; every step of the process was fantastic thanks to your hard work. More than anything, if you read this book, thank *you*.

Prologue

Greta was fifteen when she made the first pact, huddled under the old gazebo with Amy and Summer. Old enough to be considering the future, and making plans accordingly. Young enough to never seriously consider the ramifications of sticking to them. Even if some passing stranger had warned her what a hassle she was setting herself up for, she would have ignored it. They were all secure in themselves, in their foresight—and certainly knew better than to trust anyone over thirty, anyway.

The Sweetheart Dance had not gone well for the three of them, and so they had retreated to the sanctuary behind Greta's house. Summer had pulled a stolen wine cooler out of her sequin-encrusted bag and was passing warm, sticky sips around. Amy's earlier sobs had quieted to hiccups, hardly audible over the cool February rain.

"We could egg Tommy's house if you wanted," Greta offered, but the drizzle and their lethargy over-ruled it.

"Don't even say that guy's name." That from Summer, who was visibly pleased to find the attention was finally off of her lack of date for the evening's event—again.

"How could he do this to me? We're in *love*!" Amy wiped fresh tears with the hem of her pink dress. They comforted her as best they could, the rest of them hav-ing yet to suffer their first teenage heartbreak. Greta suspected that Amy was enjoying her newfound world-liness, just the tiniest bit. But dumped in front of the whole school? The sheer humiliation her friend had endured made Greta shudder.

"It wasn't Tommy's idea, you know that." Greta took another swig of the sugary drink. It was their favorite flavor, margarita. Years later, when they tasted real margaritas for the first time, they made another pact—never to speak of their wine cooler days.

"He shouldn't have gone along with it, even if it *was* entirely Lindsey's plan. He doesn't care about either one of you. He just thought he had a better chance of getting past second base with her. Tommy is a grade-A asshole." Summer had grabbed the bottle then and handed it to Amy, having recalled that women in Victo-rian novels often required a bracing drink of ladylike booze after a shock. Amy took the bottle gratefully.

"It didn't matter what he thought he was getting out of it. Asking Amy to Sweetheart and then showing up with Lindsey instead was a heartless move. He's heartless," Greta repeated, fairly pleased with her assessment.

"He isn't heartless, though! You should see some of the notes he writes me." Amy fumbled in her clutch for a tissue. And one of the notes. She kept her favorites with her at all times.

The girls assured her that they had seen all of the notes, repeatedly, and that they had long suspected he was copying down lines from his mother's romance novels. She was not inclined to believe it. It seemed that she was already making her plans to win Tommy back, and punish Lindsey in the process.

"It's better to have loved and lost, though, isn't it?" Summer had retrieved a second wine cooler and was feeling rather poetic. "At least you've been kissed."

"Oh, I haven't lost him. We are going to get back together, after a long and groveling apology. On my sweet sixteen, he'll give me a promise ring. After being crowned king and queen of prom, I'll give him my virginity in a bed of rose petals. He'll propose during Christmas break of our senior year at Golden Gate and we're getting married before we start law school. We are going to get *married*!" Amy's face was all but glowing by the time she'd recounted the familiar plans. She hadn't gotten around to telling Tommy about them yet, but she wouldn't have to. He would just know what to do, she'd reassured her friends.

"Marriage isn't all it's cracked up to be," Greta reminded them. During the moment they were silent, considering, they could hear her father yelling from the house, even over the pitter-pat of raindrops.

"But if you marry the right one, the one you're meant to be with, it's like heaven." Greta had long since stopped rolling her eyes at Summer's old-fashioned view of the world. She'd learn soon enough, so to tell her so in advance would have been mean. Amy agreed with Summer, of course.

"How do you even know, though? Like, doesn't everyone think they are marrying the right one? Otherwise why would you say yes?" Greta asked. They pondered, the truth of her words settling over them like the fog they had grown so accustomed to in the Bay.

It was Amy who had the answer. She had all the answers to everything, as she loved to remind them.

"The people who know you best. They know better than you do, most of the time." She set down the dregs of her bottle and clasped their hands. The picture was suddenly clear. Just like *her* friends knew *her* best. Her friends, who had been gently encouraging a break-up for the past whole entire month. "I'm not going to marry Tommy, am I? Because even though I'm completely love-struck, you guys know it's a bad idea to get back together with him. You tell me this stuff, even though I don't want to hear it." Resilience was another one of her self-described best qualities. The deep love she had felt for Tommy just moments before was already starting to fade into a distant memory.

"That's what sisters are for," Summer reminded them. Despite no actual blood relationship, they had considered themselves sisters since meeting in Mrs. Fischer's second grade class. That was one thing that never changed. It's why they kept their promise, despite each of them cursing it at one time or another.

"My dad didn't used to be like this. He used to be happy, when we were little. You really think my mom's friends knew things would end up this way, with him throwing things and screaming and her too stupid to leave before he hits her?" Greta could feel her face setting so she didn't tear up.

"I think he probably talked her out of having friends besides him a long time ago, G. Otherwise, yes, they'd be here now." Even Summer understood the gravity of this conversation long enough to stop Austenizing. "My mom married the wrong guy too, obviously. By the time he walked out on us, he'd driven her friends off years before. Now the only friends she has are the guys she goes out with every freaking night of the week."

"Statistically, arranged marriages are some of the most successful. If you take lust out of the equation, the people who know you best recommending a partner that suits you best is a pretty smart way to go." Amy always used statistics, even though she knew her friends thought she made half of them up. She did, but they were one hundred percent too lazy to fact-check her, and *that* stat was real.

"That's not very romantic, though." Summer, of course. "What about love?"

"But I love you guys, and we aren't romantic. Sometimes just getting to know someone intimately leads to love," Greta said, eyes cast down so no one would see her admit she still believed in love in any form, after watching her father burn things down so often.

"Seriously look at us, you guys. I got dumped in front of the whole school. Summer couldn't find a date up to her standards, because Summer has never once found a date to be up to her standards. Greta, you've been going to every event we've been invited to since we were seven—with Michael."

"What's wrong with Michael?" she asked. Amy reminded her that he was her first cousin, and certainly gay even if they lived in a state that condoned such relationships. Greta shrugged. It was a fair point.

"Honestly, I don't think I would ever marry anyone you guys didn't one hundred percent approve of." Summer met the girls' eyes in turn. Amy, and then Greta had agreed with her, and felt secure in the decision. It was so obvious then. They were so lucky to have each other. They would never find anyone who understood them like they understood each other.

And so it came to pass that they found themselves huddling around a half bottle of cheap alcohol, spitting into it to make their pact both binding *and* disgusting. There, in rain-bedraggled semi-formal dresses in a backyard reading nook, they linked their pinkies and drank that hideous drink and swore the pact they would all end up regretting but never could quite take back. Because even when they thought they themselves should be exempt, they were never really willing to give up veto power for their beloved best friends. So this is what they swore:

"We, the Sisterhood of the Valentine's Day Gazebo,

do solemnly swear that we'll never get married without the agreement of all of us." And as they giggled, newly pleased with themselves and passing the drink around, Greta's dad was leaving forever.

Chapter 1

Greta was twenty-six the second time she managed to get entangled in a binding promise with her so-called sisters. Yet again, and probably not surprisingly, there was booze involved. But, free booze was pretty much the only perk of being a bridesmaid. And the only free thing. This particular occasion was the wedding of Angie, her oldest sister. Before that, it had been Beth, her middle sister. Before that, Jennifer, her youngest sister. Before them, there had been Sheri and Melissa from school, and Paula from summer camp.

Yep, the view around this table was getting pretty familiar. Same duties, different dresses. Overpriced dresses. Amy poured another round of tequila for the never-brides, and a vodka shot for the inescapable Michael.

"To not *always* being a bridesmaid," she toasted.

"Hear, hear," replied Michael. She punched him.

"Seriously, is it just me, or do they all . . . blend together after a while? I can't remember who had the cupcake tower or the chocolate fountain. Who rented the theater and who had the live doves? Everything is just the same kind of different, and it's all boring as hell," Greta said. Although the music was better this time. And the DJ was way cuter. She grabbed a lime wedge from the bowl they had appropriated and stuck it in her mouth to cover her teeth and grinned bright green at them. None of the clever (and occasionally delicious) accoutrements meant the marriages would last any longer.

"It's all in my bridesmaid scrapbook," offered Summer, snatching the lime out and throwing it at her.

"I don't actually *care*. I'm just making a point. The first wedding was exciting. The second two were easy, because we knew what to expect. Now it's just tedious. And frankly, kind of embarrassing. Oh, here come the perpetual bridesmaids, to the singles table. Again." She glanced back at the DJ. *Way* cuter. Thank you, Angie.

"Seriously, you guys. I figured by now, I'd be married, so I could pretend to be too busy with my wifely duties to say yes to any more maid stints." Amy picked at the strap of her turquoise dress as the entire table groaned. Turquoise was a big color lately. This was their third dress in the shade. Not that they could re-wear.

The biggest lie ever told to bridesmaids was that the dresses were re-usable.

"It's not for lack of trying, I'll give you that," Michael smirked. "How many proposals have your so-called besties nixed now?"

"Only three, thank you very much. The other nine just—didn't work out." She clearly realized there was no real way to maintain her dignity through this statement, and poured more shots to cover.

"Really, Amy?" asked Greta. She donned an expression of utter innocence. "It was so surprising that the guy you were tree-sitting with didn't work out?" Sometimes her friend made it too easy.

"You weren't *there*, Greta. Rainn was so poetic. We were in that tree for sixty-two days. We shared absolutely everything. And the sponge-baths . . ." Amy smiled dreamily, recalling some of the particulars.

Michael spit some of his vodka out. "Hideous. That is hideous."

"How was I supposed to know he was already married to a girl in another tree?" It had turned out Rainn had a type. The song changed, and Greta bobbed her head. There was an air of familiarity to this song, but she didn't think she knew it. It was just a sense of nostalgia in the beat, in the surprisingly gentle tones of the girl crooning across the bass. She did *not* have a type, not like Rainn, but if she did it would be a DJ who played music like this.

"I thought you shared *everything*." Summer's eyes could not have rolled any further without getting lost back there.

"Wait, wait, remember the time you got engaged at Burning Man?" Greta added through her giggles. "To the trash collector?"

"He was a *recycling specialist*. And he treated me like a goddess. Until the LSD wore off and he realized I wasn't *actually* one." Amy seemed not to like the turn this evening was taking. "So what? So what if I've been unlucky in love? A few more times than most? At least I haven't hidden my sentimentality beneath a tough-as-nails exterior like you, Summer. Or closed myself off to it entirely, like you, Greta.

"The right one's going to come along for me. And for you, too, naysayers." She squinted at them. Greta couldn't tell if she was trying to look serious, or cut the booze-induced blurriness.

"It better. I'm about sick of being the token escort," Michael teased.

"Oh, like *your* love life is so awesome." Greta leaned over to shove him, but under-reached and hit Summer instead. She tried to move back, gave up, and stayed slumped against her friend instead.

"Ow!" Summer shoved Greta upright and hit Michael. "That was meant for you."

"Look, I'm not the one wearing my seventh bridesmaid's dress. And I *always* leave these things with at least one phone number. Which is more than I can say for any of you." He glanced out at the dance floor and winked at a groomsman.

"Well, it's not *my* fault Amy has the worst taste in men and we keep having to veto her choices." Summer was still rubbing her shoulder. She reached over Amy to grab the bottle.

"It's not *my* fault Summer thinks she can only date

fictional men." Greta held her shot glass out with a slightly wobbly hand.

"It's not *my* fault Greta thinks she's dating *us*." Amy held out her glass too.

"You three are the most ridiculous people I have ever met. If you all hate each other's taste so much, why don't you just figure it out for each other? Seeing as you guys know everything, and all. I'll be on the dance floor." Michael slammed his vodka down and went off to join a conga line behind the groomsman in question.

The girls stared at each other. Had it really been so obvious all along? Amy always picked men based on their causes, not their worth. Summer and Greta knew that. But then, Greta and Amy always knew that Summer was too scared that after the third date, no one would live up to her expectations. And Summer and Amy were extremely vocal about Greta's jaded attitude keeping her from dating at all.

Once Michael pointed it out, they knew just what to do. One by one, they spit in the tequila and linked pinkies, ignoring a nasty glare from the mother of the groom. Salt, shot, lime, and it was set in stone.

They were totally picking each other's dates from then on.

"Now that's settled, shall we dance?" Amy stood up and started doing the body roll.

"I need more margaritas if I'm going to dance. I'm not done with this—*this* yet. Let's write out our boyfriend specifications. I have a few brilliant ideas for you two." Greta had ideas all right. Lots of them. She grabbed a nearby cocktail napkin.

"I'm on my fourth, there's no way my handwriting is going to make sense in the morning. Shouldn't we have a family meeting when we're sober instead?" Summer was shaking her ass in her seat and casting longing looks at the Tootsie Roll happening on the floor. But when Greta made up her mind, she could not be swayed.

"I'm gonna—hic—even let you do me first." She was being over-generous; tequila always brought out that quality in her.

"That's what she said," Summer giggled. "Okay, then. Gimme some paper. Or . . . something. Gimme something." She snatched Greta's napkin.

Amy produced a lipliner from her fake-leather clutch. The look of glee on her face almost made Greta take back her offer. They definitely should not have had that last shot.

"Firstly. A hottie. You haven't dated in so long, you can't just say yes to the first average dudebro." She nodded in agreement with herself.

"I would not date a dudebro, Drunk Amy. That can be marked off the list immediately. But what's wrong with an average guy? They'd probably be okay with my quirks. And I am okay with *that*."

"Greta Steinburg, what you call quirks, the rest of us see for the copouts they are. When you pull this whole, 'oh I can't *possibly* go out, because my *ward* will want to watch Doctor Who' bullshit, we all know you are forcing the poor child you nanny to come watch television with you in your apartment." Amy giggled like a madwoman.

"Or how you never come to pizza night cause you have gluuuuten problems. But it's really cause you have don't wanna wear paaaants problems!" she added through her laughter.

"Not fair. I do too have gluten problems. With or without pants on." Greta wasn't entirely certain she'd made her point. Anyway, she liked staying in with Mina, so what? She actually enjoyed her job and Mina was awesome and shared her tastes in quality television shows. Not to mention that being a live-in nanny meant she tailored *her* schedule to match the nine year-old's, and not the other way around. Social lives always suffered when kids were involved, and that was how it should be. Only people like her father, and possibly Mina's, didn't seem to accept that.

"I call bullshit. You know it, we know it. Doesn't really matter what you admit." Summer always told it like it was, and when she had a few drinks, well, she was brutally honest.

Greta sighed heavily. How could it be that her friends were tougher on her than her siblings? It was Angie's wedding, but her sister was kind enough not to seat her next to an eligible bachelor the groom knew. Because Ang knew her little sister was just flat out not interested. In fact, her entire family had long ago stopped trying to set her up.

It was just her pseudosisters now. Amy and Summer,

in whom hope sprang eternal that if one of them found true love, the others would swiftly fall like dominoes.

As she formulated her rebuttal, the DJ looked up and caught her eye. Her first instinct was to look down, uncomfortable at being caught staring, but something about the searching look he gave her made her feel pinned in place. Even across the room, she could see his eyes were a startlingly green. With a deft flick of his wrist, the song changed seamlessly into something slower, and couples began to pair up on the floor.

"*Just* like that," Summer was muttering. Greta wrenched her eyes away from his magnetic gaze to glance down at the napkin, which now said things like "tall," "dirty blonde," "lean," and "DJ". Oh, no.

"Seriously, can I not even admire the view without you two reading something into it?" She wasn't just pretending to be annoyed. Drunk Amy was notorious for getting blabbermouthy, and the last thing Greta wanted was for her friend to accost this poor DJ. Poor, hot DJ. Poor, smoking hot DJ. She wasn't going to look back. Nope.

She looked back. His eyes were still on her, not lasciviously, but almost thoughtful. Maybe she looked like someone he knew, she thought. People occasionally told her she reminded them of Amy Winehouse, with her small frame, big hair, and thick eye makeup. Unlike Amy, she was completely drug free. There was one hundred percent less heroin involved in her own look, just genetics, the aforementioned gluten sensitivity, and MAC. His attention returned to the decks in front of him, and she was able to study him closer.

In the sea of semi-formal wear bobbing on the floor, he stood out in a casual white button-down and straight-leg jeans. She took stock of him, his hair was short but unkempt like he mussed it often, setting off his shockingly green eyes. His look screamed casual but he was laser focused on the music as if everyone fell away and he had the room to himself. He barely nodded his head to the beat, as if restrained by his own focus on keeping it going . . .

"You've got champagne taste, my friend," came Summer's voice in her ear, *Damn it, she had to stop staring.* "DJ Force is like *the* hottest thing on the San Fran music scene. Didn't you see his big write-up on the SFRightNow blog last week? They say he's like the Californian Calvin Harris."

In fact, Greta had stopped her subscription to that blog a month prior, after they had slammed her favorite gluten-free brewery as a hipster-catnip waste of time. She eyeballed DJ Force and idly wondered what kind of beer he liked.

"He's playing my sister's *wedding*. If this is champagne taste, I'm afraid I'm buying Andre," Greta turned to grin at the other girl. "And what kind of a name is Force, anyway?"

"He's friends with Matt. Your new brother-in-law? I'm shocked that you didn't know this. Force may not be the best name, but hey, with a face like that and the talent he's got, he can call himself anything he wants. I'm not kicking him out of bed for eating crackers." Summer waggled her eyebrows.

"I don't see why you would. He could even have some Cheez Wiz in bed with those crackers." The gestures Amy was making just a little too vigorously left no doubt that Cheez Wiz was a euphemism.

"Gross, you guys! You know I tune out wedding talk. That's what my other sisters are for. I'm just the eternal bridesmaid, that's my role. And I'm not going to bed with anyone, crackers or not, much less someone who calls himself *Force*."

"Your loss. I bet he knows a thing or two about rhythm. And its not like your disposition has been improved by all the times you *didn't* go to bed with someone. I'd *hire* you a sex partner if I thought you'd take me up on it." Summer's brows were going again. It was difficult to be annoyed at someone so enthusiastically silly.

"You know full well I'm not bringing a guy home to my boss's house. I am done with this conversation!" Greta raised her voice to be heard over the opening notes of That Thing You Do. This was one of her favorite songs, and DJ Force was creating a remix, infusing it with a few different melodies. She was digging it. Maybe those music bloggers were on to something. She pulled Summer by the arm. "Come on, let's dance!"

She chose not to dwell on the fact that the dance floor would give her a much nicer view of the unfortunately-named DJ in question.

* * *

And she couldn't dance, Jon mentally added to the list of reasons why he shouldn't continue staring at the pint-sized beauty on the floor before him. The list was actually more of a multi-circular Venn diagram, and this girl fell into the intersection of "no more girls while building career," "no dating mates' sisters," and "seriously, though, no mates' sisters."

Her arms were flailing a bit like she might break into the chicken dance, and her legs were shuffling. She knew every word to the song, yet somehow couldn't identify a beat anywhere. But she looked like she was having a blast. It was charming.

Confidence always was.

The fact that she could be confident and silly was refreshing. He scanned the crowd, taking in the confectionary bridesmaid dresses interspersed with the half-drunk guests smiling and dancing . . . or, well, trying. Wobbling was a better term than dancing after a bit too much of the champagne.

He had to admit, when Matt had asked him to DJ this wedding, he groaned. A wedding, really? One of the perks of growing fame was *never* doing weddings again. But he owed Matt a favor, after the guy had coached him through a nasty breakup, and saying out loud that he was too good for weddings was a bit shit, wasn't it? So although he would rather turn in his decks then admit it, he was having a great time. When people came to his shows, they knew they liked him. Watching people who'd never once heard his name respond to his music . . . that was a drug.

Jon knew he was talented and more than a little bit lucky, but when your star was on the rise, everyone wanted a ride. The clubs, the parties, the girls . . . all fun, all exhausting. He never knew who wanted him, and who just wanted a piece of fame. Even if it was semi-fame. He glanced over at his dancing hot mess.

She looked up at him for a brief moment before blushing and looking back at the girl in a matching dress she'd dragged out to the dance floor. That was the difference, right there. It was her seeming reluctance to connect with him. The models and wannabe singers who set their sights on him had done just that—made sure he knew they were looking. Made sure he knew they were willing to go to bed with him if he was willing to introduce them to the right people, get them into the right clubs.

It was gross, really, the transactional aspect of becoming famous. Emotionless sex-for-a step-up. How easily people were willing to trade their souls for the promise of stardom. How little that promise had to be in order to deserve their attention, their bodies. People who probably grew up with dreams beyond his, but settled for selling themselves to the lowest bidder.

What was even sadder was that Jon was so easily duped into thinking that his ex, Leah, she of the nasty break up, was different. How quickly he fell for the first pretty face that also happened to have a brain behind it; a brain that recognized his insecurities and used them to wrap him around her conniving little finger.

He wasn't going to relive that humiliation for the umpteenth time tonight, though. Tonight was a good night. Matt was getting married and he couldn't have picked a better wife, in Jon's opinion. Angie was good people.

He may have been utterly blind to Leah's true intentions, but it was clear to everyone with eyes that Angie was head over heels for his mate. For just one second, he let himself wonder what it would be like to have a woman care about him for no other reason than she liked *him*. His friend had that. Why couldn't he have that?

Despite the list in his head, the list he had carefully compiled under Matt's instructions after the breakup, he found himself gazing again at the badly dancing girl in turquoise. As though she felt it, her eyes met his. One side of her mouth quirked up in a half-smile, and it utterly did him in. She wasn't *really* Matt's sister, after all, just an in-law. And she was magnetic.

One of the other bridesmaids, clearly drunk, was grinding on poor Angie as he watched. She looked at the cute one, followed her gaze, and took off. She wound her way towards his girl—no, not his girl, he hadn't mentally agreed to—and mimed pointing her towards—him? He scratched the record. Totally pointing at him.

Could it possibly happen this easily? That a gorgeous, silly, carefree girl could just drop into his lap a mere six months after he'd sworn off women? It felt like a trap.

But then, so had his first contract.

So had his first real show.

So had every single step along the path from Jon to Force that he'd traveled since his half-assed immigration from southern England to western America.

So what reason did he have to assume this wasn't another blessing? He looked at the corner of the dance floor that Matt and Angie were occupying, slow dancing through every fast song, whispering together as though no one else on earth existed. And perhaps, for them, no one else did. He suddenly discovered that he wanted that feeling more than he wanted to hear the bass drop.

And *nothing* was better than the perfect bass drop. Jon looked away from the couple in the corner and into the eyes of Angie's mysterious sister as her friend shoved her towards him. He took a deep breath. It felt predestined, as she gazed up at him, cheeks still pink.

Yep, that was happening. This was going to be even easier than he had hoped. She'd walk up to him, introduce herself, he'd let her spin a record, she'd be impressed, he'd be suave.

But wait. Why wasn't she walking towards him? Why was she shaking her head? That was a no. A no? A no to him? A no to him.

Jon loaded the next record automatically, wondering. She'd kept looking at him. Why didn't she want to talk to him? That was new. Never mind that a few moments ago he was busily telling himself she was probably no one he was interested in. He was interested now. Not just because she so clearly wasn't.

Maybe.

Self-examination was for suckers. Right now what was important was that he had an in. She may have stolen all the attention, at least in his mind, from the bride, but the bride could answer a few questions for him. He waved Angie over.

"Love, I've a few questions about your bridesmaid." His turn to point.

"*My sister*? Oh, good luck, friend. I wouldn't put money on your odds with Greta." Angie was giggling in a way that suggested a challenge. Well, Jon had certainly never backed down from a challenge.

"I'm not opposed to a small wager . . ." He grinned at Angie. She grinned back.

And then the bass dropped.

Chapter 2

"Where is . . . jacket. I had a jacket." Amy was clinging to Greta for dear life, causing her to curse the heels
she'd worn. At least her wobbly friend was in ballet
flats, thus decreasing the possibility of a fall that would
pull Greta down too.

"Sit. I'll go check the coatroom." She deposited the
other girl in a chair and crossed the dance floor. Out
of the corner of her eye, she noticed that the sexy DJ
with the unfortunate name was no longer in the booth.
Her disappointment at not getting a final glimpse of
him was balanced out by the relief at not having to negotiate another prolonged eye contact.

She never knew what to do in a situation like that.
Smile? Stick out her tongue? Until tonight, she'd de-
faulted to Option C—look at anything else in the room
until it went away. Then again, before tonight most of
the people she'd accidentally made long bouts of eye

contact with were either making her a coffee, or being creepy on the city bus.

It was definitely a new experience to have someone's eyes laser right into her, and to lose her stomach a little bit over them. New and weird.

Entering the coatroom, Greta realized she couldn't remember what jacket Amy had been wearing. Turquoise dresses probably meant her black peacoat? Ugh, she should have asked. Then again, from the unfocused smile on Amy's face when she'd plunked down to wait for her coat, she might not remember what it looked like either.

For a brief moment, she considered just grabbing something close and not too expensive-looking and calling it a night. Her buzz had long since been sweated out on the dance floor, and she'd have to get up early in the morning with Mina. All she wanted was a bag of chips and her bed. Maybe not at the same time. Or maybe *exactly* at the same time.

Oh, there. She spotted a black peacoat, just as she'd suspected, and reached to snag it. It moved. She reached further. It moved again. She made a grab and missed as it disappeared to the other side of the rolling rack. What the . . .

In a second, it reappeared on a body that strode around the row of outerwear. Maybe not Amy's coat, then. But then Greta did a double take, because the body wearing the coat belonged to Hot DJ Dumb-Name-Force. She gave him a half smile, realizing he was even sexier up close. His perfect cupid's bow-mouth smirked back at her.

Oh, God, that meant he'd probably seen her flapping about like an injured chicken. So embarrassing. Not that she cared what he thought, totally not, just that she tried to be graceful. Yeah, graceful.

"Help you find your jacket?" he asked. His voice wasn't quite as deep as she'd thought it would be, and it was lightly accented. *Oh.*

His brilliant emerald eyes were boring into her, so she swallowed her embarrassment and annoyance that he'd flustered her and assured him she'd be fine.

"Nah, love, it wouldn't be very gentlemanly of me to leave you here." Oh, he was a *gentleman.* Of course. Because being outrageously hot, talented, and possibly British wouldn't be enough. Then again, self-describing as a gentleman pretty much guaranteed you weren't one.

"This coatroom is hardly a bad neighborhood," Greta said, smiling despite herself. He glanced around at her friends and family: tipsy, loud, and meandering in and out aimlessly. He looked doubtful, and she couldn't blame him. "But basically I'm looking for a female version of your coat. I think."

"You think?" He raised one eyebrow.

"My friend. I forgot to ask her what she was wearing, but I'm pretty sure it looks exactly like your coat." Greta started parting the other jackets on the hangers so she wouldn't have to keep feeling the things his stare was making her feel.

"I see. And what were you wearing?" He was standing uncomfortably close to her, close enough that she could smell his cologne. Something leathery and aquatic at once. She'd heard that Europeans had a different idea of personal space than Americans, and he was definitely all up in hers.

"I didn't bring a jacket." She scooted a little away. It was hard to breathe that close. She inhaled.

"But it's really chilly out." He scooted closer. Harder again. Her breath caught.

"I'm tough. I can handle it." Finally, her eyes lit on what (*please God*) was hopefully Amy's actual jacket. She sniffed it. Patchouli—definitely Amy's.

"Absolutely not. I'm not letting you leave here wearing nothing but heels and a flimsy dress." His eyes raked her over, and Greta had to stop herself from rolling her own, despite the thrill down her shoulder blades. It wasn't very *gentlemanly* to check her out so blatantly. She *knew* he was just like every other guy. Knew it.

They were all the same. They used your physical reactions to distract you from their lack of emotional ones.

"Well, good thing it isn't up to you." Greta folded Amy's coat over her arm and turned to go. She hated how disappointed she felt that their interaction was so brief and not what she'd have scripted in her imagination.

"Just . . . take mine. Please. I'll feel a hundred times better. It's really quite chilly out. Drizzly. You'll catch your death of cold." She turned around and he was holding out his own black jacket.

"You know that's a myth, right?" He winked at her instead of answering. She glanced out the window set into the coatroom of the venue. It did look fairly miserable outside. Maybe he *was* just being nice. Doubtful, but maybe. And her dress *was* flimsy, enough so that if it dampened, it could become transparent. Now *that* was a way to attract city bus creeps. For a second, just one, she regretted having turned down the after-party invite from Angie. But she only had the night off, not the morning, so staying out wasn't happening. The *drizzly* night.

"Fine. I'll take your jacket. How am I going to get it back to you?" She shrugged the proffered wool over her shoulders. It came down to her knees, but it was dry and warm. The fact that it smelled like a sexy sea-god was a bonus.

"I always keep some of my cards in the pocket, just in case. You can call me tomorrow." He grinned widely, showing off a set of perfectly white teeth with a slightly crooked incisor. Her stomach flipped a little, despite her misgivings.

"You look overly pleased about the prospect of sending off your jacket with a strange girl in bad weather." God, that smile.

"I *am* pleased. Your sister told me there was no way in hell I could give you my number, and it just happened." The grin went from cute to shit-eating in Greta's head just like *that*.

"You asked Ang about me?" At least her sister knew her well enough to tell him what was what, unlike the girls waiting for her out in the ballroom.

"Of course I did. The prettiest girl in the room was a member of the wedding party; it was a golden opportunity. I think she actually owes me a beer now, once her and Matt return from Cabo."

"You guys *bet* on me? Are you're *telling* me about it? I'm leaving. With your jacket. Which I may or may not return." As Greta turned and stalked out of the coatroom, she wished she was better at comebacks. But of course, a new jacket that smelled vaguely like she imagined a pirate would ought to soothe her ruffled feathers. Also, all the one-liners she came up with tonight in bed would go into the early morning phone call Angie was going to receive.

"What time does Pizza Pronto open?" Greta moaned from beneath her comforter, which she'd carefully arranged to cover her entire head while still allowing a tiny breathing gap. A vague memory of shutting off her alarm hovered around the outskirts of consciousness. Angie had gotten off lightly, this time.

"Not for two more hours, but I've already sent your usual order in through the online system," came Mina's cute little voice through the breath hole.

"Pineapple, olive, jalapeno?" Greta suspiciously confirmed.

"Medium for you. Small cheese for me. Are you awake yet? I know weddings are long nights." The bed reverberated beneath the little girl's jumping.

"I'm up, I'm up. Not gonna lie, the fact that you know how to order my pizza helps. You're all right, kid." Greta emerged and smiled. More than all right, Mina was awesome. What would she do without her?

She wasn't even hung over, but she was bone tired, from the early morning makeup and hair to the drinking and dancing, she felt like she could sleep for another 15 hours. Her last sister, married off. God willing, it'd work out for her. Hopefully this was the last time for a long time she would be a bridesmaid. She could hang up her dancing shoes at last.

And not a moment too soon, she reflected, thinking about a few of her moves from the night before.

Something wriggled in from the back of her mind. Agh. The jacket situation. More accurately, the frustrating-gentleman situation.

"How wrong do you think stealing is? On a scale of one to ten. And also, how long did they say the pizza would take?" Greta groped for a pair of sweats to pull on beneath the covers.

"Stealing is very super wrong, Greta. At least an eight. Two hours for pizza. That's one movie, or two episodes of a drama show, or four episodes of a sitcom." Mina was snuggling in under the sheets, and clearly ready for some boob tube. Not that Greta was arguing, tired as she was. She pulled up the TV menu and queued up their favorite Doctor Who season. She presumed it was their favorite, anyway—a thought from the previous evening occurred to her.

"Hey, Mina? You *do* like this show, don't you?" Onscreen, Amy and Rory were aboard a pirate ship, bringing back a vivid memory of Hot DJ's scent and perfect smile.

"Yeah. It's a little scary, but it has happy endings. My dad says I can't be a Companion when I grow up, is that true?" Greta's smugness that her ward did *too* like this show was suppressed by her irritation at the girl's father. It was just like Bob to squash a child's dreams. Thankfully, it seemed that Mina just might value *her* opinion more. That was an honor she wasn't sure she'd earned, guiltily remembering the snooze button again.

"You know what, kiddo? I have no idea. But I'm still hoping I can be one when I grow up, too." She ruffled Mina's hair. No one should ever tell a kid, especially a girl, that their dreams were too big. No matter how impossible they might seem. If *she* were Mina's mom . . .

"I thought you *were* a grownup." Well, she technically may have been. But it didn't necessarily feel that way, living in the apartment above her boss's garage, driving a car he provided, caring for his child. It felt like suspended animation more than adulthood. Kind of like what was happening on screen. Her life sometimes seemed a story she was telling someone else.

"Getting there. One adventure at a time." None aboard a pirate ship, sadly.

"When will I have an adventure ?" Greta's heart broke just a little bit. Mina's father had left that morning for Hawaii with his flavor of the week. He told his daughter he was going on yet another business trip.

Mina would have loved Hawaii. Running along the beach, collecting shells and marveling at the sound of the ocean reflected inside. Picking giant colorful flowers and throwing them over waterfalls to watch them float downstream. Being free, being a kid, just *being* somewhere where her dad paid attention to her.

Bob was a man before he was a father. Sex before emotion. Pleasure before business or responsibility. Something she remembered all too well from her own childhood.

"Sometimes you don't notice it's begun until you're already in the thick of it. What if . . ." Greta cuddled her up and started their favorite game. Playing what-if had gotten them through countless scraped knees, hurt feelings, and listless afternoons. "What if I was secretly a space alien?"

"What if I was a sea siren?" Mina accepted the subject change easily enough. She grinned up at her nanny, and Greta's heart clenched. Sometimes it almost hurt to imagine her growing up.

"I would be forced to abduct you into my flashy-light thingy and then tickle you until you promised to stop killing sailors!" Greta tickled Mina until she shrieked "uncle". Speaking of the sea, though—"Hey, I have to make a phone call. I'm pausing it for a minute."

She wriggled out of bed and over to the chair she'd tossed the offending jacket across the night before. Sure enough, in the pocket were a couple thick white business cards. Funny, she'd imagined a DJ would have something louder than white on their—but what was this? The card read "DJ Force" at the top, but the associated email read JonHargrave@mailmail.com. *Well, well.* Looked like he was overcompensating for his utterly plain name with the Force.

It took a few deep breaths before she pulled her cell off the desk. "I hate phone calls," she muttered to herself as the phone rang. "Hate them, I hate them, I hate—hello?"

"Hate what, love?" came that gently lilting voice down the line, and she could just *tell* he was smirking.

"It's Greta. From last night. Um, the girl with your jacket." She chose to ignore the question.

"I know."

Her eyes narrowed. "How did you know?"

"Because Ang gave me your number just in case I lost our bet. You're programmed in my phone already."

Greta was going to fly to Cabo and strangle her older sister personally. So much for having her back. Greta was beginning to think this was less about a bet and more about a setup. Angie grew up in the same house as Greta. *She* might be willing to risk it all on love, and end up losing the way their mom did, still pining after the man who'd left, after all this time. As for Greta, she'd long ago decided that wasn't happening to her. Every time she fell for someone, she broke it off. And she'd recovered just fine.

What she hadn't done was ask her sister to add more complications.

"You know I'm going to drown you both in those beers you think you're going to enjoy after her honeymoon, right?"

"That gives me a good week or so to win you over, now doesn't it?" Another question she wasn't going to answer. She wasn't sure which was worse, the audible smirk, or the fact that she was half-smiling picturing it? He just had such a cute mouth.

"Where should I bring your jacket?" Greta refused to be dissuaded from the business at hand, cute-mouth smirk or no.

"You want to meet at the Four Barrel on Valencia?" Typical. That place was as hip as could be. She idly wondered what to wear before remembering she didn't care, and also that she had pizza coming around noon.

"Fine. I'll be there at two." Greta said letting the click of her hang up say goodbye for her. She sighed, and stroked the scratchy-soft side of the jacket. As she did, a rustle in the pocket alerted her to the fact that her friends had drunkenly written down the description of the next guy she was supposed to date and then eventually marry.

"Are you going to tell me what that was all about?" Mina asked from the bed. Greta unfolded the napkin.

"Yeah, in a sec . . ." The napkin was covered in smudgey berry-colored lipliner words. Not all of them were legible (Capol? Hoobar?), but a few stood out. Besides the physical description of (course) *Jon*, someone had scribbled, "outgoing," "confident", and "hip". DJ Force Jon Hargrave certainly fit the bill for all of those things. An idea was starting to germinate somewhere in the back of her mind.

"Greta! I'm turning the show back on. Rory's about to get his black spot." She nodded at Mina absentmindedly. There was another call to make first. Details to iron out. A tangled web to weave.

Four hours later she was standing in the coffee shop wearing an adorable, sixties-style vintage dress and red lipstick. The lipstick had been Mina's idea. She had said it would make her confident. Greta secretly also thought it was the kind of lipstick that made a man stare at your lips. That wouldn't be a bad thing, as long as he was agreeing to the plan. She glanced down at the way the dress accentuated her cleavage, and back up at the man she was trying to convince. DJ Jon surely wasn't going to say no.

"So let me get this straight. You want to date me, but only where your friends can see, because you really don't want to date, and fake dating is the only way to avoid the real. Did I get that right?" Jon's face was cuter than it ought to be when it was making an incredulous look.

"Well when you put it like that, it sounds—"

"No, you've got it right," Mina interrupted. "That is exactly the plan. You're a pretend boyfriend. Only for a month, though. Then you pretend break up. It's very easy." He looked down at her and grinned. There was zero reason for Greta to be jealous of his attention on someone else, and yet . .

"A girl who tells it like it is. I like that kind of girl." His grin moved up to Greta's face. She swallowed hard. Truly, she thought, this was a brilliant plan on her part, regardless of whether or not Jon believed she was a mercenary. Though his smile looked remarkably like the one he'd had when she accepted his jacket.

In her hastily arranged morning-after meeting,

Greta had ironed out a few pertinent details of the pact they'd made the night before. Nothing less than six dates would constitute giving it a real shot, and the girls would have to see each other out to confirm. All she had to do was set up a series of fake dates, and then after a month or two, she could tell Amy and Summer it just wasn't working out—so sad, but she'd tried, their turn now. Although she hadn't exactly figured out what was in it for her partner in crime. Perhaps she should sweeten the deal.

"I am willing to compensate you for each fake date." With what? She should have thought this out.

"No kissing," Mina swiftly interjected.

"Of course not," Greta assured her, at the same time Jon said, "We can negotiate."

What *would* it feel like to kiss him? Probably pretty darn good, judging from that perfectly shaped mouth and slightly too-large ego. Too bad that wasn't happening. Not part of the deal. It would only complicate matters, and besides why was she even thinking about that? This was a straightforward situation. Fake dates don't kiss.

"With one condition." Damn it.

"I already said no kissing," Mina frowned at him. Greta was never prouder of her charge than at that moment, even more so than when she said she wanted to grow up and travel with the Doctor.

"I wouldn't condition the kissing, little one. If she does that, it'll be because she wants to. I'm a gentleman." He winked, even as Mina made a puke face. Good girl. Even if she had considered it for a half-second.

"No, my condition is this: every time you take me out on a pretend date, I get to take you out on a real one. Fair is fair." Damn, but he was good, Greta thought. She could take lessons in negotiation from him. He'd just taken this from six fake semi-public dates to a round dozen, half of which were now solidly out of her control. And yet where else was she going to find someone who fit the bill so exactly to get this farce over with? No, she was stuck, all right. Only one question remained.

"Why? I just told you I want to fake-date you. And the compensation I mentioned was more like . . . Starbucks gift cards, but I guess that isn't how you roll anyways." She pointedly gazed around at the ubercool baristas and the machines she couldn't even guess at the use of. No, he was at home in a world that was as foreign to her as a time machine.

"Maybe I might like you." Now she was the recipient of his wink, and her stomach rolled again. It was going to have to stop that. This guy had "danger" written all over his gorgeous face, and she had had enough of that to last a lifetime already.

"Not buying it. You don't know me. If you just like the way I look in a dress, well, I'm afraid you're leaving a terrible impression on my ward, and we must retract our offer." We? Our? Greta sincerely hoped Mina would not object to being involved, or tell her father what they'd spent the morning plotting. Luckily, she just glared and nodded. Good girl. There was a biscotti in it for her just for that.

"No, it isn't that. Although you do look amazing. And you should know that, and I won't apologize for saying so. Both of you." He gallantly included Mina in his hand gesture, and she stood a little taller in her own pink sundress and red cowboy boots. Greta made a mental note to try to find more appropriate male role models for the girl. Just because her dad was absent didn't mean she should fall for the sweet-talking hottie Brit.

Hello, pot? This is kettle.

"I think the fact that you aren't even remotely impressed with me is intriguing. And I must admit I like a challenge." Jon's green eyes stared into her again, clouding her head for a moment until his words sunk in. Then the anger surfaced.

"I'm not a challenge to be won. I'm not a bet with my sister. I'm more than a pawn. I'm a real person, and you know what? Forget it. Never mind. You can just forget the whole thing. Go . . . buy some records, or whatever it is that you do." Greta wasn't sure why her eyes suddenly felt hot and prickly.

Because she knew it would come to this, it always did. No man had ever failed to disappoint her, from her father to the string of ex-boyfriends that had led her to stop dating in the first place.

Her eyes were on the exit, blind to anything but escape. Suddenly his hands were on her hips, pulling her in closer, one moving to her chin to tip her face toward his own.

"That's not what I meant. You aren't a challenge to be won. You're a challenge to know, and I want to know you. Please let me." He sounded so earnest, looked so anxious. Greta wavered. It was a really good answer, but she was really unreasonably hurt by his words. Stupidly hurt. If Mina had come home with this story, she'd have slapped the responsible kid personally.

"Please," he asked gently. She cracked. Good manners had always been a weakness of hers. She nodded slightly, and Mina clapped. She'd have to have a talk with the girl later, about how she couldn't start shipping Jetta. *Oh sweet God, did I just give us a celebrity name? I'm losing my everloving mind.*

"Fine. Okay. You can take me on real dates afterwards. But I have a condition to your condition." She wasn't going down without a fight. Wait—not going down at all. Fake dates *definitely* didn't do that.

"No kissing," Jon said before Mina had a chance. It made them both giggle.

"Oh, hush, you. The sub-condition is that I get to pick what our real dates are. Shouldn't be a problem, should it?" It was Greta's turn to wink. Because of course, she planned to make it a problem. Why he evidently truly seemed to like her was a mystery, but she wasn't interested in going down that road. So if she had to arrange the roadblocks herself, so be it.

"No problem at all. I believe we've got a deal." Jon solemnly shook hands with both Greta and Mina. "If you don't mind, I'm a bit knackered from last evening still. Let me know when my first appearance is required, m'lady."

"Tuesday. I have a lunch. *We* have a lunch. You're going to meet my friends. After all, they're the entire reason I got myself into this whole mess."

"Methinks the lady doth protest too much," he said to Mina. And then he bowed—actually bowed—and took his leave.

"I want to like him," Mina announced before the door had even closed behind him. "He's very handsome, for a grownup. And he talks like the Doctor."

"I want to like him too," Greta confessed. It was hard not to be honest, now that his eyes weren't piercing her like a . . . sword. No, not that, that brought up *other* thoughts.

Anyway, how could she explain to this innocent kid what she'd learned in her life about the dark side of masculinity? The poor girl was disappointed often enough by her father. But then, that was probably reason enough not to get her hopes up. They'd inevitably be dashed. Greta didn't need to teach a course on a lesson Mina was learning daily.

"But we don't really know him. And have you noticed how much he looks like a pirate? Very cunning and rugged." Just planting the seeds that she shouldn't trust men. That was fine, right? *Goddamnit, he left the jacket again. I bet that was on purpose.*

"Isn't that a good thing? The Ninth Doctor was cunning and rugged. And he was kind of a *space* pirate. Ooh! Like Captain Mal from Firefly!" Mina's eyes were shining. Greta regretted, for the first time, training the girl in all the classic nerd television. She never dreamed it would be used against her. Gathering the offensive peacoat and her dignity, she mutely held her hand out for Mina and headed home to scheme.

Chapter 3

Jon didn't care how clichéd it was, he was never going to pass up a bowl of cioppino. He only wished his pals didn't spend quite so much time ribbing him about it.

"There's veg, and protein, and bread on the side. It's got everything you need. Like pizza," he patiently explained for the umpteenth time. "But posh." Rust just laughed.

"Pizza isn't healthy, no matter how many food groups you hit, bro. But I think I speak for everyone who knows you that we'd all rather get pizza than seafood soup every single time we go out." He stretched his long arms out and gestured around. "Or is this a fame thing? You have a *posh* quirk to mention in interviews?"

"Good lord, a fame thing? Is that what you all think? I just know what I like is all. People invent quirks for interviews, is that—is that really happening?" Jon was alarmed.

"Sure, man, why do you think people bring beer to all my things? I dropped it in a couple press things that I gargle with Belgian beer after every show. Now my fans make sure I don't ever have to hit the liquor store again." Rust smiled contentedly.

"That's just bizarre. Gargle with Belgian beer?" Jon thought for a second. "Is that why you give me Chimay for every possible occasion?"

"Oh yeah. I never have to think about presents anymore either. Honestly, you probably should mention this soup thing. It'll improve the quality of tail you're pulling if they can cook, you know?" Rust nodded to himself.

Jon was speechless.

"Mate, I'm speechless," he said. Rust just shrugged and grabbed more bread, filling his mouth and winking at some blondes making eyes at him from a couple booths over.

Rust Vee was the lead singer from V, one of Jon's favorite bands, not that he would ever tell Rust that. He thought he was a brilliant musician, and when Jon finally signed to a label, and it was the same label as Rust, he was thrilled. When a couple of artists from the label took an interest in him and struck up a friendship, he was awed. But every once in a while, he was reminded just how weird musicians and this life could be. Sometimes it was hard to stay grounded.

Rust made no effort at all, which could have been obnoxious, and sometimes was, but mostly Jon found him a mixture of amusing and refreshingly happy with his lot in life. So many musicians put on airs of being too cool, but not Rust. He mopped every drop of life up with bread.

The blondes had evidently chosen an emissary to approach, a leggy girl in shorts and a crop top.

"I bought you a Hoegaarden," she said breathily, blushing, and handing a glass to Rust.

"Thanks so much! Hey, let me introduce you to someone. This is DJ Force." The girl gasped.

"Squee!" she exclaimed, and waved her friends over as she plopped down, unasked.

You're welcome, Rust mouthed to Jon, exposing some not-quite chewed breadstick still in there. Jon just shook his head, which was sort of spinning. Did people really think he was this desperate for—what was it Rust had called it? Tail? Heavens, he had no doubt he could use his moderate notoriety to sleep with a lot of women, but that really wasn't his style.

He knew exactly who he wanted to sleep with, and her name was Greta Steinburg. She was prettier than these bottle blondes. She was feistier and weird as well, but in a good way.

He thought of Greta and the sassy little girl she was with and smiled. They would never be impressed with him just because he rubbed shoulders with guys like Rust Vee. No, he had to be an amazing date. He was surprised at how much he wanted to impress her. Yeah he wanted to sleep with her, too, he was male. But mostly, he wanted to wipe away some of the mistrust and venom he saw in her eyes. He was going to have to turn on the charm and become a magnificent date. Perhaps he'd google some pointers later.

His phone buzzed, and he pulled it from his trouser pocket.

1st fake date: meet the friends! Free tomorrow? Jon smiled to himself.

I'll be there. What time?

Bottle blonde #1 was gently rubbing his shoulder, but he brushed her off.

Noon, @ Veghead.

She redoubled her efforts, and it made him feel a little weird to have hands on him that didn't belong to the girl in his mind.

"Right, then, got to run." He slid some money onto the table and extricated himself over the protests of his friend and groupies. "Lovely to meet you birds."

"Enjoy your booty call!" Rust called after him.

Jon exited the restaurant, equally mournful over not being able to talk to his friend about the girl on his mind, and the cioppino he'd left behind. Truly, hardly an hour had passed since yesterday's fateful meeting at the coffee shop that he hadn't thought about Greta. And if they hadn't been joined by the gaggle of fans, that text would have been the perfect time to bring her up.

What was it about her that rattled him so? She spent a significant amount of time telling him how uninterested she was in him, but he saw her eyes linger on his mouth. And other areas. She definitely *was* interested in him, and the idea that eventually he was going to make out with her made his trousers tighten. Jon walked towards his flat, smiling to himself.

The last time he was this excited to be seeing someone again had been with Leah. But she was in-your-face easy. The thrill of the chase was missing from their earliest encounters. He knew he was guaranteed an entry into her skin-tight trousers, so there was a very different feeling from wondering if Greta would consent to allowing a snog.

He'd missed the longing, the little glances. The way two people shyly allow their limbs to entangle as they sit next to each other, both knowing what will happen, yet savoring the journey. That was what he was anticipating now, and as Jon punched the code into the front door of his building, he shivered a bit. He *was* going to be a perfect gentleman, but he was also definitely going to have to negotiate with wee Mina on the kissing.

Greta had to hand it to Jon—he was remarkably graceful under pressure. And "pressure" was a pretty kind word for the interrogation he was getting from Amy and Summer. Neither girl had even touched her lunch, though they had gathered under the pretext of checking out a new restaurant Summer had been thinking of applying to.

Meanwhile, Greta was nervously nibbling on everything in sight. At least *someone* would be able to report on the food quality later.

"So you quit college to DJ? Bold move." This from Amy, who'd famously quit law school to join a radical environmental protection non-profit.

"I wouldn't say my mum was all too happy with the

decision, but she respected my plan. I didn't quit until I was offered a tour with a quite famous rapper—Dee Q. I could have stayed in school, trying to study between paid gigs, or I could go to Europe for a month and make enough money to pay off all my previous years' student loans.

"We agreed that I'd finish my degree once the music died down, and by 'we agreed', I mostly mean Dad brokered that as a peace agreement. Only it hasn't died down at all since, so I'm safe from uni exams for now." He smiled that perfect crooked-toothed smile, and Summer smiled back. Her mom hadn't been too whipped on her decision to go to culinary school, either.

"So how did you go from Europe and rappers to back here doing your own thing?" Greta asked, interested despite herself. She speared a slice of maitake from Summer's untouched plate.

"The tour had gone off quite well, so Dee asked if I'd be interested in joining him on the South American leg. Initially I thought perhaps I would, because I felt like my mind had been blown a bit with the new things I'd heard in the clubs in Ibiza and Amsterdam. I wanted to start incorporating those things into my own production, and I figured I'd pick up even more in the lower hemisphere. Then I realized I'd need to update my vaccinations, and decided to just head home then and start building my own brand instead of doing backups any longer."

"Are you an anti-vaxer? Grrrr. Because you know you are basically a bio-terrorist." That was an actual growl. Amy's earlier good cheer was retreating behind her politics. Summer nodded in agreement. After the outbreak of mumps in Mina's elementary school last year, Greta had to say she was also pretty wary of this turn of the conversation.

Could you catch things like that from wearing someone's jacket?

"No, love, settle. I believe wholeheartedly in vaccines, I just wish someone would invent a pill form." Jon pointed at Summer's mushroom with his fork and cocked a brow at Greta. She gave him a thumbs up—the maitake crudo was delicious—and he stole a piece as well.

"You're scared of needles?" Summer ignored the rapidly disappearing contents of her dish to look utterly pleased at discovering Jon's weakness so quickly, and with almost no effort on her part.

"I wouldn't say scared," Jon looked pained. "I just vastly dislike them, is all. Doesn't everyone?" Everyone sort of shrugged. It was a fair point. No one actually looked forward to a shot. Although, most people wouldn't cancel a career-making trip over the thought.

"And you travel quite a bit now on your own?" Summer had the wanderlust gene, constantly taking foodcations to check out new restaurants.

"Not so much at current. The occasional festival. I'm working on an album, which is sort of slow going. I don't sing myself, so I work around all my guests' schedules.

"Tell me about yourselves, though. Summer, what

do you do?" She tossed her dark brown hair, the un-shaven side.

"I'm a chef. I've been cooking since I can remember. After culinary school, I apprenticed at French Laundry and Incanto. Now I'm just feeling a little stuck. I'm nowhere near opening my own place financially, but I need something new. I love farm-to-table cooking, but I'm awfully sick of how precious things like offal have become. I want to do something more rustic, more accessible." She sighed. "Something normal people want to eat. Being responsible, or even adventurous with your food choices shouldn't be so . . . *scary.*"

Greta had heard this one a few times, and it made her sad every time. Summer was so talented, she didn't need to spend more time languishing in other people's kitchens, getting no credit for the dishes she invented. If Greta suddenly won the lottery, the first thing she'd do would be invest in Café Coniglio, as she'd dubbed her friend's restaurant in her mind.

"Those are some pretty impressive names. I doubt you'll be working for other people much longer. I dearly hope your new restaurant serves a good cioppino." Jon really *was* playing the gentleman, saying just the right things. Despite herself, (and Summer's well-known dislike of cioppino) Greta could feel her attention being pulled to him as if there were magnets in his smile. "And you, Miss Amy?"

"I'm saving the world." A simple answer, as simple as it was to Amy.

"And Greta is an au pair. You ladies are quite the diverse team." Apparently bolstered by the crudo theft of a moment before, Jon followed Greta's lead and began to eat the vegetable tartare from Amy's plate as well.

"Delicious." He was chewing the minced carrots, but looking at Greta. *Hey, now.*

"She's not just an au pair," Summer bragged before Greta could shush her. "She's an artist."

"Oh?" He was still looking at her in that wolfish way of his, as though she was the next dish to be sampled.

"It doesn't pay the bills. Stop doing that." Talking about her art embarrassed her under the best of circumstances, but how could anyone be expected to focus clearly when a ridiculously attractive man was staring them down like this?

"Doing what, exactly?" His grin spread, exposing that incisor that undid her every time.

"That—*thing* you're doing." He ignored her, and continued doing it. Her Judases were exchanging lewd glances. That was fine. This was all going according to plan. They were falling for him, and the myth of Jetta.

"Birds, tell me about her art since she's being so retiring on the subject." They were only too happy to oblige. Stupid friends. But wasn't this what she'd wanted? And a weird little part of her thrilled to know he'd know she was more than "just" a nanny.

"She illustrates children's books. She's had two published already." Amy had probably bought all twelve copies sold of each, she was so proud. She'd given them out as holiday presents at the Green Guerrilla office last year, despite almost none of her co-workers actually having children. Amy was a good friend.

"It's not just the illustrations, though. She makes the most gorgeous watercolors you've ever seen. When I have my restaurant, she's doing all my art. If I could plate my food as well as she arranges paint, I'd already have my Michelin star." Summer was a good friend too. She was lucky. Stupid, awesome, same difference when you were talking about your soul sisters.

"I'd love to see your art sometime." He wasn't doing that thing anymore, he looked like he actually meant it. She tried to look away, but his earnestness was drawing her in. She wondered if everyone noticed how thick the air felt all of a sudden.

"We'll see." She supposed he was an artist of a sort himself, but it was still kind of like getting naked in front of strangers, showing your work to someone new. He broke eye contact, and she stared at her own coffee cup as though it held the solution to her recovery. It annoyed her.

She was more than annoyed, actually, she was pissed. Her fake date shouldn't hold real sway over her. Something started to spark in the back of her mind.

"Maybe you should let her paint *you*," Summer suggested.

"Ah, yes, I have always wanted a large portrait of myself for above the mantelpiece in my study," Jon posed and exaggerated his British accent to sound like the lord of a manor.

"I didn't mean you should be the subject. I meant you should be the canvas." Summer's smile was as wicked as any Jon had ever thrown Greta's way. Yeah, they'd definitely fallen for her ruse, imagining there was sexual tension there when really it was just aggravation and an acknowledgement of attraction. Greta wasn't going to sit around and listen to this, though, and Summer had given her a terribly brilliant idea anyway.

"Let's get out of here," she said to Jon, as her friends giggled. If only they knew. If Jon wanted to play chicken, she was in.

"Anything you say, love." He tossed some money on the table and swept his jacket around Greta's bare shoulders. It wasn't even cold out today, but she had to admit, the smell of his cologne was sort of addictive. It was like the Bay and Fog City Leather all wrapped up in one. The alluring scent wasn't enough to make her feel bad about her plan, though.

"Take it easy on him!" called Summer, while Amy did gross things with her tongue Greta tried very hard to unsee.

"Time for our real date, then. Are you taking me to your studio?" He leaned down to murmur into her ear. The shivers that went down her neck didn't even make her voice waver as she replied, proud of herself.

"Not mine."

He was obviously waiting for her to continue, but she didn't. The closer they got to her destination, the more upset her stomach felt at what she was doing, but no. He'd wanted to make her feel uncomfortable, and she was going to do the same thing right back. She squared her shoulders, and ignored Jon for the final block.

"Saint Frank Design Collective. This looks quite fancy. I didn't realize you were represented by a gallery. I'd have thought that was something your friends would have mentioned. Or is this more of a shared maker space?" Jon stared at the nondescript brick building with its hand-painted wooden sign. "Either way, I'm keen to see it."

"Not quite either." Greta pushed opened the heavy pine door, letting the staccato buzzing noise from within float out onto the bright noontime street. She held the door as Jon stepped in and then quickly stepped back out, several shades paler.

"It's not your studio," he stated.

"Nope." She held out her arm to usher him back inside.

"It's a tattoo shop." Instead of walking ahead of her as she'd intended, he took her arm and they walked in together. Even through the thick jacket, she could feel his hand trembling. Well, she wasn't going to feel bad about it. If he was foolish enough to admit he was frightened of needles, then she'd be just as foolish to ignore the addition to her arsenal.

With any luck, he'd give up right then and there, and she could go home and tell her friends they just weren't sexually compatible. Maybe she could even insinuate the fault lay in his anatomy. Though—she side-eyed his long, lean physique and confident stride—she somehow doubted that was the case.

"Looking for new ink?" asked a burly, heavily tattooed man in the corner without a client in his chair. He certainly knew how to take the focus off of Jon's jeans. With terror, maybe, but still.

"Absolutely. Both of us are," Greta said with a confidence she didn't necessarily feel. After all, she'd never gotten one before either. But Summer had a bunch, so it couldn't be that bad. Although Summer was a little tougher than she was. Okay, maybe a lot tougher. Still.

"Flip through here, let me know if you see something you like. I do custom pieces too, so don't be shy." The man handed them a thick binder filled with pictures of various tattoos he'd done. Every one of them looked fresh—which meant raised, red, and in some cases, still sporting a smear or two of blood.

Jon's eyes visibly widened, boosting Greta a bit. Maybe she wasn't as badass as Summer Coniglio, but she certainly wasn't going to faint like her "date" looked ready to. Something caught her eye, and she looked closer. Maybe this tattoo thing was a really good idea after all. She often had really good ideas, she reminded herself.

"I like this watercolor thing," she told the artist. "Can I get a couple splashes of color behind a Deathly Hallows on my wrist?" Mina was going to freak at how cool this was when she got picked up from school. "Actually, give me a sheet of paper. I'll show you exactly what I want."

Taking control of it restored Greta's confidence. She could handle tattoos if she drew them herself. It made her feel confident in this plan, no matter how last-minute it was.

"Won't that hurt?" Jon asked.

"It doesn't tickle," replied the burly man, chuckling ominously to himself as he began to assemble an equally ominous looking needle contraption. Greta swallowed, but gave a giant smile when she caught Jon's gaze on her.

"You're quite brave to go first, love." His eyes still twinkled out of his white face. How utterly irritating of him, to look so good despite feeling so bad. Likely he chalked this up to his gentleman status. Hah! She'd prove him wrong.

"I didn't know you'd be so easy to out-man," Greta replied steadily, although her heart was starting to race as the artist swiped some alcohol over her wrist and laid it down on a plastic-covered extension of the chair. He freehanded the familiar shape of a triangle encasing a circle and a vertical line on her wrist as her palms broke into a clammy sweat.

She stared straight into Jon's clear green eyes with her own brown ones as the artist tapped twice on his pedal to test his machine. When the needle broke her delicate skin for the first time, she hissed a sharp inhale and kept her face straight. *Tough. You're tough. You got this. Be a badass.*

It lasted about two more seconds before she broke.

"This feels horrible! Distract me!" She tried to keep her voice down, but *owwwwwww*. To his credit, he only half-smiled before he leaned in. Greta began to turn her head so he could whisper his I-told-you-so or words of wisdom in her ear, but his hand landed on her cheek and held it steady.

Her eyes stayed open, sure he wasn't going to do what it seemed like he was going to, but *oh* he did it. He pressed his lips to hers, as velvety and smooth as she'd imagined but somehow even more overwhelming. At first she stayed utterly still, surprised. His tongue drew a path until she relented. Was her stomach dropping out her knees because of him or the needle? She couldn't tell, and couldn't bring herself to care.

She forgot to be mad as he kissed her. She forgot she didn't like him as she kissed him back. She forgot about the loud droning noise of the machine as his lips gently parted hers. The painful vibration in her wrist turned into a hum she felt through her whole body as she tasted the faint echo of the risotto with lemon sorbet he'd eaten as his own lunch. Her other hand came up to trace the impossibly perfect line of his jaw.

Her heart was no longer racing as if running away; it was leaping in excitement. His scent was all around her, as dizzying as the citrus of his tongue. He sucked softly on her lower lip, drawing a gasp. She opened her mouth more fully, let him claim her. The moment seemed to last forever. *Oh God. What has he done to me?* Her head was spinning, and so she closed her own eyes at last, just as he pulled away.

It took a moment to register that her tattoo was complete, so sudden was the shock of his mouth's departure, and then she squealed.

"Look how pretty this is! I love it!" Greta bounced up and down as she watched her new adornment get covered in plastic and taped up for safety. She glanced back up at Jon, suddenly nervous for a different reason, not certain what to say to him. He saved her the trouble.

"My turn." As they traded places, eyes never leaving each other, she knew he was doing that *thing* again. It wasn't the tattoo he meant at all.

And what did *she* mean when she nodded? The kiss was a bad idea. It gave the impression that he *could* get ideas about her, and Greta didn't want that. On the other hand, they'd already crossed the line. And she wasn't even the one who was terrified of needles. Maybe just this once more wouldn't hurt. The first time did feel awfully good—more than good. It was earth-shaking.

"I'll have what she's having, only with different colors," Jon told the tattooist, who was changing out his gloves.

"Deathly Hallows? Are you—" Greta was surprised.

"I'm an Englishman under thirty. Of course I'm a Harry Potter fan. I've a picture on my Facebook page of myself at Platform 9 ¾. I'll friend you later so you can see. " He pointed at a couple of plastic squeeze bottles of ink that would complement her own pink and orange rather nicely.

As the paper package was ripped to expose a fresh needle, Jon's color faded again. He was trying to take deep breaths but looked too ill to gain any relaxation from them. He didn't get up and leave, though. Greta started to feel a little bad. He was definitely the tougher of the two of them.

"Just don't look at it. Right here. Just look at me."
She slid onto his lap, straddling and facing him, care-
ful not to disturb the wrist already being sketched
on. He stared into her eyes, and as the machine fired up,
she leaned in for his turn, just as he'd suggested. This
time the kiss wasn't soft and sweet, but deep and searching. She could feel his nervousness in the hand that
clenched her ribcage, holding her close against him.

His heartbeat pounded against hers, with hers, as
their tongues danced around each other. Too soon, it
was over. As they paid and received their aftercare instructions, one thought kept rebounding off the walls
of Greta's mind: how could something so off-plan have
felt so perfect?

Chapter 4

After she picked the duly-impressed Mina up from school, Greta was jittery. Too much had happened already that day, both good and bad. The conflicting emotions conspired with the inspiration she was feeling, and there was only one way to deal with the maelstrom inside of her.

"Hey, Mina, wanna do some painting this afternoon?" It was her evening off, but she'd already been out once. Twice, maybe, if you counted the restaurant and the tattoo shop as separate outings. Either way, it was plenty for Greta, who much preferred not to go out at all if she could help it.

"Can I use your good paints? The ones my dad bought me suck." Mina batted her thick baby eyelashes.

"Don't say suck. It isn't nice." Those paints totally sucked. How was an aspiring artist supposed to learn their craft with kindergarten art supplies? She would have shared her paints anyway. And she was also pleased Mina could tell the difference.

They'd only just walked in the house when Bob emerged from his room, tossing on his motorcycle jacket.

"Hey, Greta, I meant to tell you. I've got plans tonight. Might not be back for a couple days. Be good, Meens." He was halfway out the door before she unfroze her dropped jaw.

"Um, it's my off night. And tomorrow too. Remember?" Although it wasn't the first time Bob had rudely switched her schedule without prior notice, she thought after she'd explained last time just how inconvenient it was, that he'd not do it again.

"Oh, yeah, well—it's unavoidable. And it isn't like you have anything more important going on than my daughter. Right, princess?" He chuckled, and headed into the garage for his bike without so much as hugging his daughter the "princess".

Well, *he* obviously did.

Mina looked up at Greta with an expression she recognized from her own childhood. It was the look that said, "I'm really trying not to cry, but don't you dare talk about this or I will sob." Greta took a deep breath to calm herself. What an ass. What an absolute ass. What kind of a person treated their child this way?

"You know you *are* the most important, right, kiddo?" She forced herself to use her calmest voice. "And that obviously means that after painting we're going to destroy your dad's perfect kitchen with ten batches of cookies. I may even start a food fight." A bizarre idea of inviting Jon to join them floated through her head. But she stopped that thought from going any further.

"What if I was a baker that baked children into cookies?" asked Mina, with a tentative half smile.

"Then you'd probably be the witch from Hansel and Gretel. What if I was a wily hunter who found the children and set them free?" Greta threw open a few cabinets in illustration.

"What if I decided wily hunters should be baked into pies?" Mina slammed them all shut again.

"Then you'd belong on Fleet Street with the other demons. What if I was a fairy who had magic glitter-dust to make you mend your ways?" Greta opened the doors again.

"What if fairy pie was the only thing that would make the evil king happy and release me from the spell that made me naughty?" Mina carefully moved the doors to halfway.

"No one can *make* you bad, though, kiddo. There will always be people who make you want to be better, and people who bring out the naughty side of you. The real magic is in being able to tell the difference, and in being strong enough and clever enough to pick the right people." She knew she was breaking the unofficial rules of the game, but hey, teachable moments weren't something Bob apparently planned on dealing with.

"Anyways, if the only way to save you was being baked into a pie, well." Greta pushed the "bake" button on the oven and turned the dial to 350. "I'd always do that."

Mina looked like she was biting back the tears a little again. *Shit, that wasn't what I meant to do.* "I love you, Greta."

If only Greta believed in love. She knew Mina was attached to her. She was attached to the little girl, too.

"More than French fries?" She asked.

"Yep," said Mina, turning off the oven.

"More than Minecraft?" Mina pretended to consider for a minute.

"Yep." She closed the half-open cabinet doors.

"More than the BBC?" Greta led the way toward the spiral staircase at the back of the restored Victorian.

"Don't push it," Mina answered, and Greta laughed out loud. Fair enough.

Someone else's house or not, Greta could breathe easy in her own room. Her easel was permanently set up by the window, and Mina's little foldable one was easily set up next to it. They'd been working on still lifes, but nothing was ready for the impromptu session. She started wandering around, grabbing things while trying not to focus on the throbbing in her wrist.

An old, fabric-covered book.

What. Was. She thinking. Kissing a man who had no chance with her. Kissing a man at all. Okay, fine, maybe it felt good. Like really good. But that was just a lack of kissing in her life.

A flower from the farmers market, on its last legs.

Not that she wanted the kind of life with loads of kissing. Although, after reminding herself how nice it felt, maybe she did? No. No she didn't. Because as Riley Kilo said, kissing always led to more and more. And then things sucked. Well, that was paraphrasing, but still.

A half-empty wine glass from her last bath-and-book night. AKA the last night she'd spent at home. And every night before that.

Okay, so what if there *was* a distinct lack of sex in her life? She wasn't the type of girl who could one-night it. She was an artist. Emotional. There was no such thing as a one-off for her. And there was no such thing as a guy who was willing to commit. At least not the ones who had steady jobs, mortgages, and dogs. And were straight. That was why she'd *made* the decision not to date. Because every love interest had broken another little piece of her heart off, and at this point? There wasn't much of it left.

This was good, a good arrangement. The book and the flower had some nice texture, and it was never too early to learn how to paint reflections. Those were the toughies in any still, but also the ones that made the whole picture sparkle.

Greta remembered hearing a story on an art museum field trip about two artists competing on still lifes. The first painted his so realistically that birds tried to peck the canvas fruit. Determined to reveal his opponent's picture for ridicule, it took the second artist a couple of attempts before he realized the cloth covering the still life was actually the picture itself.

Although no one had made a similar mistake on one of hers yet, it was her life's goal to paint something so startlingly real that the viewer gasped. Maybe not even real. Something so beautiful. She pictured, again, Jon's lips. His bright green eyes. So beautiful. She wasn't going to paint him, though. Particularly not the way Summer had suggested. Trailing the soft bristles of her brush down his warm back, tracing the musculature . . .

"I brought the water cups," Mina announced as she broke into Greta's thoughts. "And some ice for your wrist. It looks owie."

"I'm not sure 'owie' is a word. Thanks for the water." Greta started doling out brushes and paint dabs, determined not to let those synapses fire ever again.

"Why not? Shakespeare made up words anytime he needed one. My teacher told me." Mina pulled an apron over her school clothes and backed towards Greta for the tying.

"Fair enough, kid, but I think it's a little different when you're writing them into plays for posterity. Although—never mind. It's gotta start somewhere, I guess." They wet their brushes in unison, blotting them on paper towels. Greta inhaled deeply, pulling the scent of pigment and her favorite candles in, preparing for the release she felt when she was creating.

"Are you going to marry Jon?" Mina caused Greta to choke on her meditative breath.

"Oh. No. No, no. Honey, I'm not going to marry anyone." She flooded part of the block, a bit heavier than necessary. *That kiss though . . .*

"Why?" Of course.

"Why what? Oh, here, use a bit more pigment on the edges of the book, makes it look like shading."

"Why won't you marry Jon?" Stubborn child. She wasn't adding the pigment either.

"I just don't believe in marriage. No biggie. Some people don't. *Heavier* on those edges. Otherwise you won't have any depth." Her own was lacking as well, best to take her own advice. Maybe in more ways than one. She loaded her brush with more carmine and started in.

"Why?" Mina was swishing her brush all over the place now.

"Because marriage is a contract two people make when they think they are in love. Look here, you'll want to leave that background alone for now. You can't skip out of order and end up with a coherent picture."

"So . . . why?" This was why Greta did not want kids. She idly wondered if Jon did. Not that it mattered. She was just curious. She should get to know her fake date in order to be convincing.

"Because if you fill in the back first, how will you put the shapes you want in the front without color confliction?" That should have been obvious to anyone with a basic knowledge of the color wheel, and a sense of how watercolor works.

"That's not what I was asking. Why aren't you going to get married?" It couldn't have been as simple as the color wheel. Of course.

"Because if you don't believe in love, you don't make a contract like that. Simple. I see you are still on that background I told you to stop with."

Mina smiled winningly. Greta wasn't blind to the fact that Mina's piece looked better than hers. She pretended to be, though. Cause she hadn't followed the *rules*. Otherwise, she'd happily compliment. Rules were important.

"Love is real. My dad and my mom were in love."

Oh, were they? Pretty hard to believe that a guy who had loved his wife wholeheartedly could treat their only child so callously. And be such a dick in general. Like, how could someone who didn't tip their servers even be capable of love? In Greta's expert opinion, no compassion equaled no interpersonal skills on which to even begin building a real relationship. Jon had tipped extravagantly. No that *that* mattered either. Just an observation.

"I'm sure they were." Greta decided it wasn't a lie if she didn't say explicitly 'oh, definitely.' Because Mina was creepily good at picking up on lies.

"They were very super in love. Dad says." Mina smiled to herself, and continued doing the exact opposite of what Greta had explicitly told her to. *Arrrrrg*. Also, seriously, how was it that the kid still believed her lying liar of a father about anything?

Because it's easy to believe the lies you want to hear. The thought hit her like a freight train, and she couldn't blame Mina at all. She'd done it herself, with her own father.

"You want to go change out the water for us?"

"Mine's still—"

"Go."

Her little back had hardly turned the corner before

Greta sank onto her bed. It all made sense, really. She, too, had wanted to believe in the redemption of love. Enough that she'd swallow anything else she was fed.

Dad. Just thinking his name made her cringe. Although in retrospect, maybe she should have thanked him, for teaching her that what passes for love is usually just a power struggle between people who should have dissolved their union when the shine wore off in the first place.

Except it took her a couple more men to learn that lesson. Like Tom, who'd seemed perfect in art school, but . . . wasn't. And they'd both stuck it out until it wasn't even possible to be friends after. Pointless. Then there was Oliver. Freaking Oliver.

In retrospect, she still wasn't sure exactly what it was that had swept her so off her feet that every thought she'd had after meeting him revolved around him. He was nice, but so were lots of people. He was cute, but not that cute. Maybe it was his confidence, the way he'd walked into the bar she was in and just— *owned* it.

Whatever it was, it had utterly blinded her to the fact that he had not been nearly as interested as she was. She'd moved too fast, shown her cards too soon, and he'd ghosted her—just stopped calling one day, and never answered again. And it only took a couple weeks to rebound, disgusted with herself for mistaking hormones for more. It was a rule she'd made for herself after that, not to bother with "love", or the combination of attraction and affection that passed for it. She

glanced down at her still-swollen tattoo. No matter
how good a kisser a guy was.

And again, she just didn't know how to explain this
stuff to a little kid. Especially a little kid who was too
young to hear what a shit her father was, even from
someone who knew from personal experience. Well—
maybe not. It couldn't do anyone any good to tell
her. Yet it couldn't do any good to let her get disappointed again and again, building up tree rings of broken promises. Someday her bark would be as thick as
Greta's, protecting her heart. There was just no way
around it.

Chapter 5

"So you have matching tattoos that you got while you were experiencing one of the most magical kisses of your life?" Amy was so delighted that she actually stepped on a wildflower, something that would normally never occur under even the most dire of circumstances. Although it was entirely possible that doing a postmortem on a fake date being passed off as the beginning of a relationship—while hiking, not a strong suit of Greta's to begin with—did qualify as dire circumstances.

"Basically, yes," Greta had to admit. She picked her way over some branches on the trail.

"You have matching tattoos. That you got on your first real date. It's too fast." Summer seemed decidedly less enthusiastic.

Greta couldn't tell which one she preferred.

"I want what you have. I want that." Amy spun

around just like Sister Maria in the Austrian Alps, the jacket tied around her waist flaring around her. Just like, except that they were in the Golden Gate rec area, and no one had ever accused Amy of being a nun.

"You want Britney Spears and Kevin Federline, circa 2004?" Summer stopped Amy's spinning and scooted her diminutive friend back onto the path.

"Oh, come on, Summer. It's not like that." Greta couldn't exactly tell her friend what it *was* like, though. The first rule of Fake Date was that you couldn't talk about Fake Date.

"It isn't like that, Summer, it's beautiful. It's love. And Jon is hardly a K-Fed. Wait—he isn't, right?" Amy was skipping now.

"Ha, no. He isn't. But 'love' might be a little premature, Ames. It was just our first date, after all." If she didn't say "real" or "fake", just "date", it wasn't really like she was lying to her best friends in the world, right? She was going with that.

"*Love* is premature, but matching *wrist* tattoos isn't? This is moving way too fast." Summer's eyes were going to get stuck up there if she kept rolling them that hard.

"Says the girl with loads of tattoos!" Greta protested.

"Says the girl who just got her first tattoo on her first date." Summer stopped walking and crossed her arms.

"Well, I ship it," said Amy.

"Of course you do," the other two said in unison. Summer didn't giggle about it the way Greta did. She was making her mom face.

"What?" Greta asked. "I know you think we're

moving pretty fast. It was just that it was more spontaneous than anything. And you guys know how bad I am at spontaneity." They were nodding at this. Okay. "Maybe he's bringing out a new side out of me. Wasn't that the point of picking each other's dates? Finding people to bring out the best in each other?"

"I just remember the last time you got carried away by a guy after the first date." Oh. Oh God. There was really no way to explain to Summer how trying to psych out her fake date was like a thousand percent different than falling for a tumbling dickweed like Oliver. The man hadn't even returned her first edition of *Ender's Game*, her favorite science fiction book. Who *did* that?

Point was, Greta was at a bit of a loss as to how best explain herself. She couldn't exactly comfort Summer or simmer Amy down with the fact that she wasn't actually dating Jon.

"Look, guys. I know it's either completely bizarre or utterly romantic, depending which of you I'm addressing, but you have to trust me that it's going just exactly as planned." There, another not-lie. She was discovering she was scarily good at half truths.

"Laugh at me all you want, Greta, but I see that spark between you. I think the tattoos are going to be a grandkids story. Besides, in these days of dating sites and swiping right on hookup apps, how often do you hear a story about a truly memorable first date? Guys don't ask you out the old fashioned way anymore, and like, *no one* does flowers. I think Jon sounds like a gentleman. He's not moving too fast."

Despite herself, Greta felt slightly swayed by Amy's declaration. Maybe not a *gentleman*, but there was something refreshing about going on an adventure with a date. Not that she'd been doing much dating herself, but she did hear a lot of stories at these unending weddings about couples who met drunk in an elevator, or started out as hookups, or liked each other's fanfic online.

Well, the fanfic thing was fine, actually.

But what she was thinking originally was that though she didn't believe in love herself, she did love a good love story. And she definitely preferred the swashbuckling adventure kind to the 'don't tell my mom we met on a sex site' type.

So this was fine, doing what she'd done. She did get a sweet new piece of artwork out of it, which made her look a bit swashbuckling herself, she rather thought.

"Yeah, but." Of course Summer couldn't let that lie. "Remember her first date with Oliver? They had one of those magical all-night adventures you usually only hear about in novels. Their car broke down, they slow-danced on the side of the road. They hiked to a speakeasy, and invented a drink that got put on the menu."

Greta's stomach started to hurt. How *dare* he, all over again. They'd had such potential.

"They made out next to a fountain, and he sang to her before finally cabbing their separate ways."

"It was an *epic* first date, especially considering the ending. Who knew he had it in him?" Amy agreed. "So?"

"So, imagine if there was a tattoo reminding her of it. On her wrist." Summer started hiking again.

"Oh," said Amy. "Hm."

"Oh, *fuck*," said Greta. "We moved too fast."

"Right, then, I suppose there is something to be said for that," Jon told Greta. "Perhaps it was a bit fast, but I feel I ought to remind you that it was your idea."

Crap. It *had* been her idea. Although he was the one who copied her design, she hadn't suggested that. She opened her mouth to remind him, but closed it again as he smiled at her. This wasn't exactly the time and place for an argument, and the words she had planned jumbled in her head at the sight of that crooked incisor anyway.

"Champagne?" she asked brightly, then snagged a couple flutes from a nearby table. She took a large swig of one as she passed him the other. Champagne was a kind way to describe the aggressively sweet carbonated wine they were serving.

"Thank you." The look on his face after he took a sip mirrored her own. But his was really cute. God, could he rock a suit, too. She needed to stop ogling him, but it was hard. "Well, I suppose it's in the spirit of a fundraiser to demonstrate how little one can afford, eh?"

Greta laughed, and then felt immediately guilty. The Green Guerillas, Amy's radical environmental non-profit, really couldn't afford that much. She gazed around the room, at the crepe paper and homemade poster decorations. It was like the world's shittiest prom, except if getting elected queen meant highlighting the worst animal abuse.

"Hey, it's a good cause, okay?" She didn't want him to think they'd be one of *those* couples whispering little snarky comments in each other's ears. Well, for one, they still weren't a couple. Never going to be, she meant. Oops. And for another, they were here to support her friend. If mocking was to be done, it should be done in one's own head, not aloud.

Like siblings, you were only allowed to make fun of each other. Outsiders couldn't do it. It was the code of friendship.

God, it felt good to laugh at this fundraiser, though. Greta downed her flute, grimaced, and grabbed another. Free *bad* booze meant you could get comfortably tipsy without worrying your check wasn't large enough. She allowed herself a long, judging look around the room. Nope, no big checks here.

Although that was a little sad. Bob probably spent more at Whole Foods in a week than this place earned in a month. And though some of their campaigns were slightly terrifying, most of them were entirely well-meaning.

"So, my date, tell me. What exactly is *your* pet cause? Everyone must have one, after all," Jon said. He adjusted his tie, and she had to stop herself forcibly from staring.

"The Comic Book Legal Defense Fund," she answered promptly. "And you?"

"The Amy Winehouse Foundation," he answered just as quickly. "Has anyone ever told you that you—"

"Frequently. What does her foundation do?"

"Tries to keep disadvantaged kids away from drugs and alcohol by getting them involved in music. Bit of a pet cause, innit?" He wasn't looking at her.

"Oh?" She realized that besides the few tidbits she'd gleaned at lunch the other day, she actually knew next to nothing about the guy she was "dating". Except for how nicely he filled out a button-down. Which wasn't insignificant. She had good taste in fake-dates.

"Grew up in council housing. Not a very nice place. Loads of my mates from childhood starting using or selling. I was always too busy mucking about with my keyboard, or mum's guitar. If I hadn't grown up around music, things might have turned out quite a bit differently for me as well. I still meet people like that, in the industry. Coke habits that started as teenagers, drinking they learned at the same time. You look at them and you just know they'll be gone as fast as they appeared on the scene." He was quiet again.

Greta studied his profile carefully. That was interesting. Growing up poor and giving back to make sure other kids had the same chance to get out? She supposed it *was* fairly gentlemanly of him. There had to be a catch somewhere, though. There always was. No one could be that perfect.

Her train of thought was derailed by the dull clinking of a plastic spoon tapping on a plastic champagne flute.

"If you'll get seated, we'll show our film now. We think it highlights some important issues we'd like to continue working on with your generous support.

Thanks." Amy's boss was as eloquent as ever. They found folding chairs next to each other in the last row, next to Summer. His thigh brushed hers as they sat, which affected her more than she thought it really ought to have. Well, fine, he was hot, it was okay if her body responded. Although she hoped he didn't notice how hard her nipples suddenly were.

The lights dimmed, and the title of the documentary appeared on the makeshift fabric screen. "Frackland". Amy'd had a brief affair with the filmmaker, so at this point Greta figured she had every talking point in the movie memorized. Basically, while the rest of the world was worrying about fracking's effects on humans, this dude was documenting the effects on native flora and fauna.

Definitely a good film the first time around. However, Amy had played it on repeat during her short-lived fascination with the narrator/director/producer/sound tech/lighting guy/composer/host.

Greta shifted uncomfortably in the metal chair. If she'd paid the least amount of attention to the evite, she'd have known this would happen and worn pants. Instead, she'd worn one of her signature short vintage dresses and now the backs of her thighs were melding to the chair. She wiggled again.

Her phone buzzed in her purse. She bent down and peeked inside, trying not to disturb anyone around her.

You look beautiful, btw. I hadn't told you.

She straightened up and looked sharply to her left. Jon's eyes were straight ahead, but his phone was in his lap and he was smiling impertinently.

Well. She did. She'd spent a good hour working on her hair and makeup. Not because *he'd* see her, of course, even in her head she hastened to add that. No, it was because these pics would be all over Facebook soon enough, and she wanted to look cute. That was all. *Buzz.* She leaned down again.

What are we doing after this?

Greta's smile now matched his. She hadn't exactly bothered to mention the real-date plans to him. She moved her purse to her lap to text him back.

Roller skating.

She almost felt guilty over the look of excitement on his face. Almost. Because what she still hadn't mentioned was that it wasn't just roller-skating. It was Mina's ninth birthday party. Miraculously, Bob had decided to hire a party planner to put it together instead of announcing that Greta would be putting it together last minute, as she'd expected.

Even though she wasn't technically working, she'd still feel like a heel if she missed it. But then—Greta swigged the last of her bubbly—children's birthday parties were notoriously obnoxious, so she wouldn't feel bad showing up with a bit of a buzz either. Or bad about bringing Jon to a guaranteed cock-block. And the fact that it got her out of the end of the fundraiser was icing.

So *that* was what her Cheshire-cat grin was about, Jon thought as he surveyed the rink full of screaming little girls. Greta was such a little firecracker. A good girl, though, he could twig. You could always tell what sort a person was by the company they kept.

Anyways, he was breaking down her walls, he could tell. She wasn't glaring at his innuendos anymore, she was suppressing little smiles. And she might pretend it was fake all she wanted, she'd already introduced him to all her friends and to her surrogate family. Although judging by the weird vibe between the dad and Greta, he'd wager only Mina was truly family to her.

It would be his second winning bet of the month.

Mina skated by, and he waved. It made his wrist itch. She giggled and said something to the girl she was linked-arms with. The other girl's whole head turned round to stare as she rounded the rink. She broke from Mina to link and gossip with another friend.

So word was out that Greta had a boyfriend. He allowed himself a little smirk. She could fight this all she wanted, once everyone referred to him as that, she'd inevitably come around. Especially once he made her . . . come around, so to speak. He glanced over as she was lacing up the beige rental skates. Yeah, he was going to do wonderful things to her.

His gaze travelled up her impossibly perfect legs, showed off in that short dress, to her belted waist. It lingered for a moment too long on the rounded tops of her creamy breasts before moving up to admire her— oh. Busted.

See, right there, she didn't even look mad, although Jon could tell she was trying. Yeah, it just took a little extra time, but now things were going according to his plan.

Mina and yet another kid skidded to a stop on the carpet before the bench he and Greta were on. This was it, then, she was going to have to admit to Mina and her hundred tiny friends that she *like*-liked Jon and that she was totally gonna get kissing cooties.

"Is it true? I told Mina she was a liar," demanded the small girl, fists on hips. Why was she looking at *him*?

"It's true," he responded, confused. She gaped at him, and skated off. Next thing he knew, he was surrounded by a small mob of girls and several mothers as well. Greta must have been single for a *very* long time to get this sort of response.

He flashed them his best million-dollar smile, and held his arm out to Greta.

"You're really DJ Force?" asked one of the moms. *Oh.* That was not exactly where he thought this was going. Still a quite strange sensation to be recognized, and this was not exactly the crowd he expected it from either.

"Oh, yes, he is." It was Greta's turn to flash her pearly whites. Fine then. If she thought he was going to be thrown off by some fans on wheels, well. She hadn't truly seen him in his element.

"Mina, love, where are you?" He pulled her to the front. She was absolutely glowing with pride. "Since *someone* didn't tell me it was your birthday—" he turned to narrow his eyes and received an innocent shrug—"I didn't bring you a present. Give me a moment, then?"

He glided over to the DJ, a teenager who instantly vacated the booth and pulled out his cell phone to record the goings-on.

Jon adjusted the microphone. "Mina?"

He queued up his big single, the one from the Thirst Competition soundtrack that he'd done with CeAnna, and turned off the vocals. Holding his hand out to help the child into his booth, he announced, "The birthday girl!"

As everyone cheered, she donned a very serious expression and then proceeded to rock the hell out of the vocals.

Well color me impressed. The kid could really go places with a set of pipes like that.

"It's hard to believe I had any part in making her," came a voice from Jon's left. He glanced over and was startled to see Bob had let his phone drop to stare at his daughter sashaying and singing. "Her mother used to sing just like that. And she's the spitting image . . . it's hard to even look at her a lot of days without seeing my wife."

Jon didn't know what to say. "I'm sorry for your loss, mate." The other man shook his head a little.

"Well, everyone's got to go sometime, right? Excuse me, I'm going to take this." Bob pressed the phone to his ear again and walked off, looking rather relieved at the interruption. Jon had the impression he hadn't quite meant to say all of that.

But speaking of impressions. He glanced over at the bench he'd left Greta next to. She was still there, but instead of smiling at the parent crowd, she was gazing back at him. With a fairly adoring expression, if he was reading it right. Which he totally was. He sped it up, and—

Beat drop.

Mina carried on without a second's hesitation, finishing out and then seguing right into the next track, one originally recorded with male vocals.

Greta was still giving him The Eye. Oh yeah. They were totally doing it tonight.

"We are *not* doing it tonight!" Greta panted in between the kind of all-encompassing kisses where no one can stop moving their hands over the other and neither can catch their breath and people with more talent than she had wrote songs about. "At least not in the alley behind the skating rink."

"Who ever said anything about doing it in an alley?" Jon said, reasonably. And yet she knew that's what he was hoping for. Not because she was psychic, but because he was hard and continually trying to hoist her dress up. Not a tough extrapolation, even for someone as bad at math as she.

"Yeah, you're doing that thing again," she reminded him. He broke away from her lips and stared hungrily into her eyes.

"I am certain I don't know what you're talking about, love." His voice was lilting and accented and goddamnit she definitely kissed him first that time because goddamnit it really wasn't fair that he'd speak to her like that and give Mina the best present ever and just—arg. Greta hated the spotlight more than anything, but definitely that had to be the most exciting moment for a little girl more used to being overlooked.

"That thing. Where what you say. And do. Don't

equal out." She was panting, and no longer quite as concerned about making her point than she was about enjoying this very hot alley make-out session.

Her palms were on his scruff and his tongue was inside of her teeth. Holy shit she was dizzy. Was it possible she was still tipsy? No. This was all the effects of kissing Jon Hargrave. Who knew DJ Force could have so much control over her? Almost as if he was using the Force himself—no. *This is no time to let your nerdgirl out. Just enjoy the moment.*

Her tongue rasped against his, and then he pulled back and nipped her slightly. She delved back for more as his hands tangled in her hair, and more again as her own slid up his back. Her fingers tangled in his shaggy blonde locks, while the other hands' nails sank into his muscular delts. Ugh, his muscles were so tight, ridiculously so for a man who made his living with a turntable. He must work out. She never knew why women went in for that look until now.

Her fingers kneaded into him. It was almost like a collapse, the way he just surrendered to her. It was so sexy, even though she knew it probably had a lot more to do with the fact that he likely had massive knots than that he'd been somehow waiting for the right girl to touch him in the right way.

Jon rewarded her with his thumbs on her nipples, hands down the top of her dress, those record-spinning calluses roughing her up and causing her nipples to react almost violently. He pinched just a little and she gave a little mew.

She arched into his lips, just as he bent to gently lick her breasts. It sent a thrill down her back, and she pushed further into him. His mouth closed over one dusky pink nipple and tugged with his whole being. She actually would have used the word "squee" to describe the noise she made. *Jiminy.*

His tongue traced circles around first one and then the other. Greta's breasts felt heavy in his mouth, his hands increasing pressure everywhere his mouth wasn't. It sent bolts of lightning straight down her body, and she could feel herself getting wet. Since when had foreplay been so sexy?

It was not like Greta had experienced foreplay since like—high school. That was basically depressing too, though, because who leaves foreplay behind with high school? Evidently she did. Besides Oliver, she could count on one hand the men who'd brought her to orgasm. Okay. Full disclosure. Oliver was the *only* man who'd ever given her an orgasm. In retrospect, that probably explained much of her attachment to him.

Goddamnit, all over again. That was embarrassing even in her head. She pushed Jon off. His head moved back from her chest, his eyes moved up to study hers. Why couldn't she resist that stare? With a moan, she stopped resisting.

His all-knowing fingers moved down the backs of her thighs and her back sank into the bricks of the alley wall. This time when Jon lifted the skirt of her dress, she didn't fight him. Nor did she resist when he pulled her lacey boyshorts down, and she definitely,

definitely did not make a move to stop him when he flattened his tongue against her and began to lick.

Wow. He didn't dance around, he went straight for her core, applying pressure and heat. Greta put her hand over her mouth to keep from moaning aloud. Her breath caught as he flicked over her clit.

She pushed her palms into the wall to brace herself, and hitched a leg over his shoulder. He worked his way from her entrance up to the base of her soft curls, using one hand to spread her further open. Her head lolled back as he drew circles around the spot she wanted him most.

Slowly, he drew her all the way into his mouth, sucking gently. Her legs were shaking with the force of holding back her orgasm. When he slipped a finger inside her, she stiffened, ready to come. He pulled out, holding her off for just a moment. His tongue moved faster over the sensitive nerves, and she felt his finger back inside. And another.

Greta clenched around him and came like fireworks, biting down on her hand but failing to keep all the noise inside. At least it was muffled. She could hardly catch her breath as he eased out of her, dropping one last kiss that made her gasp.

"Ssh, ssh, love," Jon laughed. "Can't be caught doing it in an alley behind the skating rink." She should have been annoyed—it was his idea after all—but she wasn't even sure she could continue standing, much less argue.

If this was *not* doing it tonight, she could live with that.

She bent down to pull up her panties when a scuffling noise from the end of the alley made her stomach drop.

There, backlit from the streetlights, stood the DJ from inside. Complete with his camera phone in hand.

Oh my God. I have a sex tape.

Chapter 6

Jon raced down the alley, as Greta contemplated the potential ramifications. Best case scenario: she became Kardashian-famous, parlaying her sexy stint into a reality show, clothing line, and signature perfume. Worst case: fired, disowned, publically humiliated.

One certainly seemed more likely than the other, but Greta had always considered herself an optimist.

-*Have unwittingly created sex tape. Unclear if ruined or need agent.* She quickly thumbed out a group text to Summer and Amy and waited. She didn't wait long.

-*OMFG CALL A LAWYER* Summer responded, just as Amy's came through.

-*if i'd known u were doing that i could have given u tips*

-*But I didn't know, that's the whole point!* The

more she thought about it, the less certain she was that fame and fortune would result.

-*Out of curiosity, though, I may need those tips later.* She added thoughtfully.

-*NOPE JUST LAWYER* came Summer.

-*i'll pm u grl* Amy typed.

Greta began to consider the pros and cons again. On one hand, it was probably good to know what one's sex faces looked like so that one could adjust them to their most attractive. On the other, her mother would most certainly kill her. And her sisters would help. And there was a decent chance her brothers-in-law would kill Jon.

But there would be a public record of the hands-down best oral ever, and she could relive it any time she wanted to. But, again, there would be a public record that any old skeeve could relive anytime they wanted to.

It was dark, and she'd been covering half her face, so there was actually a really good chance no one would ever be able to tell it was her. But what if, God forbid, Mina accidentally saw it?

Nope. The sex tape had to go. Anyway, Greta never would have survived a reality show. She was too private.

-*WTF ARE YOU GOING TO TELL US THE STORY OR WHAT* buzzed Summer's text.

-*Later. Yes.*

-*Lol i expect a copy of the tape plz* Hah, Greta thought, it'd be screened at the next Green Guerillas fundraiser, no doubt. Speaking of—she checked the time—that would be over by now.

-*Did you make any money tonight, Amy?*
-*WHY ARE WE TALKING ABOUT AMY*
-*lolol very little $ but very much fun thx for bringing hot dj*

She had to admit. It did feel sort of nice to show up with someone to these events. And it wasn't like she was showing up with just anyone. Even people who didn't recognize DJ Force still knew he was crazy good-looking, and that was pretty cool. There was a little thrill of delight that went through her knowing she was the object of other women's envy.

Tonight she'd been cornered by three different people demanding to know where she'd met him. "My sister's wedding," she'd answered, and left it at that. No doubt about it, she'd picked the best possible fake-date. She had amazing taste.

Well. Amy and Summer had. But they wouldn't have picked him if she hadn't been scoping him, so she felt she got partial credit anyway.

And she still felt deliciously warm and relaxed from her tryst, regardless of the current weirdness. Which bore some more thinking about as well. A mere few days ago, Greta had sworn she wasn't even going to kiss the guy. Then she'd had such a great experience kissing him that it was awfully easy to have done it again tonight.

And the man knew what he was doing when it came to a woman's body, no doubt about that. It had been so long since Greta had experienced that, she had forgotten to miss it.

But after this? No way was she settling back into a

dry spell. So what was a girl to do? She supposed the simplest—if anything about this could be considered simple—plan was the best.

They'd just have to be fake dates with benefits.

It would lend more credence to their pretend relationship, after all, if people saw them occasionally get a little handsy. It was becoming very easy to justify more orgasms. But who didn't want more of those? No, this was a good idea, she just hadn't seen it before.

After all, there was no danger of emotional entanglement. Not on her end, at least. She made a mental note to remind Jon that she wasn't really available.

Speaking of Jon, what was taking him so long? Was he fighting the DJ? Was he winning? Greta didn't know what the protocol was here. Should she go look for him, or stay and wait?

-In alley, waiting for co-star to return, ideally with tape. Send snacks.

-OMFG GET OUT OF THE ALLEY

-WHY ARE YOU IN AN ALLEY

-WHO EVEN ARE YOU ANYMORE

-lolololol i need snacks for this thread

-This night has really been a roller coaster. Greta realized even that was putting it mildly.

-BUT ARE YOU STILL ALONE IN AN ALLEY

-THE LACK OF HYGIENE INVOLVED CONCERNS ME AS MUCH AS THE TAPE

Just then, Jon came jogging back around the corner with a grin on his face. He wasn't even winded, and there was no visible blood anywhere. Greta was impressed with his fighting skills. He must have just demolished that kid in no time flat. Very impressive for a DJ.

"You know martial arts?" She hoped it was that, and not that he had some sort of weapon concealed about his person. Though surely she would have noticed? She'd thought he was just happy to see her, but it really could have been a gun in his pocket.

"Uh, no. I offered him some tickets to next week's show with CeAnna if he erased it." Jon looked more amused than she thought he should at the whole situation.

"So to be clear, my boss will never find my sex tape online?" She felt she needed to steer the conversation back towards the potential gravity, despite having had the thoughts she had before.

"You're safe from internet-porn-fame for now." He wrapped her into a hug, surrounding her with his familiar seafaring scent. "Shall I escort you home, then?" She nodded her assent. "And perhaps escort you out tomorrow?" She paused, then nodded again. They needed to do plenty of public dating to prove to her friends she was giving it a real go.

"I'm going to have the girls meet us," she told him. Considering he knew full well these weren't real dates, she still could have sworn he looked mildly disappointed.

"Fine, but we're continuing on without them afterwards." Greta's nipples tightened.

"No can do. I only have a little time off. Bob's got a 'business' trip." This time, she felt a little disappointed too.

-*All clear, tape destroyed, headed home.* If she didn't let the girls know, Summer would be out personally patrolling the streets soon.

-*YOU ARE WAY TOO CALM ABOUT THIS SHIT* On second thought, she might just do that anyway.

-*these texts had everything. good premise, plot twist, resolution. :)*

Well. That was true. For everywhere the night had taken her, she had to admit it was a good story.

"So your story is that you came straight home after my roller skating party?" Mina said suspiciously.

"That's my story. Yep." Greta avoided eye contact as she cracked a couple of eggs into a shallow bowl. No way was she revealing her misadventure, and not just because she was worried she'd come all over again just thinking about it.

"Because I really wanted to tell you about how Coco Barnes was so jealous that DJ Force showed up that she told everyone that Beyoncé was going to sing at *her* birthday party, only her stepmom heard her—you know, the one we're all not supposed to know was her nanny before—" Here Mina shot Greta a look that was simultaneously warning and hopeful.

Greta ignored it, and began to whisk milk into the eggs. They'd been over this story before. Obviously Mina had the fantasy of Greta being Mom too, but like hell was Greta hooking up with Bob. Nasty. Although Coco's dad was even worse. Who *were* these desperate women out there, dating all the creepy dads?

"I still can't believe your father made you invite that little twit," she mumbled, reaching for the nutmeg.

"He said if I was inviting the rest of my class that I had to invite Coco, but I think really it's because my dad is trying to get a meeting with her dad and her dad isn't returning my dad's calls." Greta paused to follow the thread, then nodded for Mina to continue.

"So her stepmom said, in front of *everyone*, that they weren't getting her Beyoncé, they were getting her a pony ride and a princess castle bounce house! Can you believe it? Do we have blueberries?" Mina was fairly giddy with her rival's public takedown. Not giddy enough to prevent her from backseat driving in the kitchen, though.

"No, I can't believe it," Greta said, though she really could. All these poor little rich girls were constantly involved in an elaborate game of putting on shows for each other. It was behavior you usually didn't see until the teenage years, at least not in the neighborhood *she* grew up in.

And it was sad.

"Well, maybe you could have believed it last night, but you were not in your bed when I jumped on it." *Busted.*

"Well, I mean. I maybe was outside talking to the girls when you went in." Greta busied herself slicing some leftover challah bread.

"Maybe. But I peeked out there too. Do we have the blueberries? And the good kind of syrup?" She was doing big-blinky-eyes now. Cute little monster was too nosy for her own good. What happened in the alley behind the skating rink was *staying* in the alley behind the skating rink, no thanks to one of the two DJ's present.

"Go look for yourself. Maybe I was in the garage." Greta was rapidly running out of hypothetical places she could have been.

"I'll look. But I guess I never know if I'll find them or not." Mina's blinky eyes were filled with faux innocence.

"Okay, *fine*. I stayed out a little bit later with Jon. Just a little bit, mind you. And I *did* spend some time talking to the girls." *About things you need never know about, little one.*

"I knew it, I knew it! You did kissing." Despite her prediction, the girl turned away from the fridge with a container of blueberries in one hand and a mini-jug of real Vermont maple syrup in the other.

"Says who?" Greta asked, indignant. Even though— well.

"Says your face."

Well *that* was impertinent. "Mina. That was very impertinent."

"No it wasn't. Your face is bright red. That's how I know you did kissing." Oh. Well. Huh. Looked like she didn't even have to relive the scene to get all verklempt.

"Okay. Fine *again*. We did kissing." Greta narrowed her eyes at Mina before tossing their French toast on the griddle.

"So?" Mina asked, leaning forward.

"So *what*?" She flipped the bread, perfectly golden.

"Was it gross?" *Good kid.* Even though it was so

beyond amazing. So amazing that she was literally floating around cooking French effing toast right now.

"It wasn't really gross. But that's only because he has his cootie shot, which boys don't get until they are eighteen, so don't think about kissing any yourself until then. Hand me your plate."

"What if I got a cootie shot early?" Mina hedged.

"What if getting it early made you come down with a raging case of cooties instead?" Curiosity was not a good thing in some cases.

"What if it didn't, though? What if I kissed Ethan Sedger?" Mina focused very hard on sprinkling the powdered sugar.

"Ethan Sedger? That little turd?" Greta broke the only rule of the what-if game. But really, that kid was such a shit. There had been the hitting incident last year, the time he mooned the teacher last month, and just two weeks ago had pulled the wings off a butterfly at recess in front of a crowd of horrified third-graders.

"He's not a turd." Mina giggled at the word. "He's cute."

"He's a turd. Remember the time he farted so much in story time that your teacher had to cancel it for the day? And he was so proud of himself. Just like a man." Greta frowned at her toast. Maybe this wasn't breakfast conversation.

"That was so gross. But at my party we couple-skated and he offered to draw me a unicorn picture and now I like him."

Greta considered. As desperately attractive as hand-drawn unicorns could be, this was definitely not typical Mina. Ethan Sedger was a blonde-haired devil. Oh. A blonde-haired, green-eyed devil. A mini-Jon. Minus the faux-gentleman schtick. Oh dear. Now she understood.

She felt guilty in some nameless way all of a sudden. Poor kid just wanted to do what Greta was doing. She was obviously feeling left behind.

Or maybe she was reading too much into it, and Mina was just at an age where farting, creepy kids were funny. Doubtful, though. Good girls like her weren't generally impressed by butterfly maiming. Odds were quite good that the promised unicorn picture would also feature flying chainsaws, or some other such nastiness.

Greta cut a piece of her own gluten-free toast, too distracted to even wish it was challah, and chewed it methodically. She'd been so certain that Jon was not a good role model for Mina, but maybe she wasn't either. And comparatively, Jon had swept the girl off her feet by performing at her party, whereas Greta had done an entirely different sort of performance. Oh, no, she was the worse one right now.

"Let's go out tomorrow afternoon, just me and you." They'd be cultural, or something. Role model stuff. It would be the perfect way to spend the day before her evening faking it with Jon and the girls.

"Can we have ice cream?" Kids. Well, as a role model, her first task was clear.

"No. We will be having Thai." She ate another piece of syrup-drenched toast, feeling rather virtuous at the prospect of curried veg.

"You don't know how to have fun," Mina grumbled. Greta considered the previous evening's misadventures.

"No, I definitely do." She was a goddamn fun machine.

"Wait, you thought a nine year old was going to have fun at the Contemporary Jewish Museum's display of Jewish artifacts?" Summer looked pained.

"I'm the biggest museum-goer I know, and even I know better than to take a small child there. A small gentile at that. Didn't you think to check the exhibit first? Shame the Amy Winehouse one is over. You're an artist, why didn't you just take her to the MOMA?" Amy said. "I mean. Really." She stared at her friend. Greta closed her eyes briefly. If even *Amy* couldn't find a way to be on her side, than she had certainly been misguided in her attempts at role modeling. Oy vey.

"It was a good idea, though. I mean, the girl has no mother. I thought maybe it would be a way to impart some of my own heritage on her. Loads of cool chicks from history are featured there. My intentions were good!" Greta protested. It could have been solid. If the exhibit hadn't been dryer than stale matzah. Even *she* was bored, but then again, she had interesting things to think about.

"And we all know what the road to hell is paved with." Summer took the edge off her comment with a grin. Greta stuck out her tongue. She might have been working on being a better adult, but that didn't take away any of the satisfaction a childlike response gave her.

Amy just laughed at both of them, as per her usual.

"Now, birds, she quickly realized the error of her ways," Jon chimed in with her defense. Annoyingly, because at least one of her friends should have done that. What was the saying Amy always used? Uteruses before duderuses. She giggled at the thought, then silenced herself before anyone asked what was so funny.

"Not the error of *all* her ways, Logan O'Toole," Summer said with a wink. Greta was pretty sure she was talking about a porn star.

Greta was delighted to see Jon's face pale a bit. Did he really think she didn't tell them literally everything? Oh. Okay, well maybe she *had* set a precedent for not telling them *everything*, exactly.

"I'd prefer Ron Jeremy, then, if it's all the same to you." He recovered quickly, she'd give him that. Yup, definitely porn. Greta blushed.

"Ew! Why?" Amy said what they were all thinking, as usual. "Logan O'Toole is the cute one."

"And he loves food," Summer added dreamily.

"Because Ron Jeremy has been around forever. I'd like to think I have staying power, myself." He lifted a single brow at Greta as he spoke. Innuendos, again. She kicked him under the table. Missed. Hit Amy. Shrugged at her.

"More margaritas?" she asked, hoping to change the subject from porn and peen and Jon. Hoping even further that at some point she would stop thinking about those things herself. When Summer had texted her this afternoon to ask measurements, Greta was surprised to learn that she was disappointed she didn't yet have the scoop on Little Jon. Naturally, she'd texted back a gif of zipped lips.

Yet. It was inevitable, even she could see that. Once she had decided they could be fake-dates-plus, it was only a matter of time until she saw him naked. And from what she had felt, it would not disappoint. Now that she knew it was indeed his manhood and not a gun.

Jon signaled the waiter for another round. Her eyes lingered just a moment too long on the shape of his arm in the air, muscles clearly defined beneath his ultra-thin cotton shirt. Amy kicked her beneath the table, evidently thinking it was a "look at him" move. Better than her realizing it was a "shut up already" move, so Greta went with it, winking at her friend.

"Anywho, Mina was bored like three minutes in, so I said we could just go to Ripley's Believe It Or Not instead. I did *not* cave on the ice cream though. So, like—half role model? Just the role?" She made a silly face.

"More like just a model," Jon said, that well-shaped arm suddenly just in front of her and his finger tracing a line down her cheekbone. Greta flushed, and glanced away. Her friends were both looking on approvingly, so she turned back to Jon and favored him with a smile. It *was* pretty cute. He was good at this.

But that was another thing that bugged her. He didn't know her well enough to really *like*-like her, so it had to be acting on his part too. And he pretended it wasn't. The signs pointed towards a man who wasn't the gentleman he claimed to be.

Although for the life of her, Greta couldn't pinpoint a single ungentlemanly trait about the guy. And damn it, she was trying. The first sign of impropriety meant she could stop with this charade.

Okay, maybe she wasn't trying that hard. They hadn't gotten to the benefits bit yet, after all. Might as well leave the party with a parting gift.

"I used to get the Ripley's show on telly back home. I quite liked it, actually. I'd say young boys always gravitate towards the macabre, but really, I think people in general do. It's just that some people indulge themselves, and then there's those who pretend they are above it."

Everyone sort of nodded. For them, it was Greta who embraced it, Summer who secretly did, and Amy who stuck her fingers in her ears and sang 'lalala' when anything gross or weird or scary came up.

"So when we moved here, literally the first thing I did was make mum take me to the museum."

The way he said it was 'LIT-rah-lee.' His accent *literally* obliterated an entire syllable. It made her want to kiss him again. Badly.

Oh, fuck it. Fake date with bennies, right? She cut him off mid-sentence and pressed her lips to his. Amy cooed, and she could even hear Summer do a little "aw". Mostly, though, all she could focus on was the feel of his soft lips, the way they smirked—she could feel it—when she kissed him, but how quickly he returned it, as if he'd been waiting.

She didn't quite want to French him in front of her friends, but the chaste lips-together kiss wasn't enough. What was the 90's movie thing? Church tongue.

Jon's mouth opened, and she gave just enough of hers to allow a brush of his tongue against hers. Even though that was supposed to keep things comfortable, it felt like a tease. A tease that made her squirm a little in her chair, longing for more.

"So was it everything you hoped it would be?" Amy asked as they parted.

"And more," Jon replied, but he was looking at Greta and she had to admit. That Thing he did was growing on her, just a little.

As long as she remembered it was all for her benefit that they kept up the act.

As long as she remembered what happened to girls who fell in love.

When you fall, you eventually hit the rocks at the bottom.

Jon was being annoying. He could tell, even to himself. His poor friends were waiting at the beer bar they favored, and even Rust had told him not to bother showing until he was done humming to himself and checking his phone endlessly for the messages that weren't quite coming yet, but were surely forthcoming.

In the space of a few dates and one ill-advised back-alley hook-up, Greta had gone from an interesting *bet* to be won, to someone he was desperate to win *over*. Every new thing he learned about her made him crave more.

He hummed some more, something silly from the radio that had been on once when they were in a restaurant, and now was inextricably linked to her in his head. He was going to text *her*, was what he was going to do.

-Hey you.

He hummed again, this time throwing a few dance moves into the mix. Oh, here was a good idea, he should call Angie and cash in on the beers she owed him. Surely she and Matt were done honeymooning by now? They'd been buddies for a while now, but now they were taking on a whole new sheen as people who knew everything about the girl he liked. He was desperate to hang out with them and talk about her. Since she wasn't exactly making herself that available and all.

But the fact that she did that—it had been exactly four minutes since his text and there was no response— was something he respected. She had her own life, she didn't rely on him for things. He sent a group text to her sister and brother-in-law.

-Matt, Ang. When can I collect my beers? I'm ready to get sozzled on your dime, as Greta and I are now an official item.

-Oh, my friend. Good luck to you. Came an immediate response from Matt.

-Not only do we owe you beers, you're going to need them. How did-nvmd. Toronado in 30. Angie was only marginally more diplomatic. That didn't matter. Maybe she didn't understand quite what a catch her little sister was. It can be hard to see family the way everyone else does.

-Is our end of the bet over so fast? We all know "an item" will last like a week. Matt could be very cold.

-We really only put beers on the "can't trade numbers" thing tho. And he'll tell us deets soon.

-I know for certain you two are sitting next to each other having this conversation about me in front of me. Call a cab already, I'll be at the bar. For heaven's sake. The cute couple thing. He could see how it was annoying, particularly to a man like Rust, but wasn't it just a tad bit appealing, too? Having someone who sat next to you, had your back, laughed at your stupid jokes. How was that not a thing to aspire to?

It helped, of course, if your intended was a tiny, gorgeous brunette who could paint like a master and kiss like an angel. Jon hummed his way through the Uber summons. It didn't even matter she hadn't written back. She was busy. That was cool.

Later, at the bar, Angie and Matt were slightly more specific with their concerns over delicious sour beers. Of which Jon may have had a couple too many, which may have prevented him from truly ingesting what they were trying to say.

"She *is* an amazing girl, we aren't arguing that," Matt had said.

"She's just not the dating kind of girl, is what we're getting at," Angie had chimed in.

"She's not really into men, is the thing," Matt started, but Angie hit him.

"She's not gay!"

"No, no, not gay, but not into men. They don't have to be the same thing, exactly. How do I explain this?" Matt looked at Angie.

"By saying she had a really difficult time with our father leaving? And then she quickly decided after a few boyfriends that all guys prefer to love and leave. It isn't that hard to explain. You're such a typical dude. If she's not interested in dating, she's probably into chicks, you think." Angie hit him again, but this time more gently, and with a soft look in her eye.

Greta might have been sour on men, but this sour beer was definitely affecting Jon. It was so flipping cute to watch his mate and his girl argue gently over *his* girl. He sighed. So she hadn't texted back, it didn't mean they were right. Although, it probably did mean he should text again. After all, if she thought all men loved and left, she was probably just ignoring him because of the hookup. She probably expected him to ignore her back. It made him a little sad.

-Busy tonight? Or tomorrow. We have real dating to do. I am going to date the shit out of you. And by dating, I mean third-dating.

There, that should give no doubt as to his meaning. The alley wasn't nearly enough. Jon was ready to take his time with her, show her exactly how amazing he found her. He gazed over at his friends, still bickering, and held up his glass for a refill. What a night. What a life! Who knew playing weddings could lead to such an opportunity?

-Nope.

Well, okay, that was an emphatic no. That was fine.

-The next day then. I am going to third-date you like you have never been third-dated before.

Yep. Greta could hardly even handle him. Matt and Angie would be in awe of his lady-skills. Both of them would suspect it was what was in his trousers that had swayed Greta as he had, but neither of them could prove it. He may insinuate they were correct, even, but it was definitely his charm. And his gentlemanly ways. The trousers were merely a bonus. Jon was drunk.

-Nope.

Hard to get it was, then. This called for more beer. He looked down at his glass. Still full. He drained it, and ordered another. This called for another bet, then.

"How much beer do I get for marrying her?" he interrupted. They fell silent and stared.

"Literally every beer," said Angie, in awe.

"For the rest of your life," said Matt, in doubt.

Never paying for a beer ever again. *Beat drop.*

"Wanna shake on it?" He asked.

Chapter 7

Greta plopped a fizz bomb in the tub, and turned on the tap. She'd been out too much lately. Making sure her friends kept seeing her with Jon, and then actually being with Jon, and then trying to be more involved with Mina was just exhausting.

The whole point of not dating was that she wanted to keep her alone time.

She couldn't even remember the last time she'd gotten to read a book in the tub, and that used to happen at least three times a week. Well, four. Okay, five. Whatever, it was her happy place. There was a door slam from downstairs. Bob's feet clattered up the stairs and back down. It sounded like he'd gone back out. Probably forgot something. Her day was done, though.

Stretching, Greta yawned, and pulled her dress over her head. Yes, this was long overdue. She eased into the steaming, jasmine-scented water, and sighed. She reached for the glass of wine balanced on the edge of the tub and took a long sip. Perfect. Well, almost perfect—she grabbed the paperback waiting for her on the other side of the tub. Now it was perfect. And then her phone buzzed.

-Decided to take a trip. Left Mina $ on my desk. Back soon! From Bob. *What the hell*? Greta wasn't even sure what was making her the most pissed about this.

-Where? Back when? And you haven't paid me for last week yet. She waited, getting more and more annoyed. This was so typical. He obviously knew he was going to take this mystery trip in advance, why was it so hard to tell *her* in advance too? And he had been late on her last three paychecks running.

Another sip of wine, followed by a heavy sigh. She turned back to her book, but read the same paragraph several times before tossing the book over the edge and back to the floor.

So much for relaxing.

Buzz.

-Mexico. Back next Saturday. Sorry about that, forgot. Forgot. Right. More like was too busy lusting after whoever it was this week—Cyndi, she thought—to consider what his responsibilities were. It was utterly beyond Greta how the man managed to run a successful company. She supposed he just delegated all of his work responsibilities the same way he delegated the home ones.

Her wineglass was suddenly, inexplicably empty. The water was cooling down. The book remained unread. This relaxing evening in seemed to have done nothing but spike her blood pressure.

Maybe she should have gone with Jon after all.

No, no, that was not what she meant. She meant maybe she should have grabbed the wine bottle, perhaps a top off on both the drink and the bath would soothe her.

Except now she was on the clock, so a second glass was kind of out of the question. May as well hop out and check on the kiddo. She flipped the drain with her big toe and reached for a towel. The good news was that she got paid extra when Bob was gone, so even though it was going to be a late check, it would be a big one.

Fantasizing about the fresh art supplies she could buy at Flax calmed her considerably, even when she recalled that Wednesday was supposed to be a day off for her that had just been unceremoniously revoked. Again. She pulled on a camisole and shorts and wandered down the hall towards Mina's room.

The hall clock showed that it was after her bedtime, but there was a light under her door.

"Mina?" Greta called softly. There was a little sniffle from inside, so she turned the knob and peeked in. Mina was sitting up in bed clutching a stuffed bear. It was pretty clear she'd been crying.

"Hey, kiddo. What's wrong?" Greta sat on the end of the bed.

"He left without saying goodbye to me," the little girl said, fresh tears rolling down her cheeks as she said it.

"He probably thought you were asleep. I thought you were, too, I just came to make sure you were all tucked in." Greta hated that she felt compelled to make excuses for Bob, but it seemed like a better alternative than Mina knowing how little regard he really seemed to have for her.

"He knows I'm awake. I said, 'Dad, where are you going?' when I heard him pulling his suitcase, and he said, 'Not now, princess,' and left." She squeezed the bear tighter.

And then sometimes it was absolutely impossible to make excuses for the man. It was one thing for the people around him to notice that his daughter was an afterthought, but this was basically him telling her that. No wonder she was crushing on the school bully. She was desperate for someone to pay attention to her.

If she were Mina's mom, she'd make sure the kid knew someone cared about her every single moment of every single day, not just when it was convenient.

Even at the birthday party Bob threw, he spent the entire time in a corner talking on the phone, hardly even making a cameo for the candle blowing.

"You know what, we're going to have more fun without him. We'll have so much fun, he'll wish he'd stayed home." Greta had no idea exactly what it was she was going to do that would be that kind of fun, but she'd figure out something—and resign herself to the fact that she wasn't getting a relaxing bath night again for at least a week.

"Really? That much fun?" Mina's tears appeared to be drying.

"Yep. I'll be a fun machine this week." Greta made a mental note to do some googling about how to pull that off. Her track record was bad, and it seemed bad form to give Mina wine and a book for her bath. *Give it a few years, kid.*

"So what you're saying is, I get ice cream." Damn, but she was good at this.

"You get ice cream," Greta confirmed. "Now go to sleep. It's your last week of school, and we aren't going to have oodles of fun if you're overtired." Mina snuggled up to the bear and allowed Greta to switch off her lamp.

"I love you," she murmured from her blanket nest.

"Sweet dreams," Greta answered.

"Bad news," was the first thing Greta said when she answered.

"What?" Jon never knew how to react to a statement like that. People should color code the badness of the news like fire-danger levels, he'd often reflected. Bad news could mean anything from running out of coffee to finding a lump, depending whom you were talking to. If one's companion said, 'Bad news—orange' it gave one a better idea of how much to brace.

"Bob up and left town in the middle of the night, so I'm on duty all week. I know I told you we'd do our date sometime this week, but I can't now." Was it his imagination, or did she sound genuinely sorry? He *knew* he'd been wearing her down.

When she'd kissed him at happy hour in front of her friends, that hadn't been planned. He could tell she was genuinely charmed by his childhood love of Ripley's. What a girl, that confessing his utter fascination with things like shrunken heads and giant robots would get her excited. She was something special, all right. Jon sighed with satisfaction, before recalling what she'd just said.

"It's okay. I'll go out with you two this week, and we can do a twofer when Bob arrives home." He quite liked that little kid she watched. She fancied shrunken heads and giant robots too. It made him wonder, if he and Greta had a child one day, would it be like wee Mina? Kids had mostly been an abstract concept to him before dating a nanny. Something to consider in the future, but watching the tender way Greta cared for Mina made him wonder if someday mightn't come sooner than later.

A memory of making a marriage bet with her sister slammed into him, and he almost groaned out loud. He didn't regret it—Greta was absolutely the type of woman he'd like to settle down with—but she'd absolutely murder him for betting on her again, wouldn't she?

"A twofer?" Greta giggled. She had a great laugh, one that sort of exploded out. She had a habit of tossing her head back when she did it, as though her mirth would not be contained.

"That's right, you may attempt to torture me with your bizarre choices twice in a row. And then you can pretend you haven't spent the whole time fantasizing about me laying you down like a record." He could almost hear the blush spread up her cheeks.

"Jon Hargrave. I do not fantasize about you." She didn't sound very convincing, so he kept going.

"Lies. You spend all night dreaming of me. I can tell." He trailed a hand lightly down his torso. Just the thought of her tight body, wearing some sort of skimpy nightie, lying in bed thinking of him caused an immediate physical reaction

"I do not. I can't fantasize about a man who calls himself DJ Force." What? Now those were fighting words. His hand stopped moving south.

"Do you mean to tell me that you aren't a follower of the One True Religion—Star Wars?" He'd thought she was special, but this could be a deal-breaker. His ex-girlfriend Leah hadn't enjoyed any of the classics either, and he'd sworn never again.

"Wait, your DJ name is a *Star Wars* reference?" She burst out with that cute laugh again. "Thank God! I thought it was meant to be some sort of reference to the power of dance, or something silly like that."

Oh, dear. Was that what people thought? He hadn't considered that angle. But then, if Lady Gaga could go by that moniker and be that lauded, than he supposed it truly didn't matter what anyone assumed of his own stage name. In fact, one could suppose that the more pedestrian one's name sounded, the more likely the average Joe was to give it a listen.

"Well. No. And anyways, it's rather difficult to invent a DJ name, isn't it?" True story. Anyone could come up with a semi-reasonable band name, but finding a one or two word construction to toss behind "DJ" was nearly impossible.

"I can't say I'd know. Although I'll admit, I'm judging you less harshly in my mind right about now." That was his cue to pick back up.

"That means you've mentally added another inch to my todger." He unzipped his jeans and pulled it out. In fact, he'd been told on a number of occasions that it was excellently sized. His words, not theirs. "Excellently sized" would be an odd thing to say whilst in the throes of passion.

"That was not even remotely what I was thinking." She was silent for a moment.

"But now you are, right?" She sighed heavily at his question.

"Yes." *Score.* He felt himself twitch a little, dick growing in response to her attentions. His hand began to stroke it gently.

"I can confirm your suspicions any time you'd like." Even to his own ears, his voice had deepened with desire. He was fully erect now, fingers wrapped around his shaft. Imagining Greta imagining him, maybe even touching herself in the same way he was . . . he pumped faster, letting out a short puff of air as the first wave of pleasure rolled through his body.

"Jon? What are you doing?" Her voice was suspicious. Perhaps he'd misread the situation slightly.

A gentleman never kisses and tells. Or jerks off and tells. He hung up on her.

Freed of that, he set the phone down and closed his eyes. Leaning back in his desk chair, he let the fantasy play out before his eyes.

Greta, lying on his bed, fingers busy working in and

out of her tight pussy. A quiet moan escaping her lips as she watched him watching her. His fist moved up and down as he pictured her nipples hardening, breasts bouncing as her hand moved faster. She'd lick her lips. Those lips, so full and soft, that he wanted wrapped around his cock. Her little pink tongue swirling around the head before drawing him deeply into her mouth.

With a load groan, Jon came as hard as he imagined he would when his fantasy became reality. He was still panting when the phone rang.

"Oh, I'm glad you called back. Got bad connection here, lately," he lied. "When shall I meet you, and where?"

Greta leaned back against the fountain in Ghirardelli Square. It was easier than she thought to be the Purveyor of Childhood Fun when she realized Mina had never really done any of the classic San Francisco things most kids repeat yearly for every out of town visitor.

"Dad says the Square is a tourist trap," Mina had explained.

"Well it *is*, but you can't live here and not have experienced our hometown chocolate. It's appalling."

"Dad says it's mediocre at best." Her hopeful expression said that she didn't believe in the concept of mediocre chocolate. Who did?

"Your dad doesn't even eat chocolate. What does he know? And guess what you can buy there," Greta said, having successfully smothered the urge to call *Bob* mediocre at best. "Ice cream." That had clinched it.

Mina was so excited she'd almost forgotten to make kissy faces at the news Jon would be joining them. *Almost* forgotten.

The sun was beating down. Greta had given her charge a handful of coins to wish on in the fountain as they waited. Idly, she wondered what the wishes were.

Personally, most of hers would involve a lottery-like windfall that would enable her to buy a small loft with a huge bathtub. Some built-in bookshelves, a wine cooler, and a sternly protective doorman would be necessary as well, of course. Loads of sex with Jon without ever needing to follow up on it. Just the simple things, really.

Her own personal Fortress of Solitude, it was basically all she'd ever wanted.

A shadow fell over her and she opened her eyes to see Jon, with Mina already clinging to him like a barnacle.

"Hullo, love." He smiled. Ugh, but he was gorgeous. The usual uniform of a short-sleeved button down and jeans was more endearing every time she saw him. And the slightly crooked smile when he saw her was definitely working its charm on her.

"Hey," she said, stretching out a hand for him to help her up. Her tattoo shone in the sun, and it gave her a little start to realize what a couple they'd look like if anyone noticed the matching design on him.

"Nah, stay there. Little One and I are going to pop in for an ice cream, we'll be right back. What's your flavor?" He winked a jade-colored eye.

"I'm fine, thanks. Not big on the ice cream. Let me give you some cash." She started to fumble with her purse, but he stopped her.

"A gentleman always buys the ice cream. Life lesson, darling, you'll not want to accept a second date from anyone who doesn't pay for the first," he addressed Mina. They ambled towards the chocolate shop as Greta closed her eyes again.

Regardless of how upset Mina would be when Greta got rid of Jon, it was really nice to see her this happy. And Greta also supposed that as long as he was behaving himself, there was nothing wrong with Mina seeing what a proper relationship should look like, unlike the weird, brief affairs her father was always having.

After all, he was completely right about paying for dates. Even uber-feminist Amy didn't fall for guys who asked her out and then wanted to go Dutch. Gentleman or not, at least he was imparting the rules of spotting one.

She caught herself and almost laughed out loud. She was holding up her fake relationship as an example of what a real relationship should look like. God, this was a complicated ruse she was pulling off. The hardest part was that there was not a soul she could confide in about it—except for Jon.

And he was hoping to get her mind changed about him, so he was biased already. It had only been a couple weeks since Angie's wedding, and her life had gotten infinitely more complicated—and annoying.

She cursed that damn pact every day. And the tequila

shots that made her feel it was a good plan. And come to think of it, she had a few choice words for her fifteen-year-old self as well. Plus a gazillion things to tell her big sister, once she'd gathered her thoughts.

Amy and Summer were lucky they all had such a history together, or she'd have told them to go take a long walk off a short pier after last week. Oh, who was she kidding? You can't dump your kindergarten besties. But you can tell your sternly protective fantasy doorman not to let them in. She pulled a nickel off the bottom of her purse and flipped it into the water, wishing fervently for a winning lotto ticket as it sank.

Her companions returned with double scoops of chocolate, and they began to wander around the square. It was crowded, and prime for people watching. Greta often considered that her favorite pastime, just behind painting and reading. And wine baths. And naps. Certainly a top-five pastime, anyway.

"Want some?" Jon offered his cone, dripping chocolate down onto his hand.

"Nah." Though she couldn't deny that the temptation to lick the stray melted custard off his hand had crossed her mind.

"Come on. Share with me. It's so hot." He winked at her again.

"It's getting to the point where I don't even know if you *know* you're doing that thing, Jon." Greta obliged him with a little lick of the cone. It was better than she'd thought it would be, rich and creamy and deeply chocolate.

He took a lick and handed it back. She took another. The third time, he surprised her by joining in. His tongue's heat startled against the smooth iciness. The sheer sexiness of him licking her while she was licking the cone made her shiver. Of course, she pretended it was the cold of the cone when Mina caught her eye.

Then Mina made the kissy face. *Busted. Again.* She simply had to get control of this Jon situation. It was spiraling quickly out of control. Just the previous day, she had been certain he was touching himself while he was talking to her. Of course, it was just a bad connection. But she couldn't shake the image, and by the time she'd locked herself in her room for the night, she hardly made it to the bed before bringing herself to orgasm picturing it.

That was not at all where her mind should be going, even if she had tentatively agreed with herself that sex could happen on occasion. Allowing thoughts of it to interrupt her day was completely antithetical to the idea of not dating seriously.

The whole point was to keep her life free of distraction, to keep things the same, the way she liked them. There was nothing at all comfortable about being forced out of one's comfort zone.

She refused the next lick.

Chapter 8

Greta was beside herself with irritation. Bob had come back earlier that afternoon as promised, but the whole week of fun she'd offered his daughter had left her broke and exhausted. Jon was calling in his date night, and she had run out of excuses to put him off.

If she were being honest, she'd even say that the thought of making out with him was starting to seem like a reward for her rough few days. After all, she'd decided that benefits were okay. But he'd just seemed so eager to jump into bed with her, and she had a lot of reservations about that. What if he went back on his word after? What if he really was, as she feared, just like every other guy?

If her fake relationship fell apart the same way as her real ones always had, the depths of her humiliation would be unmeasurable.

But wallowing in worry wasn't going to change the future.

The one bit of good news was that one of the childrens authors she had previously worked with had sent an email indicating he'd like to put together a proposal for another book. The standard on those was a storyboard with rough drawings indicating every page, and one or two finished illustrations.

The story itself looked just like something Greta would have loved to read as a child, about sisters whose house turned into a magical adventure land each night when their parents fell asleep. She had a hundred ideas about plants that would become people, shadows turning into cats, furniture becoming castles. A prince in disguise. Basically everything she'd lain awake at night imagining when she was small herself.

But paintings didn't create themselves, and when she wasn't working from life, it took even longer. Planning a composition wasn't quick work for a single page, and creating all thirty-six meant she needed every spare second she had to work.

How would she ever get out of Bob's house if she didn't get her career started? And how would she get it started if she couldn't devote herself to her art?

It was altogether frustrating. She could see that she'd brought all of this on herself, but she wasn't totally sure how anything could have happened differently. No amount of piratey British charm was going to improve her mood, and she had determined that Jon shouldn't have a good time either. So she'd purposely picked a date she could hardly participate in. It would hopefully be long and boring and thus deter him from calling in the second part of their doubleheader. If she got home before ten, she could work until one and still be up with Mina in the morning.

Now that school was out, she'd hoped the girl would take to sleeping in, just by an hour or so, but her previous experience with children had taught her that was usually a fruitless hope. She opened her closet and stared at the options.

Jon seemed to be very entranced by her vintage dresses, so she dressed very carefully tonight. In jeans.

He could hardly accuse her of doing it on purpose to dampen his ardor, because of the date she had arranged for them. It was hardly sexy. In fact, it could be called downright frumpy, she felt. She waited patiently outside the venue until he strolled up in his usual cloud of leather and lust.

"What's on the menu this evening then?" He asked, leaning in for a kiss. She was having none of it. It was time to begin unraveling this thing. *Before* the sex. Stupid idea, that, to think they could extend this to a physical situation. It was just too risky. She turned her head so that his lips landed on her cheek. Rather unfair, then, that even that bit of contact made her breath catch. Of course, *all* her poor decisions had been made while she was in close proximity to him.

"Funny you should phrase it like that," Greta said. "We're attending a baking class."

"I've always loved pie," he immediately said. "Especially apple. It's so . . . American." The way he was eying her left no room for doubt that the jeans had failed to rebuff him. Well, they *were* kind of sexy. But she didn't have any others. Even when she was painting, she tended to do it in sweats, or even just an old tee shirt.

"Not pie. Bread. Good old-fashioned San Francisco sourdough." She smiled and held the door for him. He trailed a finger along her tattoo as he walked inside. She shivered, but kept going.

Enough was enough. The weak-kneed feeling she kept getting over him was just that—weakness. She could be strong, and stick to her original plan. As long as she focused on the task at hand and not on the pleased grin he was giving her. He didn't know what he was in store for yet, but it *wasn't* going to be pleasing. He didn't yet seem to realize that a gluten-sensitive girl was going to make him do all the work but reap none of the rewards. In fact, calling it a date at all was a bit of a long shot. Greta planned to just watch him take the class and then take half the credit for the loaf she brought home to Mina.

"I can do sourdough. My lunch today was a toasted cheese on sourdough. Wouldn't the lads at the studio be impressed with me if I strolled in tomorrow with home-baked bread for snacks?" His optimism was boundless, and contagious if she didn't watch out.

She just wanted the evening to be over, her mind already conjuring up the images she wanted for each page of her proposal.

On the tucking-in scene, she'd have the magic world already popping up out of view of the parents, shadows of normal objects already distorted into their night-time shapes, maybe some mushrooms beginning to grow out of the corner of the closet—he'd said something.

"Huh?"

"I said, would you like an apron?" He didn't bother to wait for a response before settling the canvas cover-up over her and tying it behind her. He also didn't bother trying to disguise how much pleasure he took in groping her ass a little while he was behind her. Greta reminded herself that it was not okay to back into him and give a little wiggle.

She did it anyway, but she definitely also reminded herself it wasn't okay. This struggle between her mind and her ladybits was getting old real fast.

Seriously, she had walked into this bakery frustrated and anxious, muscles tight. A few tiny little moments of contact between them later, and her spirits were rising like yeasted dough. And it was all well and fine for him to be a pick-me-up, but if she *needed* Jon for that, there were a couple things wrong.

For one, she absolutely knew better than to rely on a man for her happiness. Even her own father had chosen not to make that a priority, so why would anyone else? After all, Amy and Summer made her happy too. Watching reruns of Sherlock with Mina made her happy. Being alone with her Kindle made her happy.

Why invite heartbreak in when she had so many other options?

For another, if he became the source of relaxation in her life, she'd truly never have time for painting, or reading, or a second (third) glass of wine because she'd always be chasing the next orgasm.

She sighed audibly, remembering the last one he'd given her, and the one she'd given herself thinking about him. The only way to move past that was to dust off her vibrator and spend some time with her Tumblr account of Tom Hiddleston and David Tennant pictures. *Uh oh*. Did she have a type? Oh goodness. She did. Tall skinny Brits were her type. She snuck another glance at the tall skinny Brit next to her.

Nothing wrong with that, she supposed, it was an extremely attractive type. Greta had always prided herself on her impeccable taste. She nodded to herself, and—he'd said another thing.

"Huh?"

"I said it's entertaining to watch you have conversations with yourself, but it would be more entertaining if I was involved." Like she was going to tell him about her Tumblr account. Or how she'd just realized he was totally her type.

"I'm thinking about an art thing." Unfortunately, Greta had underestimated how interested he was in her art.

"Tell me about it. Since you never showed me your paintings like I asked, Amy showed me a few. You're spectacular, of course, quite spectacular." *Et tu, Amy?* Jon surveyed the workspace they had been ushered to, next door to a pleasant looking older couple. His arm settled around her waist as they waited for the instructor to finish talking to another woman.

"Since when do you talk to Amy without me?"

Greta tried to maneuver out of his arm without being obvious. She failed, and he pulled her in closer. He was so warm, and she could feel the precise lines of his bicep against her back, and it was so sexy. This was exactly what she had been hoping to avoid, but pulling away now that she was enveloped in his soft, masculine scent and his hard, manly muscles was not happening.

The mental battle lasted mere seconds before she surrendered. For now.

She might want the evening to end early, but damned if she wasn't going to enjoy herself while she was here.

Despite everything she'd promised herself.

Didn't she say from day one that this hot DJ screamed trouble? He leaned in to take a selfie of the two of them in front of their dough.

"We're Facebook friends, aren't we?" He said comfortably. As if that didn't cross a line. As if friending her friends didn't make them like an actual couple. As if she should just be fine with this. *Et tu, Amy?*

But then, this was exactly what her friends would expect. And were probably surprised to see that Greta herself wasn't friends with him online. Outmaneuvered, yet again. This was necessary, she told herself. If they weren't leaving a footprint, then what was even the point of fake-dating? They had to do it out loud, in front of her friends, and with plenty of photographic evidence. Pictures or it didn't happen, as Mina would say. Pulling her phone out of her front pocket, Greta accepted the request she'd been ignoring since their tattoo date. Before putting it back, she glanced up. The instructor was still occupied, so she used the opportunity to stalk a bit.

He didn't have nearly as many friends as she'd imagined he would, but a couple cross-posted statuses showed her that this was a private account, and not the Force page he used to interact with fans.

But the real joy in any new online relationship was flipping through the other person's pictures, so that's what she did. Jon was looking down at them as well, of course, so the real judgments would happen later, alone. In the meantime, she just opened the album of profile pics and scrolled through.

There was Jon on stage, behind the decks. Jon taking a big-eyed selfie on the Golden Gate. Jon and CeAnna giving each other bunny ears—it was so easy to forget that he actually rubbed shoulders with people she'd only seen in tabloids. He was so down-to-earth that Greta usually forgot he was actually sort of famous. She supposed it probably helped that the DJ was never as recognizable as the singer, so most people who sang along on the radio had no idea the guy beside them in the checkout line of Trader Joe's had created it.

A couple of the older photos showed Jon and a model. Greta wasn't familiar with the girl's work, but only a model had that height, that weight (or lack thereof), those cheekbones. Ice-blond hair was casually pulled back to show off huge blue eyes, spaced just a tiny bit too far apart. Her heart-shaped mouth was slicked with metallic gloss, the kind no one in real life wore.

In both photos, Greta noticed, Jon was leaning into her, smiling widely at the camera. The blonde, on the other hand, was looking off camera both times, never smiling.

"Old girlfriend?" she asked.

"Mm," Jon affirmed, sort of. He clearly didn't want to talk about her. Good. Neither did she.

Greta immediately had a mini-freakout, just as the instructor asked them to begin adding flour and water to the starter on their workstations.

She let him sprinkle flour over the surface of their marble counter, before she dumped the shaggy lump of starter dough on top for him to work. Gluten or not, she'd love to be the one putting her body weight into the kneading rather than watching him and just standing around feeling awkward.

Jon Hargrave. The guy she was dating. Well, using and abusing, really. He hung out with celebrities and dated women who were like eleventy times hotter than her. And here she was all, "I'll only fake date you, cause I have trust issues." Was she insane? Was she giving up an amazing opportunity to date a man as talented and successful as she often dreamed of being? Or was she dodging a bullet because real dating a celebrity was an even bigger invitation to disaster than dating a normal guy was?

And the biggest question of all—why *her*?

He'd called her a challenge. Was it the bet with Angie that it all came down to? But Angie was her sister, for heaven's sake, and she wasn't mean. It wasn't some sort of *She's All That* situation, where the popular guy had to turn the nerdy girl into a prom queen. Was it? Angie surely, understood how much nerdgirl Greta would never in a million years transform into some sort of shiny Hollywood Girlfriend type.

Right?

Or did Angie think this would be a good thing for Greta, like, transforming her into someone bigger and better than the Girl Who Spends Saturdays in the Tub? As children, they'd spend hours on end playing House, in which Greta was always the doll-baby. Each of her older sisters got to take turns playing mom and dressing her up, making her exactly what they wanted. Who they wanted.

And every one of them wanted her to be girlier, sweeter, more docile than she was. Most of the games would end when Greta fled, only to be discovered hours later hiding with a book in a spot the older girls couldn't fit, like under the kitchen sink, or with a flashlight buried by clothes in a hamper.

So really, twenty years on, could Angie really be involved in a real-life game of House? And would she really believe Greta wouldn't be hiding in the grown-up version of a hamper?

And was any of this real, or was she just losing her shit because this whole charade was too hard and it felt like a house of cards that she'd never been steady enough to balance? And when they all collapsed, what would suffocate at the bottom? It could only be the friendships she'd stacked on and under the lies she'd been telling.

The timer went off, and he covered their little

breads-to-be in plastic wrap before taking a break. Besides the occasional worried side-eye, Jon hadn't said
a word about the fact that she'd spent the last thirty
minutes staring at the dough with her arms crossed as
he did all the work. So now they had time without the
distraction of the class. An hour for the dough to rise
meant an hour for the two of them to be blessedly,
dreadfully alone.

Screw that. She needed to think. She needed to
be alone. She needed to set fire to the cards once and
for all. If everything ended now, her friends would
forgive her. Jon would go away. And she could drink
enough wine in the bathtub to figure out just exactly
what *she* really wanted, without input from anyone
else.

Greta looked at the shelves of baked bread, and
made her decision.

Jon suggested a walk, and Greta agreed. There was
something up with her tonight, more than usual, and
he didn't know what to do. Things had started weird—
well, honestly, there hadn't been a truly normal moment
between them. The actual start had been weird, and
only gotten weirder.

A chance meet at a wedding? A proposition and a
pseudo contract? A sex tape? Fake dates and fooling
around in alleys? A marriage bet—oh, but she didn't
know about that one. Right, then, he supposed all of it
was inexplicable in general.

But tonight was particularly odd. He could have
sworn Summer had mentioned a gluten issue in Greta,

for one, but he supposed they wouldn't be practically drowning in flour currently if that were the case. Her attitude was another thing he couldn't quite wrap his mind round. She'd showed up in a snit, hardly meeting his eyes.

As he tried to be gentle and cute with her, she'd alternately ignored him and cuddled with him. Then after finding a couple pictures of him and Leah online, she'd just sort of stopped doing anything. He'd kneaded the dough all alone, wondering what to say and coming to no good answers. *So . . .* Jon really didn't know what to do. If she'd talk to him, they could work it out, he knew that much.

The thing about getting out of a bad relationship was that you've got to work out exactly where you yourself had gone wrong, and Jon hadn't learned how to communicate until afterwards. Now, though, now he prided himself on it. Rust Vee wouldn't mock him so relentlessly about being 'Therapist Force' otherwise.

But Greta was moody, not the communicative type at all. It was going to be a difficult future between them, if he had to pry every time they had a problem to sort.

Luckily, Jon was nothing if not optimistic. If he could learn how, so could she.

They had an hour. An hour of free time to turn this evening around. An hour to convince her that she should have a nice time tonight. An hour, in other words, to try and get those smoking hot jeans off her, because they'd both have a better night after some loving.

For heaven's sake, he knew many woman felt it ladylike to wait three dates before allowing a man into
their bed (something he'd not quite ever understood;
men loved sex! They should have sex all the time to
win a man over! Ladylike was utterly overrated in
comparison to frequent sex. He planned to write a self-
help book about this topic someday.) but he was on
the verge of losing track of how many dates they'd
been on at this point. And he'd already promised to
third-date her like crazy.

Fake relationship or not, he was ready for a real
good time. And despite the frown on her face, he
was willing to bet Greta was too. How else did you
show a woman how deeply into her you were besides
getting . . . deeply . . . into her and complimenting her
profusely?

"Let's take a walk while the bread rises, shall we?"
He offered her his arm without giving her any time to
answer. As he walked her out, she grabbed a roll and
tore off a bit to eat.

God, but it was sexy to see a woman who wasn't
ashamed of her appetite. He'd never once met a man
who believed women should live on salad, but he'd also
never once met a woman who didn't believe men truly
thought that. She continued to eat the roll as they
walked out, and he continued to appreciate her. Jon
planned to eat her even more ravenously than she'd enjoyed her roll.

Once outside, it was only a short walk to a nearby
park he knew of. She was silent for the walk. Jon wondered if this was about her seeing the pictures of Leah

on his Facebook page. It was all so confusing. Yes, his ex-girlfriend was fetching, but she was also cruel, and had a severe addiction problem besides.

Surely Greta wasn't jealous? Or feeling inferior? But why would she? She was so . . . everything. Girls were utterly complicated, he'd given up on understanding them almost as soon as he'd discovered he liked them.

The park was deserted, much to his delight. Time to show her how much he wanted her. How cute she was in jeans, even ignoring the fake date *she'd* set up. How, even though it was a bet she didn't know about, he truly wanted to consider a future with her, this talented, snarky girl that had no problem mocking his fears and dancing to his songs. The kinds of things that he couldn't put words to, only melody.

Jon didn't ask her how she was feeling. He didn't ask her what was wrong. He just held her close and kissed her deeply, kissed her with all the feelings he was having. If she wasn't willing to tell him what was bothering her, he'd simply make sure she didn't think about whatever it was for the next hour. And if, as he'd suspected, the issue was his ex-girlfriend? He'd make certain she knew he wasn't thinking about anyone but her.

Jon's arms encircled her and Greta immediately forgot about all her prior irritation and insecurity. Which only irritated her further. She chose to act out in the best way she knew how—by kissing him even harder.

Their lips crashed together, fighting for dominance.

She bit him, and he bit her back. His hands tightened around her back, digging in exactly the way she'd done to him in the alley outside the skating rink. Just like he'd done, she collapsed into his arms. Now, she understood why, though.

There was something indescribable about allowing someone else to have dominion over you like that, to master you, to touch you in a way that says they see you. They feel you. They desperately want you.

God, she really wanted him too, and pretending she didn't was exhausting.

Her right hand grabbed his hair and tugged on those shaggy blonde locks even as her fist pulled him closer to her face. His tongue was inside her mouth, fighting hers—no, dancing with hers. It tasted like fresh-baked bread, which was something she'd never associated with sexiness before now, but suddenly did.

How would she ever taste bread again without imagining this moment, with his hands halfway up her shirt, hers tangled in his hair, both of them pressing as tightly against each other as humanly possible while still remaining, somehow, vertical?

The closeness, the heat they generated, the wet she felt in her center mirrored by the hardness she felt in his made it hard to breathe.

Greta slid her tongue along the length of Jon's one more time, marveling in how beautifully they fit together and how turned on she was right now. It was so hard to breathe.

His palm closed over her breast and she inhaled sharply, hoping no one else was in this park, but also wouldn't that be kind of hot? She'd never done sex things in public. He squeezed sharply, and it hurt but it felt good and oh god it was hard to breathe.

And then suddenly—she remembered. In her haste to avoid this kind of meaningful moment, she'd guaranteed a way out. She'd eaten a roll. It wasn't hard to breathe. It was near impossible.

Suddenly, her scrabbling hands were involved in pushing Jon off, not pulling him close. Greta collapsed to the ground, head between her legs, breathing as deeply as her tightening throat would allow her. But his arms weren't going anywhere, they were still around her, giving her support, but why?

She couldn't worry about that, she had to focus on breathing, which at this point came accompanied with some dry heaving and a lot of hacking coughs. The sexiness turned to scary in a matter of seconds.

Lungs, overworked. Chest, pained. Throat, closing. Why the hell had this seemed like a good idea? Oh, yeah, because she was supposed to be showing Jon how much he didn't want to date her. Well, that much had certainly been accomplished, she decided, as she sat on her butt in the middle of a gorgeous park with a gorgeous view and a gorgeous man while hacking up something decidedly not-gorgeous.

It wasn't celiac, her doctor had determined at a pretty young age. But the gluten sensitivity was real. It affected her the same way other people felt when they were around too many cats. Nothing life-threatening, but it was horrible and disgusting and honestly, a little bit frightening from both ends. As much as she didn't like what was happening right now, Jon had to be freaking out.

"I'll call the hospital, you're fine," he was crooning and digging around for his phone. Why was he so stupid nice? She was so not nice. Just the stupid part.

"No," she managed to croak out between labored breaths. "No need. I'll be fine in." A few breaths. Maybe a hundred. "A little while." She could tell he didn't believe her. She couldn't blame him. "Give me. A minute."

He rubbed her back, held her hair back. He was so damned gentlemanly. Where was the catch? She'd been waiting for weeks for a catch to this guy and hadn't found one. It was just as hard for her to swallow his undivided, sweet attention as it was to swallow gluten. He wasn't supposed to do this. He was supposed to run. They always ran. He was supposed to be horrified by this, if nothing else.

But there was the rub. On what could have been one of their best dates yet, she'd decided to show her trump card. So now there was no chance at all at Jon didn't know she was playing the saboteur here. Because she knew full well Summer had mentioned her gluten issues, and she'd definitely eaten that roll in front of him.

And behind him. And next to him. Anywhere she could enjoy him in a pair of jeans, truly, but it wasn't a secret that she'd eaten the stupid roll. So now he knew.

Greta Steinburg was an asshole who was so scared of real feelings that she would even ruin fake dates.

And weirdly enough, Jon's arms were still around

her. She could kind of breathe now, but she wasn't ready to let him know yet. He was murmuring in her ear. Soothing her. In other words, a perfect gentleman. Just like he'd said.

How was that even going to be possible? How could he see exactly what she was doing and not just . . walk away? Maybe she hadn't given this guy enough credit. Maybe she hadn't given herself enough. Because something super-strange was happening here. It was like he saw exactly who she was, and stuck around. No, that couldn't be right—was it?

She let out another gasp. Not because it was hard to breathe. The inside of her throat wasn't as clenched as it had been a moment ago, but Greta wasn't ready to tell Jon that yet. Once she told him that, he'd want to talk. They'd *have* to talk. She'd have to to admit that she'd done exactly what he thought she did. She'd have to tell him she was trying to call his bluff. She'd have to tell him that letting him break off the fake date was preferable to her than telling him how she really felt—as in, she needed some time to sort out *how* she felt, but she was a little worried that he wasn't the caricature she'd painted him as in her head. She'd have to be honest. It was going to be terrible. She let out a deep sigh.

"Just like that. You okay, love? I'm here." He was peering into her eyes, she tried to avoid it. A gigantic twenty foot-tall wave of shame was washing over her, she couldn't look at him.

"Okay. I'm here too." And she kind of was. Not ready to admit that he was someone she needed, but ready to admit that she owed him a few explanations. And possibly an apology, though she'd drag her feet on that one. Who was dumb enough to date *her*, after all? She'd told him she didn't date. She'd told everyone.

Chapter 9

Walking back to the bakery was quiet and strained. Greta knew, that Jon knew, that she knew that he knew. It was like a bad game of Telephone. Or an exceptionally good one, but either way, she looked the bad guy.

Mostly, she supposed, because she was, indeed, the bad guy.

So much was spinning through her head, and it didn't help that her head was literally spinning. Their last free twenty minutes were silent and fraught with tension, until Jon suggested a tentative truce. She'd give him all her bread and not for one second consider cancelling on his bit of the date. And instead of the romantic evening he'd hinted at having, they'd have a Talk, about Feelings.

Ugh. Those things were only good in the fiction she read in the bath.

Once back at the workstation, firmly tied back into their aprons, they fell into a rhythm. Greta sprinkled more flour as Jon dumped the now-puffy pieces of dough out. She shaped large loaves and small buns, he transferred them to the baking stone that would go into the wood-fired oven throwing off heat and deliciousness on the back wall.

The older woman working next to them watched silently for a moment, and then leaned over.

"Newlyweds?" she asked.

"Oh dear God no," Greta replied, as Jon said, "Hopefully soon."

Oh what in the actual hell. Was he—he could not even be serious right now. She had done nothing but actively try to dissuade the man, and after a handful of dates with no sex he was thinking a wedding was in order? She had learned, as had most kindergarteners, that first came *love* and then came marriage. She anticipated neither.

Obviously her dissuasive tactics weren't working. Maybe she was too good a kisser. Maybe she should have chosen a date that would bring her gastrointestinal distress instead of mere respiratory. Certain burger joints had been known to bring that on. As she floundered internally, she noticed Jon wink at her.

Oh. He was joking. Oh.

Well, she didn't feel disappointed he didn't want to marry her. Not at all. And it definitely wasn't because there was something wrong with her. No, something was totally wrong with him. She was fantastic, and didn't want to get married anyways. So there.

No disappointment at all, just the remnants of her allergy attack giving her that unsettled feeling. Sometimes her breathing affected her heart. Maybe.

"I was telling Henry earlier that if you weren't already, it was only a matter of time. He said within the year, I said within six months." The woman smiled sweetly at them, the lines of a life lived well creasing around her eyes and mouth.

"We even went ahead and bet on it while the bread was rising. Guess what I get if I win," Henry joined in. His wife's face turned a delighted shade of pink, and she grabbed a wooden spoon to threaten him with.

"Don't you dare, Mr. King!" Greta grinned despite herself. They were awfully damn cute, but for real, was there something about Greta's face that made people unable to resist the urge to bet on her? About her?

"What Mrs. King is trying to say, is that you two look just like we did when we first fell in love. There's a spark when you look at each other. You don't see it in a lot of young couples these days."

"Particularly not in any of the girls our sons bring home," interjected Mrs. King.

"Goes without saying, dear. But you lovebirds are going to make it. You don't get to our age without being able to see what makes a happy marriage."

"Like what?" Greta asked. Purely for curiosity's sake, to test their theory against the couples she knew.

"Well, beyond the spark, you have to enjoy being close. The two of you don't let more than a couple of inches get in between you, that's obvious to the whole class. When you stop kissing each other, the rest isn't far behind. Why, Henry, remember Sheila and Walt? She said his mustache was too tickly, but once he shaved it, she admitted she just didn't like to kiss him anymore." Mrs. King laid her arm on her husband, who swiftly relieved her of her wooden spoon.

"They didn't last more than another two months, after that," Mr. King agreed.

"Sad to see people divorce," remarked Jon.

"Oh, no, dear, they died in a car crash," she said.

"I—I did not think that was where that story was headed," Greta said to Jon. His vigorous nod told her he felt the same.

"They'd given up. At least this way, their grandchildren never had to see them separate. Do you two have children?" Mr. King inquired.

"Um, no. Not married, remember?" said Greta. She was not entirely convinced these two were altogether in their right minds. A lack of kissing did most certainly not lead to a car crash, or she'd have been dead years ago.

"You don't need to be married to give your parents grandbabies these days, dear. I tell our sons that all the time, but do they listen? They never have." Mrs. King looked prepared to wind up into a monologue about babies, so Greta interjected.

"What are the other happy marriage tests?"

"Oh, of course. Working well together. Laughing at each other's jokes. Appreciating each other's jobs and hobbies. Arguing respectfully."

"Because you'll always argue," Mr. King put in.

"Just remember you sleep next to the person you're arguing with, and that's a vulnerable position to put yourself in. Why, Mrs. King has been a gardener for longer than you've been alive. She probably knows ten ways to poison my morning coffee."

"Twelve, dear." They smiled into each other's eyes. Greta and Jon were smiling too. Poison. They were a charming couple. Could Greta be wrong, that love did exist after all? That some men enjoyed more than the physical benefits of a marriage? Mr. King certainly seemed to be genuinely happy in his commitment.

"That was how we met, in fact, in my family's garden. I was planting my tomato starters—"

"And I walked by, on my way to pick up my date to the pictures, when I saw her, the future Mrs. King."

"He walked up my front steps, rang the doorbell, and asked my father for permission to take *me* to the pictures the next weekend. Then, after he'd satisfied Daddy that he was a successful young man with honorable intentions, he walked back and introduced himself to me. Then he helped dig holes for my plants before heading off to pick up his date."

"He still went on the other date?" Greta didn't see that one coming, either.

"Of course I did," Mr. King said. "It wouldn't have been very gentlemanly of me to stand her up, would it? But I told her about Hild while we waited in line for popcorn, and she understood. To tell you the truth, I think she only agreed to go out with me because our mothers were on the Ladies Committee together. She was always sweet on Bobby Thompson."

"Speaking of couples that are lovely together," Mrs. King said.

"Did your date marry Bobby Thompson?" Jon was so into this story Greta could have laughed, except that she kind of was too.

"Oh heavens no, Bobby married my brother! Just this past year. They waited all this time, can you imagine?"

"But they followed all the rules, and that's how they stayed happy," his wife said. "Now tell us, how did you meet? I do so love a happy beginning."

"And I love a happy ending," her husband told her, as she flushed again. It was a good thing she no longer had the wooden spoon.

"We met at a wedding," Jon started. "Greta, do you mind?"

She did not. It would be interesting to hear his take on their meeting, and besides, she wasn't entirely sure this old couple would entirely approve of her shenanigans.

"I was sitting in the back of the temple when the most gorgeous creature came waltzing by. I thought to myself, I reckon she's the best thing that's happened in this city since it's been founded. Once I realized she was the bride's sister, I gathered all the information I could and cornered her in the cloakroom.

"She tried valiantly to resist me, but I won her over with a combination of British charm, this accent, and the fact that she hadn't brought her own jacket. And aren't I a lucky bloke, she's been agreeing to be seen with me in public ever since." Jon finished and bowed.

Well, wasn't *he* the clever one. Not a lie to be had

in the whole story, except for the hyperbole of her being the best thing to happen in San Francisco. Everyone knew the best thing that happened in the city was the filming of *Harold and Maude*. He wasn't a local, though, so perhaps he didn't know. She'd be certain to bring it up later, perhaps while they watched said movie, which he likely hadn't done either.

Wait, wait, wait, she was not in charge of his pop culture education. She was annoyed that he was spinning tales to impress this sweet old couple in his unending quest to convince her that she should fall nose over tail for him.

Annoyed.

Although, as Mrs. King petted her and Mr. King murmured something undoubtedly not quite kosher in Jon's direction, Greta wavered for a moment. Was this the kind of thing she could look forward to if she let her walls down? Could she spend her golden years enjoying new activities with her best friend, while imparting her hard-earned wisdom on the younger generation?

Generation—that was what it came down to, she realized. It was absolutely something she could have aspired to, were she born fifty years earlier. Sometime in her parent's generation, there had been a cultural shift.

Mr. King, she could say with utter certainty, was a true gentleman. Possibly the last of them. By the time her father came along, that wasn't what boys aspired to be anymore. They grew up with television, not with real-life heroes. They thought they were entitled to things, something they then taught their children, and by the time her own generation was born, it was just a hot mess.

Guys were savvy enough to play the game, but the emotions weren't real. It was all theater, setting the stage for a relationship, but when you moved in, you realized the food was made of plaster and the furniture of cardboard.

So when she considered learning new skills and enjoying activities with her best friend in her twilight—it was Amy and Summer she should be picturing in the role. They fit all the criteria. They were respectful, interested, appreciative, etc. Basically, all the things a husband would be except the sex.

She'd gone this long, though, with merely her left hand for company, and she'd been *fine*. Granted, the sex tape was hot as hell, but sex was always the first thing to go. Just look at Sheila and Walt.

She would admit this, though—having met the Kings, it was the first time she felt nostalgic for something she'd never really had: true love.

Jon could tell she was feeling reflective, and possibly even embarrassed as they finally left the bakery, with loads of home-baked bread and the address of the Kings snugly tucked into his wallet.

An address! To which he had promised to mail postcards! It was terribly old-fashioned, in all the best ways. Lovely couple, that.

He'd often thought the fault was in modern literature. There were no good love stories these days, at least not ones men read. Sometime between his grandad's time and his dad's, things had changed so far as marketing marriage to menfolk.

Romance was now merely slotted into action stories, giving the general impression that if one merely blew enough things up, or was proficient enough at racing automobiles, a disproportionately beautiful woman would wander through by happenstance and hurl herself, nude and panting, into one's arms.

He wondered if Greta even knew the kind of love story he liked, or if she, too, was a victim of Hollywood. It could explain her cynicism. _Harold and Maude_, that was a good one, and filmed here even. It wasn't about sex or looks or sheer manliness winning out. It was simply the story of two humans, utterly opposite in nature, finding each other and irrevocably changing each other's lives.

Well, he could bring that up at a later date; right now there was a mystery to solve, and that was why she was so determined to turn all their best dates to rubbish. He supposed if he began with his own last failed relationship, she might feel comfortable enough to relate her own concerns.

"I hadn't wanted to go to the party," he began.

It wasn't at all his kind of scene. Agency shindigs were all about seeing and being seen, while imbibing as much free Dom and CIROC as humanly possible while still staying inside your designer duds. At least while the cameras were there.

If you'd asked him a week later, he'd have wondered why he ever considered skipping it.

If you'd asked him nine months later, he'd have asked you how much for a time machine trip back to have stayed home that night.

But there he was, freshly signed to Rice and Associates, and feeling obligated to RSVP yes to every invite thrown his way.

Feeling entirely star struck, Jon kept to a corner of the room. He wished he could have brought a friend, but he didn't have quite enough clout at the agency to add a plus-one to his invite. All around him were extremely attractive people wearing fancy clothing. It was uncomfortable.

Jon tugged on his rental tux. He knew full well he didn't belong here. The only reason he had been signed to such a prestigious group was the fact that Dee Q had invited him to tour, and then repeated the invitation. He could tell there were eyes on him, wondering how he snuck in, no doubt. He did a ferret around to see if anyone he knew even remotely was there.

All he saw were people who seemed sort of like himself, only less edgy. He was beginning to twig that really successful people actually didn't show to the agency parties when a tiny hand landed on his arm.

"Do I know you?" came a breathy voice. It floated out of an ethereal-looking blonde waif, who was startlingly pretty.

"I sincerely doubt it." No doubt this was a case of mistaken identity. Jon had often been told he resembled a blond Mark Ronson. But one glorious tour did not a Mark Ronson make. He started to step away when her grip tightened.

"I think I'd like to," she continued. He gave her another look. That was weird. He'd roll with it. She was definitely the kind of girl his mates would be impressed by. A selfie or two and his evening could be labeled a success by anyone who wasn't present. What to say back, though? Because he was still rather certain she hadn't meant to glom onto him. Perhaps she was pissed. He leaned a bit closer to catch a whiff of booze, but nothing. Nothing at all, which was a bit odd too.

Jon had never met a girl that had no scent about her; it had long been a girly mystery from about the time he'd noticed them, why they all smelled so good.

"Well, that's all right then, innit?" He really didn't know what else to say. As it turns out, it didn't matter, because she'd spent the remainder of the evening introducing him to everyone in a rather proprietary manner.

It felt a bit comforting to be herded about.

Hollywood was tough. He was quite more pleased than ever he'd chosen to continue making San Francisco his home instead of succumbing to the siren song of Los Angeles. Up close, a siren song could sound more like a banshee scream.

But here was this perfectly lovely pint-sized girl leading him about as though he were a prize to be won, and the longer it went on, the more chuffed he was. It was a vast difference from the "*Please love me*" attitude one typically had to assume around industry types. He met a hundred (it felt like) other tiny-yet-tall beauties that evening, and was so pleased at his new-found fortune—or rather, planning just how to spin the

tale later—that it wasn't until much later he recalled
how many trips to the ladies' room Leah had taken.

Her name was Leah, he'd gleaned that second hand,
as it hadn't occurred to her to introduce herself. Leah
had always taken the approach that everyone must
know her. Most had.

They'd both drunk an inordinate amount of bubbles
that evening, as he hazily recalled.

Next thing he knew, she was pulling him into a cab
and giving directions back to her place. She shared a
decent-sized flat with about eight other girls, all of
whom rotated in and out at regular intervals, he'd later
learned. Evidently it was part of the agency contract,
housing was.

They'd slept together, that first night, on an air mattress in a room where another girl was passed out co-
matose on another, and an empty one awaited a late
reveler.

In retrospect, Jon noticed that the only truly memorable thing about their first time was the room they
were in. That and the fact that he was extremely un-
used to women who looked like her being interested
in removing their clothing for an average bloke like
himself.

He'd gone to bed (mattress?) single, and woken up
Leah's boyfriend.

The next few weeks, months even, had been a bit of
a blur. There was party after party, night after night.
About eight weeks in, he'd gotten enough confidence
in his paychecks to lease the flat he currently resided
in, and then they began to stay there instead.

He'd never asked her to move in, it felt a bit too sudden for any such move, and yet from the signing of the lease, her things had taken up more and more of his space.

Only a week into his new, fancy life, he realized he could no longer utilize the closet, as it was filled with filmy scraps of cloth he was unable to recognize as outfits until she put them on. His bathroom, usually so austere, was cluttered with a thousand products. She insisted on calling them only "product", something that both confused and amused him. Why not pluralize something that appeared to multiply daily?

At this point, Jon was privy to the fact that cocaine was entirely responsible for her ability to stay up all night, and drink so much champagne. It was her beverage of choice, and in fact one of the more interesting things about her was that she had once slept with a bartender who had taught her to sabre open bottles.

A sabre now resided in his tiny cook space.

It was a peculiar life he was living, and one he wasn't a hundred percent comfortable with. But Leah reassured him frequently that she didn't do anything everyone else wasn't doing, and that anyway he was lucky to have her. She knew him, knew the right people to introduce him to, knew more about this life than he. And who else would have him?

For a while, longer than he'd like to admit, it was easy to believe her.

"So . . . what happened?" Greta asked, and Jon realized he'd drifted in reminiscence and quietened down.

"I hadn't wanted to go to the next party, either. Leah had, though."

"Just for like an hour, Jons, pretty please?" she'd begged, but by now Jon knew that it was bollocks when she said an hour. If she wanted to attend a party, it was because there was someone she wanted to impress, or else she'd gotten wind of the fact that a drug she was after would be making an appearance as well.

"Nah, then, I'll only be making a cameo," he'd told her, over and over. "Not even close to your hour." At that point it was still a running joke between them, that her hour was his whole night. Looking back, jokes based on her copious drug use seemed less amusing. After all, by now she'd gotten knackered enough to tell him her story.

Leah Livre was born Lee Booker, in a rough-and-tumble area of East Hollywood, to a mother who—as Leah put it—entertained men for a living. She was somewhere in between a prostitute and a professional girlfriend. A hooker middle-class, if such a thing existed.

Her mother had been a mail-order bride from the Ukraine, and her father had left just as soon as he'd realized she wasn't as enamored with his manhood as he was. It hadn't taken the former Mrs. Booker any time at all to realize her accent and carefully-tended figure were a hot commodity.

The most startling thing about Leah and her mother's relationship, for Jon, was the amount of respect Leah had for her mother's career choice.

He was rather much more pleased with his own mum, though she was a primary school teacher, and made a significant less yearly sum than Leah's. He also suspected taxes may have been more accurately paid by his own. She'd never liked Leah, of course.

Lee, though, as she was then known, was struggling through primary school when her mother had found a new husband. Steve Wyant had waited only as long as it took to send her mother out for smokes before proceeding to avail himself of Lee's virginity. His compensation was a bump of the white powder he routinely served himself and his women between lawsuits.

Steve was an ambulance chaser. Lee quickly became a speed chaser. In some ways, they were exactly the same. In some ways, they were so different. For example, Steve knew full well his girlfriend cheated on him. It paid the bills, so what did he care? As long as she used a condom, no one got hurt.

Lee cheated on him, too, except that she wasn't his girlfriend, she was just a girl who was young, and hungry, and had just recently learned what she was worth.

Instead of sleeping with men for a few bills, she slept with them for introductions. And coke.

Once it had started to pay off, she had rapidly ascended the ranks. By the time she was eighteen, she'd been signed to Rice, and had an eye for the up-and-comers.

By the time she was twenty, Leah (as she was already known) was featured equally in high-fashion magazines for her modeling, and for her dates. When she told Jon he was the best one yet, he was still green enough to be flattered instead of insulted. It meant he was worthy. It hadn't occurred to him he was just the next step up on the ladder.

So the infamous party, the one he'd not wanted to go to, the one she had. It had ended just as early in his eyes as he'd hoped. Basically, he'd gone in, shaken hands with the appropriate folk, had a G&T or two, and gone about his way. Leah had disappeared almost immediately, and so he'd left solo. Just exactly as planned.

What Leah evidently hadn't planned was that the man she was fucking in their bed had only just begun when Jon arrived home.

DJ Boom had been a Guy To Watch, but Jon swiftly availed himself of every bit of clout he had to shut that down. Leah was very apologetic, but Jon swiftly availed himself of every bit of self-esteem he had to shut *that* down.

She said she was too high to realize what a bad choice she'd made. He believed her. The problem was that she got that high on any given Tuesday for it to be a good excuse. She said she thought he wouldn't be that mad, considering the business they were in. The problem was that they were in different businesses. She said that he had no real reason to be mad, as she'd wanted to attend his party for the X. He decided that he did, as drugs were not the most compelling reason to attend one's partner's event.

It was an altogether messy breakup.

She left all of her things at his apartment, and then

had the nerve to send DJ Boom to collect them. Jon had boxed them up previously, anticipating something similar, but was surprised all over again when she'd sent an inventory checklist. He'd no idea she had been so involved with the flimsy scrap collection. Models, though.

Evidently the bathroom had not been subject to the same insurance-related inventory, as long after she'd vacated his apartment, Jon was still the proud owner of one flatiron, multiple sizes of curling irons, two straightening serums, three beach sprays, and a single eye cream.

Truth be told, he really liked the eye cream. He was on his third tub.

Even after all the personal items had been redistributed, Jon had received a number of private messages on his public Facebook account. At that point, it had been the only access to him she had, as he'd changed his number and blocked her from his personal social media.

i miss u. plz tell me u do2

ur a dick. wrz my ccnut lotion

i<3 u cum ovr

Jon had, wisely he thought, not responded to any of them. After all this time—well, at least the amount of time it took to be out of her constant and overwhelming influence, it was pretty damn cool to just be Jon Hargrave. DJ Force was a solid alter ego in today's day and age, and he'd gotten to the fame tipping-point where parties could be picked and chosen based on whom he wanted to hang out with.

Too bad for Leah. His life was infinitely cooler without her.

They were back at the park and seated again on the bench she'd had her fit on before she'd digested everything Jon had said and was ready to spill her own guts in return. Just a little, though. Because how could she be sure that Jon wouldn't end up just like every other guy who'd been cheated on, growing increasingly bitter before deciding monogamy was overrated?

"I guess I can't remember a time when my parents were happy," she finally started. "I just always assumed they'd stay together for *us*, though. Even though we were miserable. Better the devil you know, right? After Dad finally left, he stayed gone. Like, way gone. I think I have at least two half-siblings, but he basically wrote all of us off along with Mom."

"That's so shit," Jon said. "I can't imagine."

Greta's laugh was bitter. "You *can* though. You lived with a girl like Leah. Imagine there were kids involved."

He was quiet for a moment. "So shit," he eventually repeated.

She leaned back and closed her eyes, searching for any happy moments. She couldn't think of any. Her sisters could, but just barely, and it wasn't anything weighty enough to erase the memories they all had of the unhappy years.

She wasn't exactly certain of the first time she'd become aware that none of her friends' houses required even an elementary schooler to tiptoe through as though the pretend lava they'd invented at recess had oozed along behind the bus and into their homes.

She did remember that by about third or fourth grade she'd realized it was the reason she was the only kid in class who didn't have birthday parties. Some of her classmates thought she was snobby, and stopped inviting her to theirs once no reciprocal invitation ever showed up in their cubbies or backpacks.

It was almost worse that most kids kept inviting her, so she relived what a happy home should look like, just around four times a year. Just often enough that she never forgot she was different, that other kids weren't scared of their fathers.

She did know kids without fathers.

She just didn't know anyone else whose mothers cowered from their fathers; mothers who sometimes woke them in the middle of the night to hide them, delirious and clumsy, in dark quiet spots so they wouldn't accidentally get hurt or in the middle of the destructive arguments that always ensued when dads came home pissed off and wasted.

In kindergarten, long before Greta, her sisters, or her mom had realized the situation was too precarious to even attempt, she had once been allowed to host a sleepover. Just the once.

Just the once was all it had taken.

Amy and Summer were her obvious guest choices, because they were her sneaker twins. At recess the first day they'd noticed that, they had started calling themselves the Secret Sissy Club. At her house that night, neither of the girls was totally okay with being away from their own mothers for the first time.

But then her dad had shown up, late, as they were just falling asleep in their camping bags on the basement floor. He was angry Greta's mom hadn't taken the trash out, no matter that it wasn't going to be picked up until the next morning. The tongue-lashing he gave her probably woke up most of the neighborhood.

Greta had hidden her face beneath her pillow and sobbed in humiliation, hoping her friends wouldn't tell anyone at school.

They'd done much better—they'd crowded around her, rubbing her back and telling her stories, all the ones they could think of and a few they had clearly made up, about princes in disguise.

Years later, it was another sleepover of her favorite people on earth when Ang had stumbled into her room to show the girls how she'd found her dad's phone. The phone he'd evidently either not locked or wanted his wife to find.

The phone that he'd evidently been using to contact his girlfriend, someone called Megan. Someone who had left messages telling him what she was wearing and when she planned to remove it. After a sleepless night of debate, the sisters showed the phone to their mom.

She'd known all along, but the thought of leaving was scarier than the thought of putting up with it.

"I'm not sure I have this sorted," Jon interrupted. "Your father sounds like an absolute wanker, but why has that affected you so much? Angie seems to have turned out just fine. And I rather think Matt's the faithful type."

Greta sighed. "That was just the groundwork. And if Matt isn't, he'll have me to deal with." She waited a beat, not sure how to say it.

"It turned out, my father had another woman all along. And once he was able to be done with us, he changed his number. He literally had a backup family."

Jon looked horrified, but of course, it was a very blatant thing for her father to have done. What she expected from guys these days was more of a gradual fade. As though the song peaked on the third date sex, and then gradually faded to static. The DJ should know as well as anyone. Although there was one other thing he should know as well, just in his best interest,

"Once Summer saw him out with the other woman. She broke his nose while Amy filmed it. They'll do it to you, too, if you don't see our shit through." It was the easiest possible way for Greta to ask him to be gentle with her heart.

Chapter 10

"Good heavens," Jon said aloud. "I'm going to want to see that video." Wait, that wasn't what he meant to say. Although he did mean it. He wanted to memorize the cheating bastard's face so that if he ever chanced upon the knobhead, he could break the jerk's nose again. His inner voice told him that wasn't very mature, but he told his inner voice to bugger off.

"But come here, then," he added, and folded the still-hoarse girl into his chest. He truly would never understand the impulse to hurt a girl like this. Because that had to be what it was—no one could possibly get to know a pint-sized firecracker like Greta and not realize she was more than any man could ask for in one lifetime.

After all, there hadn't been any room in Jon's mind or heart for anyone but her since the night she first suspiciously eyed him in the coatroom.

"It's okay. I'm okay," she was saying, and trying to wiggle out.

"I know you are. But I'm not letting you go," he said into her hair. He wondered if she knew he wasn't really talking about the embrace.

"I just—ugh. I haven't told anyone about that in so long. It's so embarrassing, and awful. I was lucky, though, learning my lesson early. And I have good friends. I never needed anyone else before, and I don't really need anyone but them now." She took a deep breath, and exhaled hot against his shirt.

"Do you really believe that?" He asked. "Of course your friends are ace, but I think you've done yourself a mischief closing off your heart." What he didn't add was, *I'm glad you saved it for me.*

"Done my—that's cute. No, I've saved myself from all the hassle of meeting people, investing in them, finding out you're incompatible, and separating from them. It's inevitable, and it's exhausting. No one has time for that kind of nonsense." He could have sworn she surreptitiously wiped her nose on his shirt.

"Actually, I think most people have time for that."

"But why? There's so many other things you could be doing with your time. You didn't get successful while also juggling dates and breakups, did you? After all, your last relationship sucked too." She pulled back a little, so she could look at him.

"Leah was during my early success, actually. When you're trying to work it out with someone, you find time for them *and* for your career." He pushed a stray hair behind her ear. Poor girl was so nervous about getting hurt again. He wondered again how she couldn't realize her own value. He could name a dozen guys who'd treat her like a princess.

They weren't allowed to, though, because he was intent on making her his queen instead.

"I just don't understand how you could get cheated on too and not even see what's so clear to me." Her brown eyes were searching.

"The difference, love, is that I realized Leah wasn't right for me. Her values weren't aligned with mine, and regardless the circumstance, it wouldn't have worked out between us. One relationship doesn't stand for the rest, though. It's like polling, you need a larger sample size." He gazed steadily back at her, willing her to see the truth in his eyes. Because it *was* truth, he firmly believed it.

"But I have so many other examples. Like *no one* stays together. Even Kermit and Miss Piggy broke up. If those two crazy kids can't work it out, what hope did the rest of us ever have?" Jon thought he could detect just a tiny bit of longing in what she said, as if she thought he could reassure her.

"For every example you have of a failed relationship, I have one of a successful couple. With enough communication and determination, you can overcome anything." He'd reassure her forever. Weirdly, seeing how damaged she was made him more sure than ever that he was exactly the man to show her what happiness was. Her trust was clearly broken, but that didn't mean her heart had to stay that way.

"You make dating sound like mountain climbing," she said.

"I have a better workout in mind," Jon said, as he leaned in to kiss her. He'd made up his mind, the newest bet with Angie and Matt wasn't just drunken swagger. He was going to change her opinion on love. It would change her whole life, actually. Because what kind of a half life was she living without love, or even the possibility?

He had thought she was a challenge before, but now he realized she was more of a quest. And he was a valiant knight, determined to save the day. It was a good thing he was British, he reflected. All the good heroes always were.

What a relief, Greta thought as she walked into Jon's apartment for the first time. It was nothing at all like the cold, sterile coffee shops and restaurants he favored. This was an older place, full of character and quirk. It smelled like mochas and spice. The cozy living room just beyond the front door prominently featured a green velvet couch covered in pillows, a massive record collection, framed photos on the walls of people who could only be his family, as they all had the same startlingly green eyes, dirty blonde hair, and rakish grins.

Greta realized she'd never really asked about his family, beyond the little he'd told her at the fundraiser. Clearly he had at least two sisters, judging from the small gallery she'd drifted over to look at while he turned on lights and nervously surveyed the cleanliness situation.

Luckily, everything appeared in order, although she supposed the true tell of a man's hygiene was only to be found in the bathroom.

"Wine?" he called from the small adjoining kitchen. Wood creaked beneath his steps as he rummaged in cabinets.

"Please," she said, worried that her voice had betrayed her own nervousness. She was in his apartment. She was totally going to sleep with him. All the build-up, all her mental back-and-forth hadn't prepared her adequately for the experience itself, though. What if he wasn't any good at it? What if *she* wasn't? What if she'd forgotten completely how to go about having sex?

Surely it was like riding a bike. The basic physicality of it was straightforward, after all.

And worst of all, what if it was the first *and* last time?

"I hope Barolo's okay with you," Jon said as he slipped a half-filled jelly jar into her hand.

Oh, of course. Because she wasn't already comparing this to every other experience she'd ever had, her dad's favorite wine would naturally make an appearance. On the other hand, it *was* really good wine, much more so than the lower-shelf pinots she tended to buy herself.

And Greta really needed some wine right about now. She took a nervous gulp, then another. Jon leaned in close to her from the side, and trailed his lips lightly across her throat.

"Savor it, love," he commanded her. The wine, or the experience? That Thing again, but it was a whole lot harder to be annoyed when goose bumps were skittering down her arms from the gentle heat of his mouth dragging up and behind her ear. His lips parted and he breathed out, hot and ticklish before tugging gently on her earlobe with his teeth. She could feel the crooked one and it made her half-smile.

She took another slow sip of wine as Jon moved behind her and his arms came around to encircle her chest. The flutters in her belly began to subside as he drew soft fingers over her, lingering instinctively over the spots she liked best, only to be replaced by a blossoming of excitement.

Another sip of wine, and his hands came back up, drawing her shirt along with them. She set her cup down long enough for the fabric to rustle over her head and arms. She picked it up and settled back into his embrace. There was skin on skin, he must have tossed his own shirt while she was grabbing her glass.

She guiltily recalled having wiped her nose on it earlier, but pushed the thought aside at the sweet sensation of his chest pressed against her back, nothing but her beige lace bra between them.

He was murmuring into her ear about how beautiful she was, pulling her hips back into him to feel the ridge of him against her ass. Greta sighed as she sipped again, almost moaning as his lips met the back of her neck. *This is a really good glass of wine.*

And that time, it was *her* doing the Thing.

She rocked back against him for the pleasure of

hearing his breath catch, for the pleasure of knowing she was affecting him just as much as he was affecting her. The jitters of earlier were fading as she realized she remembered exactly how to do this. Although she could already tell from his worshipful attention that she'd never experienced a man like Jon in bed before.

His hand left her waist, and interlaced with her own, pulling her around in a masterful move that would have been right at home on a dance floor. With a tug, she understood they were heading to his bedroom. He led her through another door, into a lamplit space filled with books and quilts, towards the bed in the corner. She longed to go through his shelves and assess his taste in literature, but he was taking the glass from her hand and dipping his finger in it.

With a little push from him, she fell back onto the blankets. There was the take-charge guy she knew. Using drops of wine as ink, Jon began to trace shapes on her stomach with his fingertip.

She realized, between little shivers at the feeling of air cooling liquid, that he was painting her the same way Summer had once suggested.

He drew a heart, then he leaned down and she gasped at the sudden warmth of his tongue, licking it off. The next pattern was more involved, and it took a moment for her to realize he was painting his name across her belly, then tracing it off with his tongue.

He carefully undid her jeans, and scooted them down her hips. She kicked them off as he unzipped his too, revealing the outline of his hardness beneath his boxer-briefs. There was no time to admire his body, though, because he had the wine again and was painting lower, lower, until he abandoned the wine altogether. Soft as a feather, he brushed his tongue against her wetness and she cried out.

When he spread her open and applied himself in earnest, Greta understood that the amazing alley scene was only a preview of his artistry.

With every slow movement of his tongue, she wanted more. Her hips undulated against him, showing him her enjoyment, and he rewarded her by pulling her into his mouth. She fell apart, calling out, but he didn't stop. Again and again he brought her to the brink and pushed her over, until she forgot everything but his name.

It took a moment to realize he was moving back up, kissing his way towards her waiting mouth. When he claimed her lips, she felt practically drunk. Her legs fell further apart as he pressed between them.

He pulled back to look at her as he angled himself against her opening.

"Are you ready?" he asked, concern evident in his expression. She nodded, not trusting her voice. She was *so* ready.

She expected him to nudge gently inside, but instead gasped in shock as he pushed all the way in with one thrust. They stared at each other, getting used to the feel of her tight sheath around his large cock. After a moment, he pulled all the way out, before plunging deeply back in.

"You feel . . ." he started.

"Perfect," she finished.

With another long stroke, he told her he agreed. She found his rhythm and moved in synch. Her legs wrapped around his back to allow him deeper, she pulled him close with every movement. After a lifetime without Jon, all these nights alone, Greta finally realized what she'd been missing.

Everything.

Jon grabbed one of her legs and swung it around until she was lying on her side. He sat back on his heels and gazed down at her as he pushed back in. In that position, all Greta could do was lie there and enjoy it.

"Touch me," she commanded him, and he grinned at her.

"I thought you'd never ask." With that, he pressed two fingers to her clit and sent her over the edge again. Her core clenched around him as the waves rolled through her. When she opened her eyes again he was still staring at her with a look of awe on his face.

"What?" she asked, worried she had made a weird O-face or something.

"I've never seen anyone look as beautiful as you do right now." He smiled again, melting her a little before the tension started building up again as he continued his motion against her. This time, he used his other hand to fist her hair back and pull, hard. The top of her body was immobilized as he sped up, pounding her.

"Are you ready?" he asked again, this time with a growl. She couldn't nod with his hand holding her head so tightly but her pussy spoke for her, her inner muscles beginning to tighten again. When they came together, Jon was still staring directly into her eyes, not allowing her to slip away.

He stayed still inside her for a long time, releasing her hair and stroking it before finally easing out and lying down. There was nothing spoken, nothing needed to be.

As Greta drifted off, she had a final thought that if this was what a pirate did, she would let him pillage her village any day.

Light breaking through the curtains roused Greta from a dream about food. She was somewhere enjoying sushi and miso, and it was quite the disappointment to realize she was actually in a bed and not a restaurant. A stretch later and the evening came flooding back in a rush of memories and soreness.

Oh, shit. She had to get out of here, she had to get home, she had to get Mina ready for school. Flipping over, she saw Jon still out cold next to her, nude. Okay, maybe she could wait just a minute before rushing off.

The night before was so overwhelming, and then she'd fallen asleep so quickly, she felt like she hadn't really had a chance to study her lover. Her lover! She had a lover. It sounded extremely sophisticated in her head. Cosmopolitan. European, even. There was a little morning scruff on him, and his hair was rumpled even more than the bed sheets.

Her eyes travelled lower, to the sculpted chest and its fine covering of hair. Lower still and she realized he had the much-coveted V on his abdomen leading down to his dick. Summer was going to be very super jealous. She sighed happily. Her lover was so hot.

"Hey, creep," her lover said, apparently having been awake and watching her the whole time.

"I gotta go," she replied, with as much dignity as she could muster, and wrapped a sheet around herself to start the process of collecting the trail of clothing they'd left scattered about the apartment.

"We could do another round first, though, if you'd like." The rising tent of the blanket left no doubt but that he would also like.

"I really can't." It wasn't even just that she had to go, she wasn't sure she could physically do that again so soon. For all the associated joys with a well-endowed lover, it also took a bit of recovery.

Her bra had apparently never made it off, so there was that. Her panties were under the bed, her jeans had been kicked off and onto an armchair on the other side of the room. She knew her shirt was still in the living room, she'd deal with that in a moment.

"So, um . . . what *are* you doing?" She could hear the smothered laughter in his voice.

"Changing," she called.

"Underneath the sheet? You look like a stumbly ghost." The laughter was slightly less smothered as she lost her balance for the third time beneath the navy sheet. It was darker inside her little tent than she'd expected.

"I am trying to change in a ladylike manner," Greta informed him, knowing full well that it had been a badly considered decision for someone already missing her dignity.

"We shagged last night, I can probably handle watching you button your pants, you know." It took a moment of howling laughter before he got it out, but she appreciated the sentiment. The thing was, she probably wouldn't have retreated into a high thread-count cave if they *hadn't* shagged. It wasn't even that she was so shy, but the intimacies of the previous evening made her feel a little bit vulnerable.

Just a little bit. Just enough to make her want to change in there, and not make more eye contact with him knowing that when the last time they had stared into each other's eyes, they had been as close as two people could possibly be.

"I'll walk you out, at least," Jon said, hopping up without a trace of embarrassment as she emerged from her cocoon. "No time for breakfast? Coffee? I've a proper espresso machine that I rarely get to impress people with."

"Extremely tempting, especially since I was dreaming about food, especially since I am dying for coffee, and even more especially because I am dying for coffee. But I really have to get to Mina." Truly dying for coffee. And maybe just a tiny bit for a little more time with her lover. That word was never going to get old.

"Dreaming about food and not me?" He didn't sound genuinely offended, but she reassured him anyways.

"It was the chirashi at ICHI."

"Enough said," he told her, picking up her t-shirt and carefully turning it the right way out before handing it over. "I can't compete with that. Let's go out tonight."

Greta pulled the cotton over her head and stayed inside for a moment. Was going out a euphemism for more sexing? And did she mind if it was? And would he save the rest of the Barolo for her?

"Okay. I'm having dinner with the girls, so just text me where to meet you." Her head popped out, and she pulled her hair into a quick pony before leaning into Jon's chest for a totally awkward goodbye. But how did one deal with Mornings After? She honestly had no idea, having not done it with anyone who wasn't a real boyfriend. And rarely even them.

"Take some bread home for the little one. Unless you can't just call in and go back to bed for just a little longer?"

"Well, I'm pretty obviously not sick, so . . ." She grabbed the loaf he offered and stuck it in her purse.

The little flutters in her tummy at the idea of more betrayed her logical urge to go hide in her own bed for a while to process. But alas, Mina awaited. Her cell showed several missed texts and calls, including one from Bob from just a moment before. She had half an hour to make the fifteen minute trip back to his Victorian, sent him a message indicating as much, and headed out to hail a cab without a look back at Jon.

Once safely inside, Greta heaved the giant sigh that had been building up inside her since she'd woken up.

"You okay, miss?" asked the cabbie.

"Love is dead," she told him. It was, had been since Camelot, likely, but her evening with Jon had convinced her of one thing—he still believed. He actually thought he could show her the error of her ways, and that was really sweet. She gasped loudly as another thought suddenly occurred to her.

"You okay, miss?" asked the cabbie, again.

"Chivalry is not dead," she told him. Because if he really believed in love, and really wanted to show her how to believe again herself, that meant he really *was* a gentleman.

Huh. How to reconcile that with her own belief that neither of those things existed? She decided to allow it—Jon was misguided, so that didn't make him some sort of knight. What a day. And it had only just begun.

When she walked in the front door after tipping the concerned cabbie a little extra, Mina was waiting to grill her. The sound of a slamming back door was the only noise from Bob, but at least there was a check on the counter.

And a note, not so typically. She jammed it into her pocket to read later. Probably a grocery list.

"I see you staring at me, child. Say what you want to say and get it out, because I bet you haven't had breakfast yet, and we have to leave in half an hour." Greta spent a moment longer than she should have wondering if there was enough time to just stop for sushi before school before resigning herself to eggs.

"I'm not saying anything to you, Greta, that you probably haven't said to yourself," Mina said accurately.

"I hope you plan to get a cootie shot while I'm in school today." Less accurate, though a morning-after pill wouldn't be a bad idea. Same thing, right?

"Why do you assume I need a cootie shot?" Greta avoided the accusatory glare as she melted butter into a pan with a little bit of garlic paste.

"I think we both know there was kissing last night." The silence was broken only by the sizzle of the garlic and the fork clattering against the bowl Greta was beating eggs in.

"I'll invest in cootie-ridding measures while you're at school today. Maybe more than one form." She poured the eggs into the pan and immediately started scrambling. "I mean, if I *were* to have done kissing I would; I'm not telling you that I for sure did."

"Was there more than kissing?" At that, Greta turned off the heat and turned around to see Mina was now the one avoiding the eye contact.

"What—exactly—do you mean by that?" Those little hooligans at her school told her about sex? It was too early. She was too young. When did Greta learn how babies were made? Okay, Amy had gigglingly shown them all an informative book in first grade. But she'd never held herself up as a shining example.

"Coco says that when grownups kiss a lot sometimes they do a special handshake too and that's what sex is and so I haven't let Ethan Sedger get anywhere near my hand just in case." She was blushing, and Greta had a hard time not smiling in relief.

"I would definitely not want Ethan to shake your hand, Mina. You've got a good policy there. In fact, I can be totally honest with you and say that Jon and I absolutely did not do a handshake last night. Do you want chives on your eggs?" She scooped some eggs onto a piece of toasted sourdough, courtesy of Jon, for Mina.

"Okay." Nothing more was forthcoming, so Greta assumed she was both off the hook on the *special handshake* and on the hook for chopping some chives. As she spooned salsa onto her own bowl of breakfast scramble, she sighed again.

Bob was probably never going to be the one to do the sex talk with Mina, but she also felt like it really wasn't her place to go buy a copy of the book that had equally grossed out and intrigued her and her friends in elementary school. If she were Mina's mom . . . but she wasn't.

That talk was definitely outside of her comfort zone anyway.

Once she'd gotten Mina safely off to school and parked in the Safeway lot, she unfolded the note from Bob. It was not at all what she'd expected, in fact, it was such a surprise that she forgot the engine was still running and almost walked in with the keys still in the ignition.

G~

You probably don't know tomorrow is the anniversary of my wife's death. I don't talk about it much. Every year I plan to do a thing with M, but she just looks too much like her mother. Hard to be around her. Off for a while. Light a candle, will you? M will appreciate.

The letter wasn't signed. Greta could have stayed in the lot, staring at the letter for a year if the California sun hadn't suddenly broken through the clouds and reminded her that daylight was wasting. So Bob wasn't evil after all, just brokenhearted. Who would ever have guessed? Were other people this obscure? And if that were the case, how could anyone possibly know what other people were thinking?

Later, at the pharmacist, she collected a morning-after, along with a refill on her lapsed birth control prescription.

"Grown-up cootie shot, amirite?" she asked. The other woman stared at her.

"That's what I call antibiotics, ma'am."

Oh, fuck. We moved way too fast.

Chapter 12

Greta practically floated into the restaurant. It was absolutely amazing what a little banging could do to improve one's outlook on life. It turned out that everyone had been right for the past few years. She *did* need to get laid.

Amy and Summer were already at the table, so she bypassed the hostess stand and headed over. They'd had the foresight to order her a glass of wine already, which was waiting at her spot. She started, for a moment, to feel the now-familiar twinge of guilt in her tummy at the thought of deceiving such lovely ladies, but then she remembered—

She was now officially sleeping with the guy they'd picked out for her. So the whole "fake boyfriend" thing was really just a technicality, one they didn't need to concern themselves with.

Greta was certain her justification wasn't indicative of a failing moral compass.

But really, friends with benefits was an ideal situation. Because Jon was amazing and fantastic and sexy and accented, and this way she got to take advantage of every part of him, without any expectations of anything else.

She wasn't even going to bother hinting at trouble on the horizon to the girls today, because there was none. It was smooth sailing as far as she could see.

"You're glowing," Amy remarked before she'd even gotten settled in her chair.

"She is. What's that about? She hasn't glowed in years." Summer assessed her and added her two cents.

"She can hear you," Greta reminded them. Years? Really? Sheesh, she was going to have to make sex a regular part of her routine. So many conclusions she had come to after a nice bath and a nap, and quick trip to the clinic. Oh, Mondays.

"And as it so happens, it turns out there was a reason I hadn't glowed in so long," Greta said primly.

"Wait a minute—what? You guys *just now* had sex?" Summer had a combination of confusion and surprise on her face that was mirrored by Amy.

"How is that even possible? You guys have been dating for weeks."

"It just . . . didn't seem right before now." Greta drained her glass and flagged a server to bring another. Years? She decided not to believe that. She paid good money for makeup designed especially to give her a glow.

"I know what it is," Amy said.

"No you don't," Greta promptly replied. Wait—she shouldn't have said that. Now she'd have to make something up.

"Yes I do. Summer, she's in love. She made him wait so it would be extra special. Oh my God, I ship it so hard!" Now Amy was the one glowing. Bitch. But that was actually a better answer than whatever she was going to have to lie and say, so.

"I did make him wait." She blushed a little.

"Do I even want to know what was on that sex tape, then?" Summer always cut right to the chase.

"Technicalities?" This was embarrassing.

"What *kind* of technicalities?" Amy, of course.

"I go to Catholic church, so I know this. It was butt stuff," said Summer.

"Oh my God!" Greta needed to shut this down. Though in hindsight, this also probably explained a few things about Summer. "It was not butt stuff!"

"It was butt stuff," Amy whispered knowingly. She and Summer fist bumped.

"It was not butt stuff! He just went down on me in an alley, was all!" Naturally, this was the moment she raised her voice, and naturally, this was when the server had suddenly materialized with a second glass of wine. "No judgies," she told the blushing guy.

"None here. I enjoy some butt stuff myself on occasion," he said, and beat a hasty retreat.

"I'm leaving that guy my number," Summer announced.

"I don't want to be here anymore," Greta said.

"You can go, but I'm staying. I really like this conversation. Did you butt stuff Ian Davis? Because you guys dated forever, but you were still a virgin, or so you *claimed*." Amy was apparently prepared to make an afternoon of it. Well, that was fine, but Greta wasn't leaving without a burger. Sex made you hungry, it turned out. Luckily, it also burned calories. Sex was really awesome, it turned out. Sex, sex, sex. She sighed happily.

"I was in eighth grade, Amy. I did not butt stuff Ian Davis. I didn't love him like Greta loves Jon."

"That's disappointing," Amy said. "Can we talk about me now?" Apparently a lack of butt had killed her interest in the conversation.

"Can we please?" Greta was not even remotely upset the focus had shifted away from her and Jon and the love they supposedly shared. Sex, though, she definitely loved that. Sex with Jon. Sex, sex, sex. Good times.

"I am soon to join the world of unemployment!" Amy announced grandly.

"I would not have announced that so grandly," Summer said. Greta fist-bumped her. Maybe that was a little insensitive, but whatever. She was glowing, she could do what she wanted.

"I mean, what's happening? Didn't you save enough puppies?" Greta asked.

"Maybe the tree she sat in got cut down."

"She wore lipstick tested on animals."

"She forgot to order the vegan beans at Chipotle."

"*She can hear you.*" Amy was significantly less

pleased when it was her that was the subject of conjecture.

"So what's up?" Summer smothered her giggles long enough to ask.

"Since that last fundraiser was such a shitshow, we aren't meeting our budget requirements. So my hours are getting cut. Specifically, all of them. My position is going to be volunteer starting next month." Amy was slightly less grand in relating the details, which obviously hurt her. It wasn't just the paycheck for her, she really thought she was making an important difference in the world.

"What are you going to do?" asked Greta.

"She could go back to law school," suggested the ever practical Summer.

"She is *not going back* to law school," Amy said. "Also, I see why that bit was annoying to you now, Greta."

"Do you have any, like—sister organizations or anything?" Greta was feeling a little guilty.

"Not really. We fell out with Green Planet after a difference of opinion on snail-based moisturizers. My boss said I can move into the office, though, since I won't be able to pay rent on a volunteer's nonexistent salary. So that's pretty cool. It'll be like tree-sitting without any issues of balance or plumbing." Amy was shockingly optimistic.

"Can she stay with you?" Greta asked Summer, horrified. "That sounds miserable."

"I live in a studio apartment as is. That wouldn't be as big of a deal except that I still have a two-bedroom's worth of crap jammed in there from Jean-Luc." Summer's roommate had accepted an internship at a New Nordic place in the Arctic Circle. Since he'd be gone for an entire year, she'd downsized while he was overseas, and he paid her a little bit of money to store his furniture.

"I wish I could help," Greta said sincerely.

"I'd rather live in a cardboard box than deal with Bob's smarminess," Amy announced. Greta did not feel slighted; she'd had the same thought often enough herself. If she hadn't formed such a bond with Mina, she'd have left a hundred times.

Probably. There *was* that note. She felt no need to mention it right now.

It *was* a super convenient arrangement, after all. Being a starving artist was far more palatable when you lived in someone else's mansion.

"Speaking of Jean-Luc, though, I have some news too," Summer said, a little grin starting to spread across her face.

"You're banging Jean-Luc?" Amy immediately began to clap.

"He's in the North Pole, Amy." Greta thought for a second about some of the graphic texts she'd received from Jon. "You're phone-sexting Jean-Luc?"

"You get laid one time and immediately forget there's anything else in the world that can be considered news," complained Summer.

Not true. Totally not fair and not true. It was just the only kind of news Greta really cared about in her newfound orgasmic haze.

"I applied for a new job, and they called me back for an interview today." Summer brought her back from her yet again drifting thoughts.

"Oh, yay," said Amy in a dull voice, clearly disappointed about the Jean-Luc letdown.

"Tell us about it! Is it one of the places we've eaten at recently?" Greta kicked Amy under the table for her insolence. Although she secretly agreed—Jean-Luc was a beautiful specimen of a man, with his Roman nose and French accent. But then, who needed a French guy in her bed when she had a perfectly good British DJ? She wished *last* night was the one that got taped. Her panties went wet all over again at the memory that flashed across her mind of his face when he came.

"No, it's more of a private chef-type thing. Cheftastic would let me write my own menus and work alone, but they'd handle all the marketing and accounting. It's all the things I love about the idea of opening my own place, with none of the things I dread." Summer was practically glowing herself.

"That actually sounds really perfect for you." Amy was far more sincere now.

"The best part is how much control I get while still getting a steady paycheck. You have to have so much money saved to open a restaurant. No one turns a profit for at least a year, sometimes closer to two or three."

"Paychecks. I remember those," Amy said wistfully.

"Me too," Greta agreed.

"Is Bob late again? How many times in a row is this now?" Summer made a fist and pounded it into her opposite hand. "I swear if I ever see him alone at night . . ."

"It's a lot of times. But hey, I don't pay rent or a car payment, so it's okay."

"It's not okay, because that's not how you treat your employees. Do you think he 'forgets' to pay his employees at the tech place? Guaranteed not. Are you looking for different jobs? Someone told me the chef-owner at Thai Me Up was still looking for someone to nanny for the baby she's having in a few weeks." Summer had mentioned that one a few times, actually, but babies were *exhausting*, Greta thought, so no.

Plus there was the issue of abandoning Mina.

"I don't want to talk about it right now. We've got enough to deal with here. Plus, I'm meeting Jon in a little while, and I don't want to be all verklempt." Amy immediately began to make kissy faces at the table. It was shades of Mina all over again.

Next thing she knew, there'd be handshake talk. Although honestly, she wouldn't necessarily mind discussing the details of her special shake. It was just such a good handshake. Probably the best one ever. Yeah, she was definitely angling for another one tonight.

"We can't take her anywhere," said Summer.

"You can take me anywhere you want. Home, for example. I would not mind watching Jetta do it. I bet they have really intense, dramatic sex, with like—lots of staring into each other's eyes." Greta wasn't sure if she was more annoyed that someone else had applied the celebrity name, or that Amy was entirely correct about their sex life.

"Oh, you can always come here," their server muttered as he delivered the burgers just in time to overhear again.

"Jetta?" asked Summer.

Greta read the address again. This was definitely the place, it just looked pretty shady. She walked further down the alley, while wishing fervently that she'd tossed some pepper spray in her purse just in case. A couple was most definitely in naked compromising positions in the shadows of the building next door, and she was torn between wanting to stare and wanting to flee.

This was exactly what must have run through the kid's head behind the bowling alley. She totally understood him now. With a smile for the couple, she skipped along to the entrance, which was no small feat in heels. A giant metal door set deep into an alcove and spray-painted purple loomed before her.

"ID and twenty bucks, darlin'," said the six-foot something woman in leopard print waiting just outside the door. "Is that MAC's Rocky Horror lipstick? I tried to get that and it sold out."

That was not actually a woman.

"You can usually find some on Amazon, I've found," Greta confided. "Here's my ID but I think I am on a list? Of some sort? My not-boyfriend's playing here tonight."

"*Honey*. You should have *said* you were Greta! We've all been dying to meet you. I'm Nevaeh, by the way. Lordy be, she's managed to see our Jonny-boy naked *and* she wears MAC," the drag queen exclaimed to the sky. "We love her. We really do. Wait, what do you mean, not-boyfriend?"

"It's complicated, I suppose," Greta said, stepping forward as Nevaeh opened the door for her, bicep flexing in a way that reminded Greta she should totally work out more because she didn't look that good in a cocktail dress. And usually she thought cocktail dresses were her thing. You learn something new every day, she supposed, and today it was that she'd been out-womanned by a man.

"You think you can tell a woman like me anything about complicated? *Pedro*!" She suddenly roared. "Cover me, I need to buy a lady a drink! Follow me, honey, and watch your step on the stairs." What had she just walked into? There was a faint pulsing beat, and a narrow hall. It felt like more of a mistake than an entrance. Then they rounded a corner, and suddenly the whole club opened up. There was the kind of flirtatious courtyard covered by what looked like a glass dance floor. And if she wasn't mistaken, that's what she was being led to.

They walked up multiple flights of steel industrial stairs, passing doors to rooms with what looked like extremely interesting entertainments inside. At the top, a small bar beckoned from the left of the balcony that had a view of the dance floor below. It was covered in roiling bodies, glow sticks and glitter reflecting off the sheen of skin everywhere she looked.

So it wasn't the floor—it was the heavenly view of it she got. *Well, played, Neveah.*

"It's pretty amazing, isn't it? Have you seen him perform before?" Nevaeh had walked up to her leaning over the rail and marveling at the circus beneath. She handed Greta a glass of something blue and potent. That was why the song sounded familiar—sure enough, there was Jon in the DJ booth, headphones on and the crowd in the palm of his Force-ful hand.

"No," Greta said. And goodness but it was amazing to watch. A flick of his wrist in the booth changed a beat that sent a ripple through the crowd as though they were on strings. "And . . . wow."

"Wow is right. You are one lucky bitch. Now drink up and explain to me how the man who does all this isn't your boyfriend? I'd be angling for a ring, myself. Have you not seen him? Delicious." She touched plastic cups and they both drank up. Greta's mouth filled with saliva as the drink burned its way down her esophagus. Blue was just a pretty disguise for grain alcohol, evidently.

"I don't believe in boyfriends. Jon's my lover." Oh, that was just as much fun to say as it was to think. And she did sound totally cosmopolitan. Hell yes.

"That sounds slutty," said Neveah.

"Are you sure it isn't cosmopolitan?" She had another tentative sip. A pleasant side effect of the drink's high ABV was that it sort of numbed everything it touched, and the second swallow was significantly less painful than the first.

"Maybe," Neveah said doubtfully. "But if you were my person, I'd just assume that meant you wanted an open relationship. Which is fine, of course, we love our polys around here, but that doesn't really sound like what's happening here."

"Oh! No. It's more like how my friends want me to settle down and I'm like I *have* settled down, except that it's with the BBC and my bathtub, but they insist so I pretend Jon's my boyfriend, which he totally isn't but he *is* my lover, so we've got that. No big deal."

There was dead silence for a long time. Nevaeh turned back to the dancers, now enjoying a club remix of something Madonna.

"Straight people are fucking weird," she finally muttered. They stared off into space for a while, not seeing each other or the dance floor.

Greta smelled Jon before she saw him, the mix of ocean brine and leather enveloping her a moment before his arms did.

"Hey, you. Oh hell, are you drinking the Jungle Juice?" He turned accusingly to Nevaeh, who suddenly had very important things to look at everywhere but at Jon.

"It's not bad, once you get used to it. Want a si— oh, never mind, I drank it all." Greta was ready to dance. So ready. "I'm dancing, you do what you need to," she told him.

"I'll help you down. I've buggered up my ankle on these damn steps more than once after a few cups of Nevaeh's Jungle Juice." He grabbed her arm and gave her ass a little smack.

"Not so fast, Jonny-boy. You owe me fifty bucks over the Giants game." Neveah towered over Jon in her chunky heels and held out her hand.

"Does literally *everyone* have a gambling problem?" Greta wondered.

"Yes." Neveah passed out another round of blue lighter fluid and gently tucked Jon's money into her ample cleavage.

"So how do you guys know each other?"

"We work out at the same gym," Jon said.

"And you know the gay clubs are the best dance clubs around, so it just made sense to start booking him." She smiled fondly at Jon as she adjusted her bra around what Greta now saw was a sizeable roll of bills.

"You didn't know I was a DJ when you tried to hire me the first time."

"Well how was I to know go-go dancing wasn't something you were interested in? We figured out an arrangement regardless, now didn't we."

Greta's eyes were pinging back in forth between them. This was better than television. Well, American television anyway.

"Speaking of go-go dancers, I believe there's someone here to meet you, DJ Force." Neveah smiled at someone over Jon's shoulder. A slinky young blond guy in a jockstrap and athletic shoes sashayed around Greta. "This is Jack. He works a box on the floor."

"Jack," he extended his hand and visibly caressed the palm of Jon's hand with his middle finger as he shook it. Greta grinned. Would she ever grow tired of seeing Jon through other people's eyes? Tonight had been so surreal, so magical, that she'd almost forgotten to keep her guard up. As Jack looked over at her, she saw herself through his eyes, too—a girl this talented, gorgeous man had picked out of a crowd. As someone worthy of his time. A fairy tale. She tried holding her own hand out. He took it.

"Jack," he said, trailing his finger in the exact same way. It was pretty sexy. If Jon had been the one to do it to her, she'd probably have let him move right into the other special handshake. As it was, she planned to try it on him pretty soon. Because it had already been almost an entire day since they'd had sex and she was ready for more.

Ready to keep pretending the fairy tale was true. Ready to give up, just for a little while, the sheer exhaustion it took to keep Jon at arm's length.

From the looks Jon kept sending her way, it was clear he was ready too.

"Who's ready for lap dances?" asked Jack.

"We should probably get out of here," Greta said, at the same time Jon said, "We can negotiate." Her eyes widened until he grabbed her butt again and pulled her in.

"I want to give you a personal lap dance, that is."

Earlier in the day, she'd thought they had moved too fast. But as she skipped the goodbyes and hustled Jon down the metal stairwell, she thought that they couldn't possibly move fast enough.

The cab back to his apartment was nearly as frenzied as the dance floor had been earlier. Twice, the driver had to remind them that clothes were to remain on in the vehicle. If they'd gotten kicked out, Jon would happily have carried Greta the rest of the way.

Matt had once sworn to Jon and Rust over beers for the conversation to come up, that the sex he was having with Angie now was even better than the sex they'd had five years ago when they'd met. If that was the case, then soon enough Jon and Greta were going to be lighting up the Bay with dynamite every time they so much as kissed.

It took real effort on his part to stop kissing her as he unlocked the front door, but finally they made it in. She started heading back to his bedroom automatically, but Jon stopped her.

"I believe I promised you something." She looked shocked and delighted at the prospect. She'd be even more delighted in a minute, he thought as he pushed her into an armchair. Being a DJ meant he lived for music, for the beat. He knew how to hypnotize entire crowds with pulse pounding melodies, and he knew how to move his body to them. Dancing was part of the territory and he was a freaking fantastic dancer. Plus all the time he spent at Nevaeh's club meant he'd picked up a trick or two. "Sit on your hands."

She obeyed, and he put the needle down on a Mark Ronson record. When the beat started, he began to move his hips. Slowly at first then as the beat picked up more forcefully. He caught her gaze and dared her to look away, but she was transfixed. Moving closer, he nudged her legs apart as he danced between them moving closer and closer to her.

She started to pull a hand out to grab him and he froze until she put it back in place. He gave her a smirk and waved a finger at her. "Don't touch."

Jon went lower, his head was now between her thighs. He slowly moved his arms round her waist and under her arse, and then in one swift movement stood, so he was holding her as she wrapped her legs around him. He kept moving, channeling his best Magic Mike, until she was squirming against him and he was so hard he thought he'd pass out.

She slid down his body like he was a fireman's pole and she was on her way to a fire. It only took seconds for them both to divest themselves of their clothes and then it was Greta's turn to push Jon down onto the chair.

"I feel like I should tell you that I spent today taking precautions so neither of us gets . . . the cooties."

Jon burst out laughing. "I've a copy of my last test if you want to see it, too. I am certified cootie-free." She looked placated, and just in time. As pro-responsibility as he was, he didn't think he could possibly wait any longer to feel her skin on his.

He settled back into the chair and Greta rewarded him with a flick of her tongue over the tip of his cock. Oh God, it was even better than his fantasies. Jon watched through lidded eyes as her tongue swirled over him. It flattened out and swiped up his length, and back down until he was begging for her to take him in her pretty mouth.

She did, ever so slowly. It was an agonizing sort of pleasure, and he had to restrain himself from pushing back, to let her lead. This was her show.

When her lips reached the base of his shaft, Jon thought he actually could die happily.

After that, she sped up. It was a blessing and a curse, because with every perfectly executed forward motion, Jon had to think about the Giants to stop from coming too soon. It only took a moment or two before he had to grab her hair and pull her back.

Her hair, he had lately decided, was one of the wonders of the world. Thick, dark, slightly curly—it was like a mermaid's long locks. Or a sea siren's. She raised off her knees and kissed him deeply as she climbed up to straddle him.

Jon broke the kiss to watch her face as she lowered herself, ever so gently, onto his waiting cock. The growl rose from the back of his throat as he felt again how tight she was, how wet and ready for him. He fit so perfectly, she was everything he never knew he was missing.

They were made for each other.

Her hands came up to cup his face. She kissed him again, in perfect rhythm with her hips. They lifted until he was almost completely out, then slammed back down to join their bodies completely. Jon softly wound her hair around his hand once, twice, then pulled hard. She moaned so loudly he remembered for the first time that he had neighbors. Oh well, they could enjoy the free performance.

With one fist still tangled in her hair, he pulled Greta's head back to expose her breasts for his mouth. He feasted on each of them in turn as she ground against his dick, held in place by his other hand heavy on her waist.

He could feel her inner muscles fluttering around

him, her climax imminent. As much as he wanted to give her a hundred before allowing his own, it wasn't going to happen. Right now he wanted to come with her, for her, in her. He wanted her to know how his body responded to hers. He wanted to tell her he loved her.

So he did.

His words pushed him over, thickening inside her and filling her with the most intimate part of himself. He felt her follow a moment later, as he still pulsed inside her. She collapsed on his shoulder and bit it gently.

"Wow," she murmured, half giggling. "That was amazing."

He knew she'd heard him, and he knew it was too soon for her to respond. But as for Jon Hargrave, he was definitely in love with Greta Steinburg and he didn't care who knew it. So he carried her into his bed, cleaned her up, and held her as she fell asleep, writing a new song in his head the whole while.

Chapter 13

Perhaps she'd heard him right the other night, and he *did* think he was falling for her. Because Greta was beginning to have the sneaking suspicion that Jon was not even remotely put off by her sabotaged dates. For example, she really thought feeding the animals at the zoo with Mina in the sun all day would be miserable. It sounded miserable to *her*. But here was Jon, wearing a rubber trunk and ears and chasing Mina around while trumpeting at her.

Who was really being punished here? She decided not to delve too deeply into that one. After all, Mina was still having fun and that was really the whole point of this one.

Bob had texted her earlier that he had double-booked dinner with different women that evening, and would she mind telling Mina he wouldn't make it to her school play? *Actually, Bob, I mind plenty.* Some day, some day when she was more financially stable, she was going to tell that tumbling dickweed just what she thought of him and his terrible parenting.

Today was not that day.

Although the thought of that reminded Greta that she still had a painting to finish before she could send off her piece of the proposal to her author. It was going to be her project while Bob was at the play—Greta had gone to the dress rehearsal, so she wouldn't feel guilty missing the big show.

After the play wouldn't work, because Greta was heading straight to Jon's. An addiction was forming, she knew it, but she couldn't bring herself to care. Sleeping with him was the best decision she'd made since deciding to invest in Netflix, and that was pretty much the highest praise she had for anything. Luckily, he hadn't brought up that thing he'd said that night again in their texts, so she was willing to chalk it up to the heat of the moment, and carry on with the benefits.

"I'm coming for you!" Jon warned as he charged again, and Mina shrieked, but she wasn't his target. Greta was unwittingly swept into the air and over Jon's shoulder.

"Put me down!" She tried pounding on his back, but it did nothing to break his grip. He was a marauding pirate elephant, and she was the booty. No sooner had the thought popped into her mind, but she felt him wind up for a smack on her booty.

"If you're ready," came a stern voice. Greta felt herself carefully lowered to the earth as the zookeeper cleared her throat. She had gray hair, khaki pants, and a resting bitch face Martha Stewart would envy.

"We're ready, mum," Jon said in his most charming voice, smiling that crooked-toothed grin and generally charming the pants off both Greta and Mina. The zookeeper, Karla, was having none of it.

"I am not your mum," she said crisply, "Now follow me." No one bothered to explain that was just how he pronounced "ma'am". They just followed.

"Who do we get to feed first?" Mina asked, oblivious to anything except the animals. She was so damn cute. Jon grabbed Greta's hand and grinned, and she knew he was thinking the same thing. It was funny how much like a family they felt all together like this. Fake, crappy animal-scented date or not, she was happy.

The difference was that a pretend family never fell apart. She squeezed Jon's hand. Pretend families probably had more fun than the regular kind too. And way better sex. She could hardly even wait until Bob's return. Sadly, Mina's presence here prevented her from just pulling Jon into a secluded exhibit and seeing how much they could get away with before someone called security.

She made a mental note to add it to the sex bucket list. Because they had a sex bucket list now. She was so pleased. It had been her idea, and they'd spent an entire night on the phone planning it out. Sex tape and lap dance were probably the top honors on other people's—assuming other people actually did stuff like write a sex bucket list—but Greta and Jon had set their sights higher.

There was church sex, inspired by a naughty Catholic novel called *Priest* Summer had forced them all to read last year. *Forced, suggested, same difference.* There was museum sex, because Jon had a real hard-on for history. It was one of his finest qualities. The Mile High Club was Greta's idea, the Golden Gate club was Jon's.

Best of all, showing the list to Summer and Amy solidified the appearance of a relationship. They had fully accepted him as her boyfriend, so there was no real reason to carry on with the date charade if she didn't want to. They could just ride out the remainder of their time together in bed.

"Dolphins first, they're the easy ones," Karla announced. "I've got a bucket of fish and you just toss them. No one's squeamish, I hope."

"Can I go first?" Mina asked, clapping. *Mina.* She'd miss the dates. Maybe they should keep fake dating. For the kid.

"My bucket of dead fish is your bucket of fun, little one," Jon said. Greta had never actually planned on touching one of the nasty little things to begin with, but made a show of allowing Mina to have hers too. It took a couple tries for the girl to figure out exactly how hard you had to grasp them so they didn't flop back into the bucket.

"Slippery little blighters, aren't they?" Jon said, grabbing Mina's small hand in his own and helping her figure out a better method so the poor dolphins would

actually get a meal. They were all gathered in antici-
pation around the little bridge. When the first fish
flew through the air and landed neatly in a cetaceous
mouth, Mina looked ready to cry tears of joy.

Even Karla looked slightly mollified with the response. It was beyond Greta why this wasn't something Bob made time for, but she'd spent enough of
her time and thoughts today thinking rude things
about the man. His loss was her gain; this was turning into a pretty cool day despite the sun and the
outdoors and the animals and the weird smells and
the no-alcohol stipulation. Well, as cool as something
like that *could* be. She made a mental note to hint to
Jon that a bottle of wine and a bath together might not
be out of line.

"Do we get to do tigers now?" Mina asked hopefully.

"Unfortunately, the zoo has deemed that too dan-
gerous for civilians." The look on Karla's face left no
doubt as to her preference for feeding civilians to the
tigers. "We'll do the hippo instead." A slow grin spread
across her lips.

"Is Mina going to be safe doing that?" Greta was
immediately suspicious.

"Oh, the child isn't going to be feeding Cyrus.
Your . . . gentleman friend can do it." In *that* case,
then, no big deal. He could handle it.

They approached a large enclosure containing a single greyish lump. The path surrounding the hippo
area was raised up about six feet and bordered by a low
cement barrier. As they walked closer, the grey lump

lumbered to its feet and headed straight towards its servers.

"Hippos kill so many people every year. So many people," Karla mused. "Their mouths open 180 degrees. Then they just snap shut. It's beautiful." She demonstrated with her hands, making a brisk clapping noise that Cyrus didn't seem too impressed with.

"What's he eating, then?" Brave Jon asked.

"He loves fennel. Apples, too."

"Ah, a man after my own heart, eh, chap?" Jon tentatively reached out to pat Cyrus's monstrous snout, then seemed to think better of it. "Where's the fennel, then?"

"Oh, we're all out. You'll feed him grass." Karla pointed at a bale of green a few feet away. Jon was a much better sport than Greta would have been, hoisting the bale and yanking tufts out to offer the prehistoric beast in front of him. "Wave it in front of his nose, he'll lift his head and you can toss it in."

"I want to see his mouth do the giant thing!" Mina whispered, thrilled, to Greta.

"Me too, actually. It sounds disgusting." She could always google pictures later if the animal didn't comply. Jon did, though, taking a large handful of grasses and waving them in front of Cyrus. His head moved forward as he sniffed. Jon moved forward too, prepared to deliver the animal's salad.

In the blink of an eye, Cyrus's mouth went full open, as widely as the keeper had promised, revealing enormous yellow teeth and emitting a heart-stopping roar. Jon shrieked as loudly and at the exact same pitch Mina had earlier during their game and fell over backwards. As soon as he hit the ground he began crab-walking backwards, scuttling as quickly as he could away from the pissed-off hippopotamus.

Greta and Karla clutched each other as they howled with laughter. Mina was holding herself so as not to pee. Jon turned a shade of red not normally found in nature.

"There's today's life lesson, Mina," Greta finally choked out when she could breathe again, wiping tears from her eyes. "Even tough guys sometimes meet their match." *I so wish I had videotaped that.*

"How did no one videotape that? It would have been YouTube gold!" Rust could not have been more disappointed if the whole of Belgium had stopped making beer.

"That would have ruined my credibility, mate! You'd probably be the one to send it to the media too, you scoundrel." Jon was certain his red face would never fade back to its normal shade. He fervently hoped for it to cool sometime between now and when Greta came over. He had to find some way to reclaim the pride he had lost.

"Of course I would have. You'd do the same to me. It's what men do—enjoy every advantage. And speaking of advantages, where's the girl?" Rust glanced down at his phone. "I got a gig later I don't want to be late to. I was late last time I played there, and they threatened not to give me my drink tickets next time. Like hell *that's* happening."

Jon glanced down at his phone too. She *was* extremely late, and hadn't sent any texts. Maybe the play hadn't started on time or something. Still, he'd have thought it would have ended a couple hours ago, so that would have been a preposterously late start.

You on your way?

"I just texted. I bet she'll be here any second. I've never known her to be late before, so I'm not worried." He was worried.

"I bet she's done with you after today's little performance. You can't show weakness in front of chicks, man. They want alpha male, all the time." Rust got up grabbed another beer from the fridge and tossed one to Jon.

"I don't think that's so. Not all the time. It isn't practical," Jon said thoughtfully, popping the cap.

"It isn't about practical. It's a sex thing. Don't you ever read, man?"

"I read all the time, but I don't know where you're getting your information. It seems a bit dodgy." The beer was cold and fresh, but he really would have preferred the wine he had waiting. Maybe just because he associated the taste of it with the taste of Greta.

"You gotta get a Kindle. Chicks write down all their fantasies about getting spanked by billionaires and shit. It's kind of hot, actually. No one talks like that in real life, so it's pretty easy to make the ladies swoon when you do it. Man, I can't believe no one's told you about this before. That's probably why you never get dates." Rust had set his beer down, animated. "And now you've ruined your shot with Gretel."

"Greta. And no I haven't." Had he? She really wasn't ever late. Shit! "And I don't have dates because I don't just sleep with every girl who crosses my path. Unlike some of us."

Rust looked very doubtful. "Huh. Do you order her food for her in restaurants? Salads and shit. Keep her skinny."

Well, there was the reason women thought men didn't like an appetite. Good heavens.

"No. No, I like to actually enjoy my food with some-one who is enjoying their food too. You order girls salads? I imagine you are singlehandedly responsible for many, many therapy visits."

"What, it was in that book! The one with the con-tract. They like it, because it shows you like the way they look and want to keep it. Oh, I do contracts now, too. Rice can get you one if you want, he did mine. Probably too late for Gretel, though. Not after you screamed like a little bitch."

Jon couldn't have been more horrified, both at the words coming from his friend's mouth, and by the fact that he was truly concerned he had ruined things by screaming like a little bitch.

"Better head off, then, traffic's tough of a Friday night and you don't want to get cut off before the show even starts. You can meet Greta another time. Perhaps we'll pop round and catch the last of the set." If she showed. Seriously nerve-wracking, this. Luckily, Rust didn't argue.

"Perhaps you'll 'pop round' solo, bro. I'll leave your name at the door just in case." With that, he'd grabbed his leather jacket and headed off to the nameless crowds of submissive women just waiting for him to order them a salad and then pop them one on the rear.

Jon gave a heavy sigh, and started pacing the floor. He set his phone on the counter, checking for the umpteenth time that she hadn't texted. Or called. Or emailed. Or sent an owl. While Rust did have a point about today being a bit of a turning point for them, displaying weakness wasn't what had Jon truly concerned.

It was more that he'd come on too strong. He knew full well she had come into this—whatever this was— with no intentions of staying. That hadn't bothered him particularly, he'd never really gone into a relationship with expectations of forever on his mind. She was just slightly more pessimistic than that. Jon was an optimist himself, and he had blind faith in his ability to wear her down.

Now he had to wonder if he'd read the situation wrong. Maybe he wasn't wearing her down, but wearing her out.

Maybe she just needed a reason to run, and all these plans they were making gave her one. Maybe by pushing her to get close, he was actually pushing her away. A little voice reminded him he'd known it was too early to say the L word, but he shoved that voice down. She'd ignored it, and they'd carried on afterwards.

That wasn't going to stand, though, not without discussing it. He tried calling, but the phone only rang fruitlessly in his ear before the voicemail lady came on, reciting the number he'd reached and inviting him to leave a message.

"Bit worried about you, love, ring me back when you get this." He hung up and tapped the phone against his palm. What if something had happened to her? He texted Amy.

Greta . . . ?

She'll call u

The reply was immediate and terse. Oh heavens. She was going to break up with him. Jon felt a bit sick to his stomach. After all the moments they'd shared? He'd truly believed she was falling for him.

And he knew with utter certainty that he'd fallen for her.

He paced some more. What did one do when one was preparing for heartbreak? The couple other times in his life he'd been dumped, he'd either seen it coming or hadn't cared for longer than a few beers at the pub with his mates. If this was it for Jetta, he was about to be leveled like an old building.

He wondered if he'd told her he secretly gave them a celebrity name, if that would have charmed her at a crucial moment. Possibly it could have caused her to dump him on the spot though; it was so difficult to tell with these things. He replayed a hundred conversations in his head, trying to isolate the moments that had led to this. He'd had such certainty that she was opening up to him. The last time they'd had sex—no, made love, the night he'd told her so—she'd seemed different. Softer, somehow. Like she was showing him her heart.

It kept coming back to one thing though—today had almost certainly been the tipping point. The blooper reel went through the loop in his mind again.

Leaning forward, dangling the grasses, simultaneously seeing the depths of the digestive system of the beast, hearing its ungodly roar, and smelling the sulphurous stench rising as though it was hell's mouth that yawned before him and not Cyrus the hippo.

Falling backwards, becoming slowly, humiliatingly aware that the high-pitched keening noise echoing throughout the park was being emitted from his own mouth.

Scrabbling for purchase on the hot concrete, logically knowing Cyrus could not leap from the pit and swallow him whole, somehow unable to communicate that bit of knowledge to the lizard brain powering his motions and screams.

On the whole, it could have been far worse, Jon reflected, as he could have soiled himself.

Yes, it was certainly an undignified business. He found he couldn't blame Greta for being reluctant to shag this evening. But a break up felt a bit unnecessary. How could he salvage the situation?

He paced the floor, racking his brain. If she truly thought that men always left, he would have to find some way to show her that he was staying. He needed a way to prove to her that not everyone was like her father. To prove to her that she meant so much more to him than a series of bets and dares.

The phone rang. It was her, at long last, and he was ready for this moment.

"Greta."

"I'm so sorry." She sounded like shit on rye. Perhaps she'd already decided against the break up. What a relief.

"You sound upset, love, are you okay?" Such a relief. Not that he wanted her to feel bad. It was okay to have second thoughts.

"No. I just got done with the police." His blood ran cold, and all the snarky thoughts disappeared in his concern for Greta.

"Are you okay?" he asked again.

"I'm okay. But Bob's been in a car accident. The cops came to tell us he was killed on the scene."

Oh God, the little one. What would become of Mina?

Chapter 14

Mina burrowed further under the covers of Bob's bed, leaving Greta's hand in midair, holding out the mug of chamomile tea.

"Just a sip or two? You haven't slept at all. You need to sleep, Mina." There was no answer from the covers. In fact, she hadn't said a word since Greta had to leave the cops in the living room, walk up to Mina's child-hood bedroom, and inform her that she no longer had a living parent. That room might hold memories of happiness before, but now it was also going to be inextricably linked to the news that her father was dead.

Greta knew that if she lived to a hundred, she'd never forget the look on the little girl's face. Disbelief, horror, and most of all, despair.

Mina had often expressed her frustration that kids had to just do what everybody said, go where they were told, eat what was put in front of them. Now she wouldn't even have the familiarity of routine. Greta had no idea what to tell her, because she had no idea what was going to happen next.

"Please just one sip? For me?" Tears continued to roll silently onto the already-soggy pillow as Mina shook her head. Greta was swallowing past a lump of her own at this point. She would have done anything to protect Mina, but no one can protect anyone from death. Watching the pain rack her ward's tiny body hurt her too.

More than she knew you could hurt for someone else.

She sent a quick text to the girls.

She still won't talk. At what point do I call a professional? Greta had no idea where the line from grief to medical shock was drawn. She never felt this type of fear before. Mina had been in her care for a long time. It often *felt* like she was a parent, but she wasn't. And even if Bob wasn't the best, he was always a safety net. Now he was gone and she didn't know how to make this better. She was helpless.

It's a fresh wound. Give her time. Thank God for Summer. The girls had offered to come over immediately, but Greta thought Mina probably didn't need anyone else around. She felt like she was intruding on the little girl's grief enough as it was, but she didn't know what else to do. Helpless was an understatement, actually.

Mina had been crying into Bob's pillow for almost five hours. Dehydration was a danger. She could work with that. She could fix it. If she focused on the physical symptoms, maybe she wouldn't have to think about the broken heart underneath.

Because that was something she'd never learned to fix.

"Mina, you're going to have to drink something, or else we'll have to get you on an IV," she said firmly. She didn't want to be mean, but maybe being told what to do would be a little less scary for the kid.

After a long moment, Mina struggled to sit up and drank the cup of tea. Then she lay back down and resumed her silent vigil, staring at the photo of Bob and her mother on his bedside table.

Greta's own tears started then. Nine was too young to be alone in the world. There never was a good time, but nine. Geez, Mina was an orphan at nine.

M slp yt? Amy would let not death nor destruction force her into spelling and grammar rules. Greta reached out to smooth the hair back from Mina's face and saw that her swollen eyes had actually closed. A moment later, as Greta stroked her arm gently, her breathing evened out.

Yes. Thank God. You guys I am at such a loss.

Go through his shit. In fact, I'm coming over now she's asleep. We'll go through his shit together. Greta felt marginally better. Summer was better at . . . things than she was. Grownup things. Greta was ready to go cry under the covers with Mina and let someone more grownup handle the whole situation. The prospect of uncovering all of Bob's dirty secrets was the only thing that kept her out of bed and downstairs waiting on the porch when Summer finally arrived in a cab.

"First things first. Has the rest of the family been informed?" Straight to business. It was comforting.

"I'm not actually sure. I always had the impression Bob wasn't close to his family, he never talked about them. The police gave me his phone, it somehow just got a cracked screen, and nothing else. But I just don't know who is who on the contact list. And I don't know if I can be the one to break the news again. And again." The feeling of being completely out of her depth threatened to overwhelm her again, and tears pricked yet again. She had to do this stuff for Mina, no one else was going to do it for her.

"Photo albums?" Summer asked. "We can match up names to contacts that way."

"Yes. Yes, Mina's showed me a couple in her room. I'll go get them." Just moving around with a purpose felt like something was happening. It felt better. She peeked in on Mina as she grabbed the albums—still sleeping, but as Greta watched, she let out a little moan and a few more tears slipped from beneath her closed lids. Even in slumber, she was hurting. Greta's heart wrenched.

She had no clear answers on what would happen next. Mina couldn't go to the state. But who would take her? Until they knew, she wasn't going to leave her side. Not for one second.

She wasn't going to be another person that left.

It only took a few minutes to figure out that Bob's

older sister was Janice in New York, and a few more after that to realize—well, for Summer to realize, she was the one to call—that Bob had been dead to her for some time. She didn't even ask about Mina. There were no living grandparents. There was nothing about Mina's mother's side of the family.

Summer broke the lock on his filing cabinet and they started the process of looking through all his legal documents. That was a little easier said than done, as neither of them had the slightest clue about what they were even looking at half the time.

Articles of incorporation were jumbled together with birth certificates and contracts and old bills and who knew what else. It felt like everything under the sun was in there except what they really needed—a will. Something with the legal directives of what on earth Greta should be doing.

She could tell the cops were totally annoyed when she'd told them she didn't even know what funeral home the body should go to. She had just finally yelled at them that she was just the goddamn nanny and she couldn't make those decisions before starting to cry. They'd taken pity on her, finally, and said she could call in the morning with what she wanted to do.

With all the other things that had likely happened to Bob's body, a night in the county morgue wasn't going to make anything worse. She fought a wave of irrational anger at him, for dying and leaving her with this impossible mess. He couldn't even be bothered to clean up his damn paperwork.

"Okay, the same guy's name is on all of these contracts and stuff. I bet it's his lawyer. Let's call him." Summer pulled up Bob's contact list. "Yep, home, business, *and* cell listed. It's basically 6 am at this point. I'm calling."

Greta leaned against the wall and listened to her friend explain the situation. She felt bone-tired, not just from the all-nighter. The weight of responsibility just kept getting heavier and soon enough Mina was going to wake up to her first day without her dad and Greta still had no idea what to say to her. How to make it better. You couldn't kiss this kind of owie away.

"Okay, he's going to go through his paperwork and get back to us in the next day or two," Summer reported, snapping the phone shut.

"So . . . what do I do for the next day or two? I don't even know who's supposed to plan the funeral." Greta blew her nose. "God, I'm so *pissed* at him."

"He's on ice, girl. He'll keep until we figure this out. And speaking of ice, you need a drink. And I'm going to make you guys some food. You just sit for a few minutes. You'll need your energy for the little one." Summer decamped to the kitchen.

'Little one' reminded her that she should probably text Jon again and give him an update. The thought of collapsing into his arms sounded better than anything else in the world right now, but this wasn't about what she wanted. She pushed away the selfish whisper telling her to invite him over and let him shoulder some of the burden.

Mina had just lost her father, it would be cruel to get the pretend family together and show her what she was missing. At least that's what Greta told herself.

A couple of days passed in a haze of tears, casseroles, and phone calls with Janice. There was not enough wine in the world to deal with her, it turned out. She came to every conversation as though Bob had arranged to get himself killed just to inconvenience her. Never mind that Greta felt the same way. Janice had an extremely busy schedule, evidently, all of it revolving around her four Yorkies.

After quite a bit of complaining, Janice had finally made it clear that she did not see it as her problem to deal with the funeral or the child. That was what she called Mina—the child. Greta's heart broke a little more every time she thought about how unwanted this amazing, talented, intelligent little girl was. No parent could possibly hope for more. If she was Mina's mom . . .

The thought had come in unbidden more than once. She had no idea how it would work, but maybe she could adopt the little girl. The idea was still germinating, though, so she hadn't run it past the girls yet. Or Jon. He kept asking to come over, and she kept putting him off. It was weird how hard that was to do. That morning, she'd caught a whiff of something that reminded her of his leather-and-sea scent and she almost moaned out loud at missing him.

But this was her problem, not his.

The doorbell rang. There was no noise from Bob's room, where Mina had basically moved in. No surprise there. She was no longer catatonic, but the only words she'd spoken were to ask for more tea and to politely refuse all but the barest minimum of food.

Meanwhile, Greta was stress-eating everything in sight.

"You must be the lawyer," she said to the tall man in the suit standing on the porch, holding out her hand. "I can't tell you how happy I am to see you."

"I wouldn't say that quite yet, young lady. May I?" He walked in and started spreading out folders on the kitchen counter. "I'm afraid I have quite a bit of bad news here for you."

"Well it can't get worse than dying, can it?" She wasn't sure if she was making a joke or stating a fact. The lawyer made a noncommittal hum. *Oh, shit.*

"The long and short of it is, Bob's company went under almost a year ago, and his savings are entirely depleted." He tapped a few papers with the end of his pen. Greta's jaw dropped.

"But—no, it didn't. He went to work all the time! He had meetings! He didn't go to his daughter's piano recital because he had a business trip!" This couldn't be true. Even Bob couldn't be that guy.

"I'm afraid it did. He'd been working very hard to land a big new client," here he tapped another set of papers, "And borrowed a significant amount of money to woo them. We'd both hoped this would work out before any of his living circumstances would have to change. I am sorry Bob didn't confide in you, although as his employee I can see why he didn't."

"I can't believe this. I need to sit down. When you

say savings depleted, you mean . . . ?" Greta's hand was over her mouth. She thought she might actually throw up. So many things were coming together—how he could never seem to pay her on time or her full salary, or why he'd stopped wearing a tie to "work".

"I'm sorry to be the one to tell you this—" *Oh God that was exactly what the cop said before he broke Mina's world apart.* "But there is nothing here. The house was double-mortgaged already, and the past several payments weren't even made in partial. I spoke to the bank just before arriving. You really probably should sit down."

She obeyed numbly.

"There isn't a gentle way to say this. You aren't the next of kin. You aren't on the deed. The bank is going to be repossessing this house within the week. I'm so sorry." He did look genuinely sorry, but that was no comfort at all.

"But I'm the primary caregiver for his next of kin! She's only nine years old! They'd just kick her out?" It just didn't make sense. None of this made sense.

"I'm sorry. Even if you were a relative, without your name on the deed, everything would go into probate regardless. Unfortunately, nothing about this process is smooth. You should start packing as soon as possible."

Greta leaned across him and threw up into the sink.

The house was quiet except for the muffled sounds of sobbing. Amy's sobbing, not Mina's or Greta's.

Summer poured more wine from the box. This was no time for mere bottles. If she'd had access to a cask, she'd likely have brought that instead. Greta had divined that when Summer had said, "I wish I'd had a cask." That was as intuitive as she was right now.

How on earth had she not seen Bob's figurative crash and burn happening?

"I was always looking at the symptoms and not the cause," she said.

"Looks like you just didn't know him as well as you thought you did," said Summer.

Amy had assured her over and over that there was nothing she could have seen, and if so, nothing she could have done anyways, but Greta wasn't inclined to believe either of them. She should have known. She could have helped, somehow. Done something. Anything.

He'd been *off* since he'd stopped paying her on time. She just hadn't wanted to delve any deeper, too wrapped up in living her own life which wasn't even her own life: too wrapped up in stagnation. In her cocoon. And now it had burst from around her too soon, her wings too wet to fly.

And Mina? Mina was too much of a baby to even consider a caterpillar. She could no longer remember a time when her tummy didn't feel like a rock tumbler, but more pebbles appeared every time her ward asked what was next.

And ward was officially the term now. It had started as a joke, like how Robin was technically Batman's ward, but mostly a sidekick. In the good old days, the so-recent days, Mina really was. Painting together, watching shows together, freaking *dating* together.

Instead of cookie-baking extravaganzas, now there was just Greta heating up soup and pleading with Mina to swallow just a sip, just enough to make up the calories it took to cry. Robin was an orphan too, she remembered now.

Although technically, so was Batman, so at least he knew what the hell he was doing.

"For someone who doesn't know what she's doing, you've held everyone together pretty effing well," Summer observed.

Amy cried.

"It wasn't *your* dad, Amy," Summer reminded her for the third or fourth time, to less avail than before.

"She's sensitive," Greta said, somewhat doubtfully. "But I'm sure as hell glad Mina isn't awake to see this hot mess."

"Do you think she's just projecting a little since she *did* get made redundant at work?" Summer asked.

"Makes sense, I kind of want to sob for a similar reason. If you pinch really hard right between your first finger and thumb, they dry up. Learned that little trick when I was a kid." More tears might relieve a little of the hot, dry pressure on the backs of her eyelids, though. After all, she and Amy were both homeless jobless wretches now.

Guilt immediately set in at the thought. Greta might not have any idea what she was going to do, but she wasn't the delicate flower Amy was. Commercials about animal abuse would have her concerned, and considering writing a check. For Amy they were tantamount to miniature holocausts, every viewing resulting in fresh waves of hysteria, phone calls, internet research, and in one memorable case, late-night ninja freedom work.

That had been her first arrest, and Amy was still very proud of it.

No, Greta was already on better footing, because she wasn't losing it, and she had no criminal record to screw up any sort of future lease.

How did you get a new lease with no income and a kid that wasn't yours?

"Can I live with you, Summer?" she asked.

"Nope."

Well, that was abrupt.

"The Frenchie?" Greta confirmed it was his room-confining things and not any sort of character flaw of her own which had caused the negative.

"Yep."

She nodded, feeling better but not actually better.

"Can we live in your office, Amy?" This was bottom of the barrel, but what else was there? A women's shelter, she supposed. It wasn't that she was opposed to the idea, but Ang was in social work, and she had repeatedly assured her sisters that death was probably preferable to a lot of the city's shelters.

For such a progressive place to live, there was always more work to be done.

"You may," Amy sniffed out. "But it's a bring your own sleeping bag situation. Also I think the building is haunted. Also there's no shower. I brought a pretty big bucket though, so we can all take turns standing in it and pouring water over." Oddly, this seemed to cheer her. "It'll be like Little House on the Prairie. The biggest will go first. Oldest, I mean. Me. You guys can bathe in the rest of the water."

"Sweet Jesus, Amy, you guys *are* moving in with me, I guess. I cannot allow this," Summer said, eyes wide. "All of you. I have running water. Electricity even, for those who don't prefer an Amish lifestyle. We can just . . . squeeze."

"Bless you," Greta collapsed into Summer's thankfully strong arms. Amy's office was starting to sound less civilized than a tent in the redwoods would have been. Now that she'd thought of it, though, that wasn't the world's worst backup plan. They could study nature, live like nature intended, just worrying about nothing but their next meal.

That would probably mean foraging and hunting though. Never mind. Fuck that.

But now that Summer had offered, they could all just crowd in there. Live like a weird little family, under one twelve-by-twelve roof. Amy could keep on volunteering, and Greta could check online for other baby-sitting jobs while Mina was in school.

They could make it work. Through the sheer force of her will, she'd *make* it work.

"Birds?" came a tentative voice, accompanied by the front door's signature squeak.

"Jon?" Greta didn't know it was possible for her heart to leap so high while still remaining contained within the safety of her ribcage. "Jon!"

He held his arms out straight, holding a wine bottle in each, while she grabbed him as though her life depended on it. She didn't realize how much she'd missed him, his warmth, his strength, his goddamn *smell*. Nothing was as good as this. Not even Summer's veggie lasagna, and *that* was amazing.

"I missed you I missed you I missed you," she muttered into his chest, crab-walking along him as he divested himself of the bottles and grabbed her close at last.

"I missed you too," he said into her hair, kissing the top of her head in the same way she'd kissed Mina's a thousand times, comforting her the same way she'd tried with Mina. If Mina felt even an ounce of this relief from her own lips, she'd kiss the poor girl a thousand times more, a million even. Because right now, there was no over-estimating the relaxation of every muscle in her back, her neck, every thought in her head.

She should have asked him over sooner. She should have but she didn't, because she was a good surrogate mom. It was just the right thing, to keep him away.

Now that he was here, though, she did feel lighter. Selfish or not, it was nicer to wallow in a pond other feet were in.

"I'm glad you're here," she said, meaning every unworthy word. Every moment she'd sat by Mina, she'd wished he was beside her. It was for Mina's good she hadn't just picked up the phone. Right? Not because admitting to herself that she was becoming dependent on him would have forced her to have a long think she didn't have time for.

Being near him now, breathing in his scent, she

realized she wanted him with a fierceness that shocked her.

And scared her.

Greta was not in a headspace to deal with him, to think about her emotions. Grief and anger and confusion and fear were a potent enough cocktail without adding him to the mix. And he had to know the way he affected her. It was so obvious. Just look at the way he'd walked in the house and immediately reduced her to a clingy mess. Of course he hadn't called first. He just showed up, knowing she'd never refuse him to his face. Using their chemistry to get his way. It was downright manipulative.

"Why are you here, anyways?" She didn't mean it to come out as combative as it did, but then she also hadn't expected him, welcome as he was, to show up unbid in the midst of the mourning taking place in this newly bereaved home. He blinked a couple times, clearly not expecting this sort of turnaround. Greta felt a twinge of guilt but squelched it, because this was *her* problem and *her* place and *her* ward and he should have waited for her to give the all-clear.

"Amy texted me, then, didn't she?" he replied, as though it should have been so obvious but it wasn't, and suddenly there was a flutter in Greta's chest. It wasn't affection, this time, it was anger.

"This isn't Amy's problem! That wasn't fair!" she cried, hearing the silly frustration in her own voice. Her fists clenched and released, clenched again.

"I can leave . . ." he said, Amy that bitch of a traitor and Summer another one, both stumbling over themselves to stop him. All the warmth he'd brought to her chilled when she thought about how he'd insinuated himself into her life via her friends. He was just like a teddy bear they'd pulled out for her. But worse, because he'd asked them to put him in when she hadn't wanted him, hadn't wanted anyone at all.

Amy and Summer were staring at her strangely. But of course, why *wouldn't* her friends call her boyfriend? Why wouldn't she want him there? The futility of the entire setup was suddenly overwhelming.

She'd been happy before him. Why didn't anyone see that but her? She had been happy alone. She and Mina against the world. It had become a mantra as of late, she'd found herself repeating it at odd intervals. Again, now, they were against the world.

She just needed a plan. Everything would be better if she just had a plan. Something to tell Mina. She relaxed her fists and counted to ten. It was fine. It was okay.

"I'm sorry. I'm just worried about upsetting Mina, is all. And the news about the house is a blow. I'm sorry I yelled." She gave a half-hearted smile to everyone, her eyes lingering on Jon's bright green ones. They were filled with compassion, and she felt more conflicted than ever.

"Okay, well, I'll call about a storage unit tomorrow, and you and Mina can take the flip-couch. Amy— I'm sorry but you seem best equipped to handle extenuating circumstances so I'm going to let you go ahead and sleeping-bag it up wherever you can find room." Summer looked extremely pained, but after

Amy's offer in the office, Greta understood why she'd jumped in.

Smashing three besties and kid into a single room was still probably preferable to letting everyone you cared about smash themselves into a squat. God love Summer. Her own room was about to turn into a shelter.

"You're all moving into Summer's?" Jon looked confused. "But . . . why?"

"Because we're all homeless," Amy sniffed. "So we're going to move into Summer's studio and live the tenement life."

"You're *all* moving into a studio apartment?" He sounded horrified. "But . . . how?"

"I have no clue, Jon. Everyone has stuff and there's not even enough room for a cat in there. We'll work it out. We'll get storage units, and new jobs, and get really good at ignoring each other, I suppose." Summer clearly already regretted her offer, but it was too late to take back.

"But . . . why wouldn't you just come live with me?" He asked, staring at Greta with a look of confusion on his face. "I've two bedrooms, the second is just my studio. There's more than enough room for Mina to stay in there. It makes a lot more sense than piling in like sardines at poor Summer's."

There was a note of hurt in his voice that she wouldn't have asked him. Of course she wouldn't have asked him. It would have been crossing an imaginary Rubicon, admitting she needed him.

But now that the offer was on the table . . .

"Summer, I'm afraid I must decline your offer. You see, Mina and I are moving in with Jon."

Summer couldn't hide her look of relief.

"That really does make more sense. Okay. I accept your declination." She turned to Amy with a hopeful glance.

"Oh, I'm still moving in," Amy assured her.

"Can't win 'em all," Summer muttered.

"I'm going to go tell Mina. Save me that bottle of Pinot," Greta said, and mounted the stairs to break yet another piece of life-changing news to Mina.

She found herself more surprised than ever to discover that Mina's tears at the news were of happiness. "If I can't be home, I'll be with you guys. That's okay, Greta."

How come every single time Greta thought she knew what was going on, she discovered she was wrong all over again?

Chapter 15

"I'll drop Mina at school on my way to the studio, will you be able to pick her up?" Jon asked, dropping a little peck on Greta's cheek and stealing her toast all in one fell swoop. She swiped at it, but he held it teasingly out of reach. When she leaned closer, so did he, and Mina made loud disgusted sighs as they kissed, long and slow.

They'd only been in the apartment for a week, and it already felt like the domestic arrangement had been going on for a year. Greta sighed too, but not in disgust. It was weird to feel so relaxed in a situation that should have, by all rights, made her very uncomfortable. Maybe it was just the comfort of knowing Jon wouldn't end their arrangement while Mina was there. He truly doted on her.

"Are you totally sure you're ready to go back?" she asked. "The counselor said as long as you're keeping up on your work, you can stay home for another couple weeks."

"I'm sure. I'm bored," Mina said with all the honesty of youth.

Truth was, Greta was kind of bored too. She didn't know for a fact that there were rules about how to deal with bereaved people, but she was pretty sure there were. So she and Mina had basically done nothing at all but eat ice cream and watch the BBC together since Bob died. Going out felt too weird.

Besides, it turned out Jon had been living without a television, and was therefore woefully behind on the latest British dramas. Greta was more than happy to park her own set in the living room and catch him up. Jon had turned into quite the Antiques Roadshow fan, too.

Every day the two girls lounged around, painting and cooking and taking full advantage of On Demand. Then Jon joined them to complete their weird little family, gathered nightly around the telly, and Mina's sudden crying jags had grown fewer, as long as no one brought up her dad or the uncertainty of the future. Last night, Mina had whispered a good-night prayer into Greta's ear—to stay like this forever.

"That does sound kind of nice, doesn't it, kiddo?" And she meant it, it really *did* sound nice. This was, she supposed, why so many people got married and had kids. The routine, the pleasure of caring for people, the little moments when her eyes met Jon's above Mina's head to silently acknowledge a joke that had also gone above her head . . . All of that was very tempting indeed.

There was a good reason so many people began families, it was just that so many couldn't finish what they started that bothered her.

"Love you, Greta," Mina had murmured. Greta had smiled back; tucked her in. Then she'd gone back out to the kitchen to have a glass of wine with Jon and talk about the studio and the girls and Mina until he'd simply picked her up and carried her to the bed.

This morning he'd tried to incite some more bed antics, but Greta was more nervous than Mina was about going back to school and got up to stress-cook.

Now, as Mina collected her backpack and waited for Greta to put her hair up for her, Jon jangled the car keys. "Don't want to be late, then, eh?"

"Are you *sure*?" Greta asked desperately one last time as Mina rolled her eyes. This was the part of faux parenting she'd never get used to, the stress of wondering if every decision was right. "You can call me to come get you!" Mina slammed the door.

"Okay, then. A whole day alone." Talking out loud didn't make the apartment feel less lonely, though. Maybe it was *she* and not Mina who wasn't ready for real life to start again. She wandered into Mina's room, where all the art supplies were set up. She gazed at the pictures on their respective easels. Mina's, a tree. It was really cool, actually, all swirly and Van Goghy. Her own held the beginnings of a new series she'd dreamed up.

Literally, the image had come to her in a dream, and haunted her until she'd managed to finish, at long last, the pictures for the children's book.

After taking that long to finish, she'd be lucky if the poor guy ever called her again. But now she could work on her own stuff with no guilt. Mostly no guilt—after all, she reflected as she filled a cup with water to get some more work done, she supposed she ought to be job hunting.

What could she possibly do? Her schedule with Mina didn't really allow her to work an eight-hour shift in the middle of the day, nor would evenings work for the same reason. If she worked weekends, that would leave Jon to schlep the kiddo around from gig to gig, which wasn't the most savory environment for a child to be in. Not to mention unfair. Much as they were both pretending, Mina wasn't really hers, and even less Jon's.

Greta dabbed a bit of blue onto the stream that flowed through the middle of her block, stared at it, then corrected with a bit of green. She guessed she could maybe find another family to nanny for, but would the parents be okay with another kid along, one whose piano lessons and play dates would always come before their own kids'? Not bloody likely.

And yet she had to do *something*, because right now she was living in Jon's apartment rent free. And if that wasn't enough to worry her, she'd recently realized her savings account was too depleted to continue with her Wine-of-the-Month club membership.

Truly, this had to be rock bottom.

Grey, that was what the stream was missing. She rinsed and reloaded the brush. Maybe she could give art lessons to other kids. Coco came to mind. *Not her, that little brat.* Not anyone who'd ever been mean to Mina. Nor anyone whose dads had ever hit on her at school functions. Nor anyone without talent whose parents only wanted an extracurricular for the CV's all rich kids seemed to be working on from birth in order to get into Ivy League schools.

When she thought about it, that basically ruled out every kid. Maybe not art lessons, then. Her brush curled and flicked, describing the flow of water around a rock. Maybe she should sell her sex tape. Not really, obviously, since it had been destroyed. But she could set up a webcam and do private shows.

The idea had legs. She could set her own schedule, and the pay would be decent. Curl and flick, the stream flowed on. She would have to be naked, though, in front of total strangers and doing the sex stuff for them. In Jon's room, while he was gone, because no way would she want him in the house. Or knowing at all. Or anyone knowing even.

Okay. She'd set up a camgirl account that involved her wearing a mask, full bodysuit, and her shows would feature mostly just dancing. Good thing she was an amazing dancer.

Who am I kidding. She really had no clue what she was going to do. Whatever it was, she had to figure it out fast. One month, she decided. One month she could continue to play house before she needed to find her own. Longer than that and Jon would forget this was only a matter of convenience. She thought he may already have. She thought she should probably rectify that soon.

"Honey? I'm home!" came Jon's voice from the front door. Would his accent ever fail to ignite a fire in her pants? She hoped not. That was still the best part of the whole deal.

"Is it time for a nooner already?" she called back.

"More like a ten am-er," and there he was in the doorway, already pulling his shirt over his head. "I couldn't wait. And with this being our first time alone in a week, I thought we ought to take advantage."

Greta placed her brush in the water before following Jon to their bedroom. "How'd you get away with that? I thought you were in post-production today."

"No one argues with a doctor's appointment, love. I very nearly felt guilty about it. Now, let's play doctor. Show me where it hurts, and I'll kiss you better." He was naked and ready. It only took a couple of seconds until she was too.

Ten am-ers would certainly take off if people knew about them, Jon thought to himself smugly. He'd just invented the greatest thing ever. He'd be a hero. If only he could actually tell the lads about this. Damn that fake doctor's appointment. He ran a finger down Greta's spine.

It was remarkable how well they fit together. Every move she made while they were making love drove him wild. It was like she was made for him.

So why on earth did everyone seem to know it but her?

The long breaths from her side of the bed indicated she'd fallen asleep. Good. She wasn't getting near enough sleep, getting up four times in the night to check on the little one. On the plus side, she was going to be an ace mum someday. On the down side, constant fatigue had made her even tetchier with him than usual.

Jon rolled to his back and stared at the ceiling, making patterns out of the little popcorn bits of plaster. There, a dog, there, a face. Her face.

He could certainly admit that this time, moving too fast was his own idea. Unlike the tattoos, she could definitely pin 'moving in together' on him. But what was the alternative? Her sisters and mother hadn't been available to take the two girls in. She could have gone to a shelter. Stayed in Amy's hovel of an office—he'd have called social services himself.

The only viable other choice was to go stay with Summer in a single room where they'd be penned in like hoarders with all the collected things that came with them. Like hell were either of those things happening on his watch. So whether or not it was too fast, living with Jon was truly the best plan.

He couldn't help it if it happened to coincide with his own relationship goals. He'd wanted a way to prove to her that he'd catch her when she fell, but apparently a house key still wasn't quite enough for Greta.

So how to win her back over? He pondered, while locating a moose in the plaster. Probably more romance. They needed more romance. Between having a child in the house and adjusting to each other's constant presence, he'd been a bit remiss in that category lately.

He rolled back to his side to watch Greta sleep. One of his fingers traced a strand of her hair that fell across her shoulder blade.

She desperately needed a night off. He'd cook her dinner. Jon ran down the list of things he knew how to cook. Things in a can, things that boil in bags, things that come on tiny plastic trays covered in wrap, toast.

Out to dinner it was, then, and dancing of course. Nothing got you out of your own mind like working up a good sweat. Hence the reason for so much of sex's popularity. Good old ten am. He rolled over, grabbed his phone, and started planning. This date was going to be epic, and for once, not prefaced by any fake nonsense. He couldn't wait.

"Right, then, this is a really cool setup. Maybe we should just stay for a round or two?" Jon asked hopefully. Greta followed his gaze to where Amy had set up the office projector to play Minecraft on the big screen. It was not that cool. Minecraft was just not that cool. Jon should be cooler than that.

"No." She turned back to futzing over Mina's dinner. Amy had wanted to order pizza, but Greta felt that Mina needed more vegetables. Always more vegetables. Growing bodies and all that. It felt like a grown-up thing to do, anyway. Amy had told Greta she'd take care of it, but all that appeared to be set up on the desk were a bag of plantain chips and a damn pizza.

"Plantains are a vegetable," Amy told her, apparently having recognized the issue from the tapping of Greta's heel upon the laminate floor.

"No, they're a fruit."

"Oh. Well tomato sauce is a vegetable." She offered a winning smile.

"No, that's a fruit too." They stared at each other at length, but Greta had a sinking feeling that it didn't really matter what her thoughts were on the matter. Mina was not eating vegetables tonight.

"Go away. After Minecraft, we're watching Frozen, so you feel free to stay out just as long as you like." Amy opened the grease-spattered box and removed a slice for herself. Pineapple, olive, and jalapeno. Perhaps Mina could be persuaded to eat a pepper? They were green vegetables, she thought. Her stomach growled.

"I think she might be too mature for that movie." She briefly wondered if Jon could cancel their reservation so they could get pizza. Hanger was setting in.

"Don't be ridiculous. No one is too mature for a sing-along to Let It Go. Anyways, I picked it because the princesses in Frozen are orphans, too, but it doesn't stop them from being badass bitches."

"Am I badass bitch?" Mina asked, materializing at Greta's elbow and reaching for the pizza as well.

"Best be off then, love." Jon hastily pulled Greta out of the office and down the corridor before she pulled off her heel and smacked Amy with it. "Reservations at Tosca wait on no man."

"This just feels like a bad idea," she muttered, throwing one longing glance back at the office door.

They made it in the nick of time, and sat poring

over the menus while Jon ordered wine. "Glasses?" inquired the waiter.

"Bottle. Bottles. One apiece," Greta clarified. Jon gave her a surprised look but what the hell. If it was a night off, it was a night off. He shrugged, and ordered a couple appetizers.

"Everything looks really nice, but I guess I just don't know how you can call yourselves Italian and not have a pizza option," Greta remarked conversationally. Jon's face darkened a bit, as though they couldn't have a conversation like that after all.

"It's a quite famous place, you know. One of my countrymen in the kitchen, and years of history on the walls. If they don't want to serve bar food, I suppose they don't have to, then." Luckily, the wine bottles arrived then, preventing Greta from telling Jon exactly what she thought about his assessment of "bar food". The server poured Jon a taste, but he motioned for a fill-up without the traditional swirl and sip.

Her cup filled as well, Greta and Jon locked eyes and drained their first glasses. She set her cup down with a smile. That was better. She felt better. He smiled back.

"Pizza is a legitimate ethnic food, though, and you can basically put any kind of fancy charcuterie on it that you want to if the traditional toppings are too pedestrian for you." No, she wasn't ready to let that one go.

"Bread smothered in sauce and cheese. Yeah, that's pretty posh, isn't it?" Evidently he wasn't either. She narrowed her eyes at him and refilled their glasses, just in time for the first round of not-pizza to be presented with a flourish.

It was pretty good, she supposed as she chewed, but twenty minutes later, as she hacked and coughed and struggled to pull breath in the ladies', she took it all back. This never would have happened with a gluten-free pie from Zpizza. If an item had bread crumbs in it, it should be clearly labeled. She chose not to dwell on the fact that in her haste to down as much wine as possible, she'd neglected to inform the server of her allergy.

By the time she got back to the table, breath still ragged in her chest, Jon looked properly contrite. "I ordered more wine to go. Let's get out of here, yeah?"

More wine did go a bit of a way towards forgiveness, she supposed.

An hour later, there wasn't enough wine in the world. So she'd stepped on Jon's toes a *couple* times. With her *heels* on, big whoop. He did not have to be so nasty about it. That toe was *not* broken, she'd wager money on it. He was just a baby.

Oh, she was drunk. So was he, though, so maybe it was his fault she stepped on him. Drunk dancing was her forte, after all. All in all, this was officially the worst date in history. Greta managed to text Amy to please drop Mina off, but her friend said they were having a sleepover with Summer and that Mina had been asleep for an hour already.

Greta hiccupped, and decided that was probably a good thing. For once, possibly the first and last time, Amy was more responsible than she at the moment.

It took Jon several tries to locate the correct house key in the echoing silence between them. Greta stomped in ahead of him, once he got it unlocked, and commandeered the bathroom. There was no comfort in there, because she'd had way too much wine to enjoy a bath. She washed her face and brushed her teeth and stomped back to the bedroom to put on sweats.

Jon went into Mina's room and started fiddling around with beats. So that was how it would be, he wasn't even going to go to bed with her. Greta's eyes pricked.

Sex could have maybe salvaged the evening, but that apparently wasn't on the agenda. She grabbed his pillow and breathed deeply of his pirate scent clinging to the cotton. It had started already. She hadn't even really let him in, not fully, and things were still falling apart. Too much time together and too little sex. Focus on the kid and not on each other. It was a story she knew all too well. It was her own parents' story. It was only a matter of time now.

This was why she'd made her vow in the first place. No such thing as a happily ever after. No such thing. She took another long inhale of his smell. She'd miss that—God would she miss it—but one more month was all she could do.

Jon would be relieved too, of course. He had to want his house back to himself. Mina—well, she wouldn't be happy about it at all, but someday she would understand. Someday.

Chapter 16

Greta woke with a start at six in the morning. She could not recall the last hangover she'd had that was this bad. Her mouth was filled with the taste of death, and her face looked equally corpse-like when she staggered out of the bed and into the bathroom. Water straight from the faucet alleviated only a fraction of the deep thirst she had.

When had Jon come to bed? She'd lain awake for hours listening to him pull a song together in the other room. If she hadn't been so pissed and distraught and sad, she'd have told him it was really cool to listen to his process. It wasn't unlike her painting, actually, working in layers, correcting each one before moving to the next.

God but she'd been a bitch the night before. Did she need to throw up? She wasn't certain. Remembering a few of the snide remarks she'd thrown Jon's way definitely made her queasy.

Then she remembered the ones he'd thrown back. All she'd wanted was some goddamn pizza and a bath and maybe a lay. Why did he have to force her into all that stuff she had zero desire to do? Greta missed her old life, the single life, the easy life.

Fucking Bob ruined *everything*.

Greta ran a hot bath, hoping a soak would relieve some of the tension in her muscles, and ideally a bit of the throbbing behind her eyes as well. She couldn't find her favorite salts, so that was just icing on her crap-cake. Plain stupid bathwater. She stole some of Jon's cologne and put that in instead. Sinking into the briny, leathery scent, Greta heaved a large sigh.

She really would miss that smell. She might not have remembered all the things they said to each other last night, but she was as certain as ever that whatever you could call their relationship was on its last legs.

A shrill ring sent sharp shooting pains through her head, and she fumbled around the edge of the tub for her phone. She didn't recognize the number.

"What?" she hissed into it, furious that anyone would assume she was up at such an hour on a weekend.

"Greta? Is this Greta Steinburg?" a voice asked frantically.

"I'm going to be honest with you. That answer is going to mostly depend on whether or not Greta owes you money." Possibly that should have occurred to her *before* she'd actually answered.

"This is Shea Hagen," the voice went on. "My sister was Mary—her husband was Bob—" Greta sat straight up in the water.

"Are you telling me you're Mina's aunt? On her mom's side? I had no idea you were—well, I had no idea about you at all, actually." This was an interesting turn of events. Greta had always just assumed there hadn't been any family on that side.

"That's exactly what I'm telling you. I'm so sorry I haven't called sooner, only Janice *just* got around to telling me about Bob. I assume her Yorkies were keeping her too busy to bother before now." Well they were certainly on the same page about Bob's sister, then.

"Okay, but . . . Mina's never mentioned you." This was just beyond weird, and Greta's head was too sore to let her think through it properly.

"She probably barely remembers I exist. Bob and Mary moved to California from Boston when Mina was three. The funeral was back here, but Bob chose not to bring their daughter. I have asked him if I can visit my niece over and over again, but he always had an excuse. After a while, I just thought maybe . . ." Shea sniffed, tears obviously creeping in. "I thought maybe Bob didn't want any more reminders of my sister, but that might mean me never seeing the last piece of her again, you know?"

"I don't know. That seems pretty messed-up to me." Greta was still not ready to pull any punches. Bob was even worse than she'd thought, denying his dead wife's family their rights to see Mina. What in the actual hell?

"It hurt, I can't deny that, but I also can't deny him his right to grieve in his own way, either. Sometimes it's difficult to understand what's in someone else's heart." Shea sniffed again. "Bob and Mary were just so in love. I'd never met a couple so happy. When he lost her, I think he just couldn't cope."

Greta felt chastened. Everyone kept telling her Bob wasn't as bad as she thought. Was it possible that she'd only seen what she'd chosen to see? If his sister-in-law could forgive him for cutting her out of her niece's life, then Greta's anger suddenly seemed inconsequential. Mina would probably be pretty happy to talk to her aunt again, if she even remembered her at all. Then came the inevitable other shoe.

"I'm so indebted to you, Greta, for all that you've done. Bob's lawyer has filled me in pretty well. I've gone ahead and filed the paperwork to begin the adoption process. Of course I'd like to be the one to tell Mina, but she barely knows me, so I think perhaps it would be best to hear it from you."

"Of course," Greta said numbly. No more Mina? But—Mina was *hers*. Shea was still talking.

". . . if we can speak again tomorrow, and I could talk to her myself then. Oh, and I know you must be in a bit of a bind, financially, with a sudden dependent, so I'm also arranging for a funds transfer."

"Of course," she repeated. "Thank you, okay. Of course. Um, I have to . . ." She hung up and dropped the phone back to the bath mat rather than finish the sentence. Greta took a deep breath and sank beneath the water.

This couldn't be happening. She was going to adopt Mina, and they were going to be together forever; it was her *plan*, even though she hadn't thought it much through yet. A little more time, that was all she'd needed, to get back on her feet. Then she'd be ready to provide, to give her the childhood she deserved, the attention she never got from Bob.

Her and Mina against the world.

Running out of air, she surfaced again to see Jon had come into the bathroom and was crouched beside her with painkillers and a glass of juice.

"If you feel half as shite as I do, you'll need these," he told her, running a hand over her wet forehead. She opened her mouth to reply, but burst into tears instead.

Greta had spent years of her life learning how to swallow her emotions, but this past fortnight, as Jon would say, had really broken down her walls. Through her sobs, she told Jon how terrified she was to let Mina go.

Aunt Shea was going to send her payment, and she was going to send this stranger the child who had her heart.

And gratitude that she wouldn't be borrowing more money from Jon, thanks to the blood money that was soon to be in her account. Because that would make her a shitty person. And Greta wasn't a shitty person. She was just confused and hung over and blindsided. That was all. She closed her eyes and let the melodic sounds of Jon's soothing voice wash over her along with the sea-scented water. After a while, he wrapped her in a towel and carried her back to bed for a nap.

Did it count as a nap when you'd only been awake

less than an hour? She supposed it did when that almost-hour had been as eventful as hers.

She woke with a start at the crack of noon. Again, the shrill ring of her phone, but this time her head only gave a dull thump instead of the knife-pains of earlier. Another unrecognized number.

"Hello?" She attempted a perky 'been awake all day' voice, but what came out was more of a croak. *I am never drinking again.*

"Greta? Is that you?" A man this time. She considered asking if she owed him money before confirming, but then decided in her newly less-deathly state that it was unnecessary. She'd simply hang up on him if that were the case.

"It is, and whom may I ask is calling?" Still croaky, but getting better with a bit of use. There was some water on the nightstand; she took a large swig.

"Greta, its Jacob Anheier." *Oh.* The author, the children's book guy. Oh God, he'd hated her paintings so much he had to call her and fire her? This day was *not* improving after all. Maybe she should still hang up. Turn her phone off. Just deal with everything later, after she'd mentally prepared.

Her finger was on the end-call icon when he continued.

"Got some really good news for you, so I wanted to call instead of email." Her finger hesitated.

"I'm listening."

"Your illustrations were amazing, Greta, you truly outdid yourself." Well. She had thought so, right up until she was positive he was firing her. "All of the publishers we submitted to agreed. We've gone to auction!"

"That's amazing!" she squealed, and then paused. "What's that?"

"It means there's a bidding war. The last bid was six figures. They're expecting this to be *the* big children's book for next holiday season. Everyone's including offers for merchandise and tie-ins along with the advance money."

She could no longer speak. *Six figures?* That was a far cry from the two grand she'd received on their last collaboration, even once it was split and Matthew's agent paid out.

"I, uh. Wow. I need a minute to . . ." She hung up on him.

Mina and Jon were chattering in the other room, meaning he'd gone and picked her up while she was recovering. That was fine, she wasn't quite ready to talk about this yet. Her portion of the advance was like—real money. Get-your-own-apartment kind of money. Support yourself kind of money.

Move-out-of-your-fake-boyfriend's-place money.

Adopt-your-ward money.

But that was off the table. Wasn't it?

This was a weird day. Greta sat on the bed a moment longer, and then made an important decision. The only decision she'd been truly confident in for weeks now. She went back to sleep.

Sunday seemed like a halfway decent day to deal with important issues, also there was the fact that Greta had slept through Saturday altogether. So Sunday was the day Jon and Greta were going to break the news to Mina about her Aunt Shea. If there was a protocol to this sort of thing, Greta did not know it.

If only she hadn't sworn off drinking. This would a most excellent time for a wine or three. Perhaps there was some sort of Bloody Mary loophole? It bore more thinking about.

"How about at dinner?" Greta hissed at Jon as they passed in the hallway.

"She needs more time than that to deal before she goes to bed. Lunch!" he hissed back on his way up from the basement laundry room with a basket of clean clothes.

"That's too soon for me to prepare my speech," she muttered as she grabbed Mina's pile for her to fold and put away.

"You have a speech?!" he followed her to grab Mina for the chore.

"Ssh. Obviously. So we'll do dunch." She stared at him for a long second. "And it'll be pizza."

"What is *dunch*?" Honestly, it was like Jon was new sometimes.

"It's like brunch, but between lunch and dinner," Mina said. "Are we doing dunch?"

"Yes," said Greta.

"I always thought we called that linner," Jon said. "But yeah. Pizza okay?"

"Pizza is *always* okay," Mina said, and Greta knew it was not very super mature to stick her tongue out, but she did it anyway because pizza really was always okay, especially on important dates. So there, DJ Fancypants, she thought.

Time seemed to drag on for an eternity while she waited for The Meeting.

"Hey Mina. Do you remember when I met you?" She hoped she sounded offhanded.

"Yeah. You let me eat candy for dinner." Mina certainly sounded offhanded. Although in retrospect, that wasn't one of her finer adult decisions, nothing won a kid over like a candy dinner. Perhaps pizza shouldn't be on tonight's menu? But no, *she* wanted the pizza. It was going to be the only cure to the intense craving she'd had since the disastrous date night.

"That's when you knew I was awesome, right?" She kicked Mina gently.

"Actually I thought my dad was going to fire you. And that made me feel sorry for you. So I lied and told him you made me eat spinach and that it made my tummy hurt and that was why I was sick all night." She kicked Greta back.

Well that was a surprise. She'd just assumed they'd been partners in crime that first day, but Mina actually was the brains of the operation. The good news was, she *had* gone on to force plenty of spinach over the next few years.

Watching *Food Inc.* with Amy had been a nanny life-changing experience.

"That was nice . . . hey Mina. Remember when I moved in with you?" Another kick.

"Yeah. You couldn't sleep so I came and cuddled you and we watched *Dr. Who* until you finally fell asleep." Hm. Again not quite how Greta had remembered it. She'd thought having a little slumber party would get Mina used to the idea of having her in the house. But come to think of it, maybe it *hadn't* been her idea. Memory was a funny thing.

She headed into the kitchen to grab some water and ran into Jon.

"Are you ready to go pick up some pizza and wine?" he asked.

"Nah. You just go." She turned on the tap and filled up her glass.

"Come with," he urged.

"I really don't feel like it. I'd have to put on real pants." She gestured down at her sweats. Obviously not going out clothes. Men knew nothing.

"Greta, love. Are you serious? Just put on some trainers." Was she serious? Of course she was serious. The most serious variety of serious.

"I'm not going. But don't forget the pineapple on mine. And did you say wine?" Perhaps never drinking again had been a rash decision. She'd simply stop drinking multiple bottles at a time. *That* was a reasonable, grown up decision.

"I did say wine." Jon folded his arms. "I'm going to pick up pizza and wine, and when I get back I will eat *my* pizza and drink *my* wine." Oh, two could play that game.

"And while you do, Mina and I will take *my* television into her room and watch *my* DVR episodes of *Antiques Roadshow*." Jon's eyes widened and he held his hands up in contrition. *Bingo*.

"Let's not be territorial, then, shall we? I'll go pick up *our* pizza and *our* wine. Then we'll watch *our* show together. And after we put Mina to bed we'll play with *our* boobs." He gave her a quick honk, a wink, and headed out the door.

"What's so funny?" Mina called.

"Nothing," Greta yelled back, once she was certain she wasn't going to choke on her water. It really was hard to stay mad at a guy like him. She felt a little rush of warmth in her chest. Jon and Mina. They'd had a really good run together, the three of them.

"Hey Mina, remember when we met Jon?"

"I knew you were lying about the kissing when I saw you look at him," Mina said. "You were already in love with him." Still offhanded. Now there she was wrong, though, because Greta was not and had never been in love with Jon Hargrave. It was slightly, *slightly* possible that kissing had been considered that day. Slightly. Memory was a funny thing.

When Jon walked back in with pizza and wine, Greta felt her tummy start to squirm like she'd been the one to eat a full meal of candy, or spinach. How had she been cast in the permanent role of Bearer of Bad News? At some point, Mina was likely to shoot the messenger.

More importantly, an upset tummy meant Greta wasn't going to be able to even eat her long-awaited pizza.

"Hey Mina, do you remember your Aunt Shea?" Maybe if she kept it casual it wouldn't be as big of a deal.

"No," as she tore off the offending crust from the top of her slice. Well, *balls*. There went keeping it casual.

"So she's your mom's sister. From Boston. She called me today. Wants to call back tomorrow and talk to you too." Squirm, squirm went her tummy, like there were worms inside it.

"My mom had a sister? Weird." Beyond a mild curiosity, it was apparent Mina hadn't the slightest idea what was coming. Time to drop another bomb.

"I don't really know how to say this . . ." Frustrated, Greta looked at Jon. He grabbed her hand.

"Little one, your aunt wants you to go live with her." Greta supposed maybe she should have been the one to say it, but all she felt was an immense gratitude for his help. She squeezed his hand back, hoping he understood.

Meanwhile, Mina was making that face again. The one Greta had hoped she'd never have to see again.

"But I don't want to live in Boston! I want to live with you!" She was clearly on the verge of hysteria. Greta grabbed her and hugged her as tightly as she could without breaking a rib.

"Ssh, ssh, I know. I know. Me too." Was there never going to be an end to the hurt she'd bring to Mina?

"So tell her! You can fix it, Greta, you fix everything. I'm not going to move, I'm not doing it." She was sobbing into Greta's arms by now, the pizza forgotten.

Could she? Could she fix it? If it was what Mina wanted. And what she wanted. And the money changed everything, of course. Made it feasible. How many times had she thought to herself that things would be different if she were Mina's mother? More than she could count.

The real question was if a judge would deem it allowable for a non-family member to take her. But of course there would be psychologists and advocates and whatnot, and they would talk to Mina and she would verify her preference. From that first candy dinner, which Greta would be sure to remind Mina not to tell any court-ordered social workers about, they'd been together every day for three years.

Every single day.

Countless snuggles, bedtime stories, piano recitals, and little games of what-if. What did Aunt Shea have? A few memories of a toddler. Nothing more. Surely even the court would see that, see how clearly Mina and Greta belonged together. This was a game of what-if she was certain she could win. Especially with all the money. She could refuse the transfer from Shea. Bob's lawyer was probably pricey, but he *was* already familiar with the case.

"I'll see what I can do, okay, kiddo?" Jon met her eyes and made a weird face.

"What?" she mouthed.

"Later," he mouthed back. It seemed like the idea of Greta's intervention was sufficient to calm Mina down, because here she was pulling back, blowing her nose on a napkin, and reaching for her half-eaten pizza again.

He sure meant later, too, because no sooner had

Mina's door shut behind her for bed than he rounded on Greta.

"What are you thinking, getting her hopes up like that?" He looked well and truly disappointed in her. It stung more than she'd thought it would.

"I'm not—I mean, it isn't like I hadn't thought about it, you know." Of course she hadn't mentioned it to him, but did he really think the thought hadn't crossed her mind? What kind of a guardian would she be if it hadn't?

"No, I didn't know. How would that work, exactly, then?" He pulled her into their room so their voices wouldn't carry.

"The same way it's been working for three years. Mina and I are a good team. She's comfortable with me." Greta wasn't ready to tell Jon about the book sale yet. After all, it wouldn't be final 'til the next day, she rationalized.

"Love, she needs to be with her family now. You aren't her family." He sat down with her on the bed, eyes tender. "It's not fair to put these ideas in her head."

"But . . . I *have* been. For three years I've been the most family she's had." *Should* she tell him about the money? Then he might understand why it wasn't impossible to adopt Mina. Something about saying it out loud was still scary, though, like it might be ripped away at any time. The promise of making a living with her art had been her carrot on a stick for so many years that it almost felt too easy to have just—*happened*.

"You know what, I don't really want to talk about

this right now." Her head was too swirly with emotion to have a logical discussion. Surprisingly, Jon nodded.

"Later, then, but I don't want you talking to Mina about it either." That was fair. The person she really needed to talk about it with was a lawyer, anyway. It wasn't as if Jon was going to be part of the process. She watched as his shirt came off over his head and he stretched. He was just pretend. Hot pretend. Really hot, accented, ripped pretend. But he wasn't family.

"Does this mean we aren't playing with our boobs?" Greta asked.

"Don't be ridiculous," Jon said, and yanked her down into the covers with him.

Chapter 17

"I swear my entire life revolves around making you casseroles at this point," Summer said as she pushed open the door with her butt, she and Amy both being laden down with foil pans of various oven-ready dishes. "I brought cookies too, where's Meens?"

"Play date with that horrible little Coco child," Greta told them, opening the wine. "I guess a bunch of the other kids didn't really know what to say to the orphan girl, but Coco was just totally normal. So now they're best friends."

"That's really sweet. Maybe she isn't so horrible?" Amy dumped her dishes and retrieved a glass of red.

"Honestly, my guess is that she's too self-involved to actually *notice* what happened to Mina." She clinked her own glass to Amy's. It felt like ages since she'd had a girl's night. She had missed the hell out of her besties.

"You're so cynical. When did you get so cynical? What happened to my nerdy little Greta?" Summer clinked in too.

"I have *always* been cynical, thank you very much, I've just only recently started applying it to children." She could feel the tension draining from her already. "What'd you bring? Is there lasagna? Jon likes your lasagna. At least enough to stop bugging for effing cioppino every day when it's around."

"Most children probably deserve it, actually," Amy said. "What *is* his deal with that stuff, anyway?"

"It's a mystery to me too. There's two lasagnas," Summer pointed and slid them into the freezer.

"This is awesome. Thank you. I actually *can* cook though, in case you forgot." Well, Summer was better at it, so she wasn't actually complaining.

"It's the Italian in me, girl. I hear there's bad news, I must immediately feed the recipient. It's just a thing."

"It's true," Amy announced. "She's fed me into five extra pounds."

"You probably needed it, Bones. How *is* the whole roommate situation going with you two?" Greta took another sip of wine. She was very curious about how Type A Summer was going to handle Type Nothing At All Amy.

"Pretty badly! We didn't speak for the past three days! Maybe even four!" Amy was obviously not put off in the slightest by the silent treatment.

"Yeah, I pretty much hate every minute of it," Summer agreed. They all clinked glasses again.

"I guess I'm just a little unclear on why we're all so fine with that?" Or maybe more than a little.

"Because she'll move out and it'll be fine. We're not going to not be friends or anything. This is something we'll laugh about later. Post-strangulation, most likely," Summer told her. Amy just giggled.

"Want to go hang out in Mina's room?" Greta asked. "I'm folding her laundry."

"Aw, are you so sad?" asked Amy. "It isn't going to be easy to say goodbye to her."

"Maybe I won't have to." She led the way to the little second bedroom, wine in hand.

"What's that supposed to mean?" Summer sounded just like Jon when she used that tone of voice.

"It means I was kind of thinking about talking to a lawyer about adopting her." Surely her friends would understand. They knew her better than Jon, they knew how much she cared for Mina.

"That's your dumbest idea ever," said Amy, current reigning queen of dumb ideas.

"So dumb," Summer lifted her glass in a silent cheers to Amy. Well, wasn't it nice that they could make up over their mutual disdain. Greta liked it much better when that was Amy's role.

"Not that dumb. I'm more of a surrogate mom at this point than a nanny. Why does everyone think this is a bad idea? Mina thinks it's a great idea."

"You didn't—Greta, you can't give her ideas like this!" Summer looked like Jon too, with that little frown. How obnoxious. This was not at all how the conversation had gone down in her head.

"You know what, I don't want to talk about it." Shockingly, it worked again. Though from the glower on Summer's face, she'd wager it wouldn't work for long. "Amy, how's the job-search coming?"

"Oh, I'm not looking," she said contentedly. "Volunteer or paid, this is what I'm meant to be doing."

"Squatting in my apartment is what you're meant to be doing?" Summer's mood was darkening by the moment.

"Um, did you ever hear back about *your* job, Summer?" Greta wasn't sure that alone would salvage the conversation, so she went ahead and topped up their glasses at the same time. She remembered the time she tried sobriety, all those two days ago, fondly. It was good that was in the past now. This was no time for a wineless life.

"Oh, yeah," Summer said.

"And? You didn't tell me that," Amy said.

"Well everyone else is having such a shit time of it, it felt really rude to be like 'oh hey guys I got the job and they're giving me more money than I asked for,' you know?"

"Is that what happened?" Greta asked. They could all really use some good news right about now. "That's amazing!"

"It is."

"I remember money," said Amy. "Vaguely."

"Well my new boss seems like a total jerk, so I'm sure it will suck like everything else. Hey, I have an idea that will cheer us all up," Summer said, looking a little embarrassed.

"What's that?" In response, her hand reached over and plucked the phone from Greta's side.

"Reading your sexts out loud in a dramatic fashion for everyone's general amusement." *Oh no. Oh, no no. Why didn't I lock my phone?*

"Let's not do that right now. I bet Amy's are better anyway," she said as she frantically tried to retrieve the phone. Damn Summer's superior height. She'd been winning at keep-away since elementary school.

"I don't know, I never made a sex tape," Amy said. "Think that's on there? Send it to me, Greta never did."

Summer was already thumbing through the texts, and Greta could see the exact moment when it all came together for her. She silently handed the phone off to Amy, who did the same thing, face gradually going from all smiles to completely empty. Greta sat, feeling like a prisoner awaiting her sentence.

"I did not see this coming," said Amy, handing the phone not to Greta, but back to Summer.

"This is totally fucked." Summer couldn't even meet Greta's eyes. "Fake-date? Seriously?"

"I'm sorry," Greta said. And she meant it. Well, she was sorry she'd hurt her friends. Well, she was sorry she got caught basically. Same thing in the end, wasn't it?

"I'm not mad. You're only lying to yourself," said Amy with confidence.

"What's that supposed to mean?" asked Summer, throwing the phone onto Mina's bed and standing.

"Summer. Isn't it obvious? She's in love with Jon, but scared to admit it. Maybe it started fake, but it got real."

"No it didn't," Greta said, bluntly. "It just got convenient."

"Greta. You might know a lot more than me about Star Wars and Tolkien. But love is *my* area of expertise. And you can't fake the look in your eyes when Jon walks into the room. You might not be ready to admit it to yourself, but you fell in love somewhere along the way."

"There is no such thing as love, Amy. Trust me on this." Greta knew her friend wouldn't believe her, but she plowed ahead. "It's just a combination of attraction and affection. And that's all I feel for Jon. All I will ever feel for Jon. And I'm sorry I lied to you guys. I just thought it was a good way to get you to lay off, you know?"

"I don't, actually. I don't know. I don't know why on earth you felt the need to lie to your best friends' faces for *weeks*. That's so incredibly beyond what I thought you were capable of. What was your end game? When were you going to tell us?" Summer's face was red, and she stood up.

"Honestly? I was just going to fake a breakup, except the whole Bob thing happened and it was easier just to keep going with it. Look, Summer . . ." She stood too, and put a hand on her friend's arm.

"Don't talk to me. Come on, Amy." She stalked out of the room, turned and came back, drained her wine, left again.

"What happened to 'we aren't going to stop being friends'?" Greta yelled after her. She couldn't resist a parting shot. "Or maybe you're just mad your matchmaking skills suck!"

"Say what you want. I know the truth. She'll come around," Amy whispered with a little grin. "Coming!" She too, finished her wine and scampered off. Greta sank back onto Mina's bed with a groan.

That was *not* what was supposed to happen. Her stomach felt as tangled up as when she'd told Mina about her aunt. Screw this, she was napping. With that, she pulled a pillow over her head and put herself to sleep.

"Attraction and affection," echoed in Jon's head. "Attraction and affection."

He'd tried to be quiet when he got home early not to disturb the girls. He knew how much Greta had needed an evening with them, so he'd found things to do around the kitchen, enjoying the sounds of giggles escaping from the second bedroom.

"Just convenient," she'd said.

He walked into his bedroom—their bedroom—and lay down on the bed. Her pillow smelled like her, that scent that had said *home* to him almost since day one, when he'd fallen for her stupid dancing and her reluctance to take his number.

Of course, that was before she'd broken his toe and made this preposterous suggestion about Mina to him. Before he'd deluded himself into thinking she'd come around. That she'd grow to see all the little things that made them fit together so well. The reasons they'd fallen in love.

Because they *had*, of course, she was just too damn stubborn to realize that was what that feeling was. The silly one that blossomed when he cracked the wine and she turned on the music and they shimmied towards each other like total dorks. Or the loud explosive one when they came together, holding each other tight. Or the quiet, soft one that wound around them like vines when they sat side by side on the couch reading books together.

It was love. It had always been love.

For Jon, it might even always be.

"Easier just to go with it," she'd said. Every remembrance of her voice, her slightly too-deep voice, sent another crack shooting through his heart.

She was never, ever going to change. She was never going to tell him she loved him back. She was never going to be the partner he thought he'd found. And his heart was shattering in slow-motion.

And it wasn't like he didn't know that everything going on right now was scary and overwhelming to her. But that shouldn't have been an impediment—it should have been an impetus. Jon had been determined to be her rock. And by his own accounting, he had been. She should have realized that this was more than a fling, more than convenience. This, what they had, was Fate.

That wasn't how she'd seen it at all.

And on that one terribly poorly planned Night of Romance Gone Awry, he saw how willing she was to sabotage herself, them, just to avoid admitting to herself that she could have been wrong.

It had occurred to him then, that he couldn't change her mind, because you couldn't change a *person*. Then the next morning, he'd woken up with an aching swollen toe and an aching swollen head and thought—nah. They'd both drunk far too much to hold the evening against themselves. Of course, the fact that he'd found Greta soggy and sobbing in the bath hadn't hastened him to think it all over too much.

He reckoned he should have seen it. She'd told him over and over that she didn't believe in love. That was where he'd gone wrong, his common sense all in the bin. If one didn't believe in love, one wouldn't recognize it if it slapped them in the face.

Like his mum and climate change.

Her heart's been through the wringer, though. "Attraction and affection," her voice in his head answered his.

His had been as well, and he chose optimism, he chose life and love and second chances. She chose solitude and selfishness. She chose her fear.

She chose it over him.

So this is it, Jon thought, holding the pillow as tightly as he could. It's done now. He had to be done with trying. And that was something in his eye, not a tear. Okay, perhaps it was a tear. Because Jon wasn't a liar like Greta.

He was first to admit he was lovestruck, and now he was going to be the first to admit he was heartbroken.

He should go into Mina's room, he should talk this out with her, but it just hurt too bad. Plus, blokes shouldn't cry in front of their ladies. It was untoward. Maybe he was a coward, but so be it. There was another way. And it was the same way Greta had basically chosen. He had a phone call or two to make.

Firstly, to his agent. The phone only rang once before Mr. Rice's secretary answered and put him through.

"Right then, I know I said no to the Vegas show, and I'm not normally a diva as such, but . . ." He didn't really know how to say he wanted to be added to the bill last minute *without* being a diva.

"You're a brilliant marketer, my man, brilliant. We'll drop you in last minute and double attendance with our surprise guest. CeAnna's going to owe you royalties! Yeah, you did a good thing here, my man, a good thing." Rice was oily, but at least he wasn't mad? This was a weird business.

"Right, well . . . I suppose you can email me call times and I'll head out in the morning?" He had no idea how to handle being congratulated for his breakup maneuver.

"Sure, buddy, sure. I'll go ahead and have who-ever works for me now cut you a check." His agent hung up.

How do you not know who writes your checks? It was the one good piece of advice his parents had given him when he started to get big—if you're making the money, always be sure you're the one signing the checks. It was likely time to start hunting for a new agent, then, wasn't it. Nothing was ever easy.

Jon rolled out of bed, setting Greta's pillow down with reluctance and finality. Time to pack a suitcase.

For the . . . she didn't want to count . . . time in a row, Greta woke to a sinking feeling. How many bridges was she going to burn? At this point, she had no idea how to stop setting fires.

And she had no clue how to fix anything she'd broken, either. They'd always been a little triad, she and Summer and Amy, but now she felt she was on the outside looking in. They lived together, albeit in an uneasy truce. Still easier than the situation she now found herself in. Was found herself the right phrase? Had placed herself was probably more accurate, but that sucked.

It would be easier to live with if there was anyone to blame but herself. Only, for the life of her, Greta couldn't figure out how to shift any of it off.

She could have said no. She could have told her friends, 'hey, not ready.' That hadn't even occurred to her. Lying and setting up a scheme was actually the first thought in her head. What kind of a person did that make her? Not the kind she had thought she was. Not the kind she wanted to be.

If she'd been in either of their shoes, she'd be furious. More than furious, she'd be ready to walk away and never go back. Just like—well, just like her father. This was betrayal on that level. She was going to be that person to them now, she was the little niggling voice in the back of their heads when someone made a promise.

Ugh, she collapsed on the bed again, *I am literally the worst*. And for once, that wasn't a figurative thought.

Of the three of them, she was the bad friend. Worse than that, though, because a friend wouldn't behave that way. This was the sort of thing that Coco would do and she would immediately ban Mina from having any sort of contact with her ever.

Mina. Sweet Mina. She'd have to make a note to remind Mina not to be this kind of a dick. Dishonesty was so uncool. Lessons learned. Teachable moments.

How had it even gotten to this point? Sure her dad and a few boyfriends had been commitmentphobes and jerks, but had she really become so wary of men that she was willing to sacrifice her oldest and best—hell, her *only* friendships—just to maintain her cynicism?

She felt like an absolute heel right about now. The pillow was going to stay over her head for a while, as she wallowed in her guilt. Worst nap ever. Somehow she instinctively knew that wine and a bath wouldn't make it any better, though. This was the worst possible kind of problem. It was the kind that must be dealt with head on.

The kind she'd spent her entire life avoiding. *Gross.*

And yet—when she replayed the entire sequence of events in her head, and she did, ad nauseam—she couldn't change the thought that even though it turned out shitty, she probably wouldn't have done it any differently.

Maybe she was destined to be an ass. Maybe it was Fate. But was it her destiny to lose Amy and Summer? Not after like, twenty years, she couldn't let that be her new normal. No, remember how Summer had said her and Amy's fight was circumstantial? Surely the same applied to her.

Surely.

But if her best friends were going to forgive her, why did she still feel so terrible? They were all she'd ever needed, after all.

When she emerged, finally, to make dinner, Jon didn't even say hello. Which was really not cool. So what if she was heating up Summer food instead of cooking her own. It was the stupid lasagna he loved so much, so he'd come around at some point. She'd even serve it on fancy plates.

Wait, so why was he eating a sandwich?

"Why are you eating a sandwich?" she asked.

"Hungry," was the simple answer. If Greta was to guess, she would think there might be a more complex answer beneath, but eff that, because she was super annoyed.

Okay, he didn't know she'd just had an awful fight with her best friends, but since when did they not do dinner together? It was normally their 'family' time.

"Are we not going to have dinner together then?" She could hear the note of rudeness in her voice, but felt powerless to stop it. It just felt like everyone was mean tonight.

"Nope." A one word answer. Well, sheesh. Of course now the only other friend she had in the world would have to be pissed about something. Well, she'd *told* him she hated washing dishes, so if his snottiness came from the pile in the sink, he would just have to deal.

Like everyone else in the world didn't just do it themselves. Or use paper plates. Or not even use plates. There was just no reason to be fussy. Was it even worth heating up an entire pan of lasagna if Mina was gone and Jon was eating a sandwich? She supposed not, but now her own dinner would have to be a sandwich as well.

And Greta did not want a sandwich.

Why were so many first world problems piling up on her? This was not fair. All she had ever wanted was her own life. The one she'd been perfectly happy with, alone with her television and her bathtub and her wine and her watercolors.

All she'd gotten was a big old hassle. She opened her mouth to have it out, and her phone rang. It was Angie, wanting to meet up in the morning, and while they made plans, Jon went into the bedroom. When she hung up, she considered going in after him but felt like the moment had passed.

So maybe everything that had happened tonight was her own fault, but Greta was not even in the mood to hash out another set of problems, so she simply went back to Mina's room. Ostensibly it was to finish packing, but instead, she just went to sleep. At least in her dreams, things could be like they were.

Chapter 19

"Hey girl heyyyyy!" shouted her favorite sister, as she wove her way over to Greta from across the park. "Have I even seen you since my wedding? I don't think I have! Squee!" She snugged up on Greta, apparently ignoring the stiffness and lack of reciprocation.

She still wasn't forgiven for betting on her sister like a racehorse, but Greta was sick of fighting. That was just going to wait for another time. She was still mad, though.

"How was . . . the honeymoon?" That felt like a weird question. It felt like she was just asking how the sex was.

"The sex was amazing," Ang said. Well, at least they were on the same page. "And yours is too, right?"

"Wait, what? Why do you know about my sex life?" Oh, she regretted coming already, and she hadn't even gotten a good rhythm going on the swing yet.

"I don't know details, prude, but of course Jon told Matt he was officially living with you and of course Matt told me and of course I was shocked because my sister Greta is as celibate as a nun." Ang's voice got louder and softer as she swung up and down. Accordingly, other parents were moving their children away before things got graphic. "Wait, you *are* banging, right?"

"Um, yes?" There didn't seem to be any alternative to just answering. *Sorry*, she mouthed at a particularly shocked-looking lady trying to maneuver her toddler out of a baby swing.

"Oh, good. Yay! Okay, so tell me what's happening with Mina. Are you so sad?" Pleased to be on less treacherous ground, Greta kicked off even higher.

"I am very super sad. Which is why I've decided to adopt her."

"Oh. No. Yeah, that's not—no." Seriously what was everyone's problem with this? It wasn't like any of them had kids. Maybe that was it. They didn't want her moving on without them.

"It just makes sense, Ang." She leaned back, legs in the air, and enjoyed the pleasant sensation of wind rushing over her hair, and slightly up her dress.

"It makes zero sense, G." Angie stopped her swing, and grabbed one of the chains attached to her sister's to stop her as well. "You are really not qualified to take that on."

"I've been her nanny for years. Obviously I already did take that on."

"Greta, listen to me. You *are* a kid. You can't *have*

a kid." Angie's eyes were boring into her uncomfortably.

"I'm not a kid. I'm a grownup," she protested.

"You say 'very super'. And 'grownup', instead of adult."

"You say 'squee' and 'yay'! I'm not seeing your point here." Greta tried to kick off again, but her sister didn't let go of the chain.

"Sweetheart, I say them ironically. Anyways, have you considered Mina at all in all of this?"

"Of course! She *wants* to live with me," Greta said. Angie sighed heavily.

"Kids her age don't get to make those decisions for a reason. You're behaving very selfishly, and it's reactionary. You aren't considering how important it is for Mina to get to know her mother's family. To be around people who've been bereaved, and understand what she'd dealing with. It really seems like you're only thinking of how to avoid change. Which is pretty childish."

Greta would have stomped her foot if she hadn't been on the swing. This wasn't fair. This wasn't what she thought she would hear. It also felt uncomfortably true.

"But Mina needs to be *happy* and I'm good at that!" she protested. She could convince her sister. And if Ang was on her side, nothing could stop them.

"So are puppies and Amy, and I wouldn't give either of them a kid either. Being a good time hardly makes you responsible." Angie was rapidly becoming her least favorite sister. "When was the last time you went to the dentist?" She abruptly asked.

"Oh, who knows? No one goes to the dentist." Greta was confused.

"Everyone goes to the dentist. And especially *children* go to the dentist. And it's going to be like this about everything. You kill plants. You never return library books. You just aren't a responsible mother, Greta. You will be some day, but today is not that day." Finally, she let go of the chain.

Ouch. Not a responsible mother. That was a really crummy thing to say to a person.

The worst part about hearing these hard words were that they were generally true. She'd only been at Jon's a few weeks and she'd already killed one of *his* plants. She couldn't show her face at any library in the county. And it was possible that other people *did* remember to schedule dentist appointments.

Hell, only a few days ago Greta had slept the day away, hung over and trying not to cope with reality while Jon cared for Mina. She hadn't even asked Amy to keep her longer, or Jon to go get her. She'd merely assumed it would take care of itself.

Which it had.

She supposed that was more a testament to her friends than to her own fortunes. There was no way around this, her sister was right and it absolutely freaking sucked. She closed her eyes for a moment, picturing Mina's face. Picturing Mina's *life*. She sighed.

"Maybe I'm not going to adopt her," she admitted after a long while.

"Of course you weren't. I bet you never even called a lawyer, did you." Damn Angie.

"I was *gonna*. But I was busy. And I kept forgetting."

"Well, case in point then. When is she meant to go to Boston?" Ugh, that part she didn't want a reminder of either. Had she left everything up to the last minute unconsciously on purpose? Maybe somewhere deep down, she'd always known keeping Mina was unrealistic. That the little girl was just the last tie she had to a life where everything got taken care of without her having to do much more than play games and take baths. And that cutting that tie meant her life was about to become a scarily blank canvas.

"Tonight. Today's her last day at school."

"Aw, I'm sorry. I know you're going to miss her." Angie stopped the swings again, this time to grab her sister in a bear hug.

"Even more now, because I guess maybe she won't come back to me." Tears were jumping unbidden to her eyes again. She'd never been a bigger crybaby than she had been since Bob died.

Bob ruined everything.

Chapter 20

"Jon?" Greta yelled when she walked into the apartment with Mina later. "Go grab your bag, I packed it for you, kiddo. *Jon.*"

There was no answer, and the house had that peculiar sense of absence to it that occurred when he was gone. *Where is he?* She thought he would like to say goodbye to Mina. Surely he'd walk in any second, probably with wine for after she got home. Which would be so very super welcome. She could use (another) friendly shoulder to cry on, and nothing was better for a good wallow than wine.

Wallows, celebrations, Tuesdays . . . wine was her best friend. She decided not to tell Amy and Summer about this epiphany. Not that they were speaking to her, anyway.

She wandered over to Mina's bedroom; there was something she really needed to do.

"So kiddo?" She asked from the doorway.

"What?" Mina was attempting to jam every stuffed animal from her bed into her carry-on. It was going as well as everything else was lately, which was to say it wasn't going at all.

"We've been talking about you maybe coming back to live with me." Her throat was closing already. This kid had been disappointed so many times, and here she was about to be another time in a long list.

"Yeah?" Mina tried sitting on the bag like a cartoon character would do to close a suitcase.

"It's just—I don't know—Mina, it isn't the responsible decision. I'm so, so sorry. I want you. I really do, don't ever think for a second that I don't want you, it's just . . ." Maybe Greta would eventually drown in her own tears like Alice. How they just kept coming was nothing sort of supernatural.

"I know." Mina hopped up from the suitcase to hug her guardian.

"You know?" This was surprising. She herself hadn't known.

"Yeah. It was just like the what-if game. But it made me feel better that you did want me. I guess I've never had a bunch of people want me before." Solemn words, too true. It was the closest Greta thought she'd probably ever get to admitting Bob wasn't an ideal father. In another year or two, only the curated happy memories would remain, probably; that was the way of things. And maybe that was only right. If he'd loved his daughter in a way she couldn't fathom, who was she to dictate what his legacy would be?

"But—okay. Yeah, I guess I haven't really either." She thought about it for a minute. Nope, Mina was definitely more popular than she'd ever been. And that was good, she deserved to feel like a hot commodity for once in her little life. As long as she also remembered all the lessons she'd learned from watching *Doctor Who*: always be kind, and be humble, and try to help when you can. And never, ever, power up a cyberman.

"I guess I just wanted to say sorry, though, because I would have had a special night with you last night if I'd realized this would be the last time we see each other for a while." She sagged into the doorframe. Angie had been right. She wasn't even a good enough guardian to make the last night in San Francisco one to remember.

"Oh, that's okay. Jon took me out for ice cream and then we went and looked at the Bay for a while and talked about things." Mina returned to the plush toy job.

"You did? No one woke me up." That was an extremely thoughtful gesture. Why hadn't she been included? A little voice in the back of her head reminded her that she'd gone to bed at an unreasonably early hour. That she hadn't picked Mina up, instead leaving it for Jon. That she'd rather go to sleep at dinner time than figure out what was going on with him, because she was upset about her friends.

Ugh, her friends. When the Mina thing was over with, she would have to try and convince them to take her back. But she could only deal with one giant emotional blow at a time.

"I try to only wake you up if I have pizza," Mina said, and Greta could not help but approve.

"Hey, anything that doesn't fit, I'll send. And if it's stuffed animals you need, I can always send them ahead of the rest of your stuff." She pushed off from the door and smiled through the lump in her throat. Maybe, just maybe, everything would be okay in the end. As long as Mina wasn't mad at her, she could keep calm and carry on.

Or at least keep calm and cabernet on. Where the hell *was* Jon? Maybe he was asleep. She headed back to their room to double check. If he'd kept Mina out late he may well have decided on a nap. Heaven knew she certainly loved a good nap herself. Even if she hadn't been up late.

He wasn't lying on the perfectly made up bed, but something else was—an envelope, with her name on it.

Sigh. He knew this was going to be a rough day for her, and he'd let her something—a letter? A poem? A gift card to a spa that served wine? She felt so much less like crying as she walked over to the bed and pulled out the sheet of paper inside.

> Greta,
> *I know it's a bit cowardly to write this instead of say it, but I can't look at you without losing my nerve. I heard you talking to your birds. I know you're never going to tell me you love me. I know you're never going to do what I thought you would—feel the same.*

*I'm not mad. I just can't go on as such. I want
more from life, from my partner. And mostly, I
just want you gone when I get back. I'll be at the
Jamz Fest in Vegas for the next several days, so
you have time to move.*

I'm sorry. I love you. I wish you felt the same.

-J

The ride to the airport was a blur of numbness. Her
time with Mina was moving too fast, almost gone,
but there was too much left to say. Her time with Jon . . .
Greta couldn't process it, she needed time to think, but
she didn't have that either.

Turned out Jon and Mina's big date was his goodbye. Turned out he didn't think *she'd* merited one. Of
course, she probably didn't deserve one.

*Attraction and affection. Convenient. You're just
mad your matchmaking skills suck.* She remembered
every word she'd said, that he'd heard, with a sinking
feeling. It wasn't like she'd ever lied to him. She'd been
as honest with him as she'd been dishonest with her
friends. And she had definitely lied to Summer about
those matchmaking skills. They didn't suck, just her.
So why did she feel like such a heel?

"You know what the greatest thing about Boston is,
is the cream pie," she turned to Mina. The child needed
her wisdom now more than ever.

"You've been to Boston?" She looked impressed
and inquisitive.

"Well, no." Greta was quiet for a minute. "But I have
had the cream pie, and it's pretty solid. I also watched

Crossing Jordan when I wasn't too much older than you, which I wouldn't advise, and I often celebrate St. Patrick's Day. My favorite Julie Johnson books take place there. So I'm basically a Boston expert."

Mina gazed at her silently, but there was an air of skepticism to her stare.

"I was kind of hoping you'd teach me what *you* learn about Boston soon." Greta ruffled Mina's hair.

"I'll email you," she promised.

"No you won't. That was why I did this." Greta had planned to wait until just before boarding to show Mina her surprise, but the cab was as good a place as any. After all, she'd never been great at surprises.

She pulled out her cell phone, opened her email, and presented Mina with the itinerary she'd bought just an hour ago. An airplane was scheduled to take her across the country, coast to coast, in just one month.

Greta had done the adult thing after speaking to Angie, and called Shea to confess all of her concerns and hopes and rants. Between them, they'd worked out a plan where Greta would play more of an aunt role than Shea had been able to—there would be trips home to the Bay on school breaks, and Greta was welcome to Boston any time as well. She planned to abuse that already. Particularly with the check that had come through that morning burning a hole in her pocket.

It was even bigger than Jacob had indicated it would be. It was kind of the only good thing in her life right now. Because if you couldn't drink champagne with your two best friends—scratch that. Your three best friends, Jon had sort of snuck his way into that one, too. If she couldn't celebrate with them, then what was even the point?

As Greta collected Mina's bags from the trunk of the car and was assured that the driver would wait, the hurt set into her heart again. At first she deflected by making sure Mina knew exactly where to go and what to do once past security where Greta couldn't help her; she knew who to ask if she got lost or confused.

Then she kind of just wanted to curl up and sob.

"Hey Mina, what if your airplane is secretly a TARDIS?" she asked.

"What if I'm a disguised Dalek?" the girl immediately responded.

"Dark, kid. Are you nervous?" Greta was nervous. If Mina wasn't, she was inhuman. Maybe she was the *Doctor Who* villain Dalek after all. *Dun dun dun*.

Mina didn't answer, she just nodded and then crashed into Greta like a burning building. Her arms wrapped around Greta's waist, and the dampness of her tears soaked through almost immediately.

"What if I hate it? What if Aunt Shea is mean? What if—what if," she sniffled so hard Greta could hardly understand it, "What if she isn't anything like I remember my mom?"

Time to be a fucking grownup. No—an adult, a reasonable adult, she reminded herself, swallowing her own inevitable tears. No one needed to see those now. They could wait.

"Mina, she won't *be* your mom. But she knows more about your mom than anyone else right now, and she's going to want to honor that memory by doing right by you. She will probably tell you more about your mother than anyone, maybe even bore you with stories. But those are the things you'll be grateful for later."

"But what if I hate it?" Mina asked again, like she hadn't heard any of the very super solid words of advice Greta had just pronounced.

"You won't. But if you do, I'll be there in a month and we can talk about it." There. Not a lie, not a false hope. Damn it, why was *now* the moment where she suddenly grasped maturity?

"Okay. Is it time to go?" Mina asked, pleading the negative with her eyes.

"Mina. Do you remember the morning we lay in bed watching the Doctor and you asked when you could have an adventure?" Greta dropped to her knees to fully impart this to her ward, in their last seconds.

"This is it. This is where your adventure begins. That plane may as well be a TARDIS, because it's a special craft taking you to the next place you are going to be. And once you get there, you're going to do cooler things than you can imagine. Everything is waiting, and it's waiting for you."

Mina hugged her again, and now the tears were flowing freely from both of them. This shouldn't hurt so badly. This shouldn't—it just shouldn't. Greta had cared for her so much, but she was being a gro—an adult. Adults didn't get this worked up.

And then it hit her, so hard she actually flinched.

"I love you!" she told Mina.

"I know. Care about you too," she said, in a perfect

parody of Greta, as she joined the security line and slowly filed out of sight.

In complete disregard for the taxi meter running outside, Greta stayed by security and waited until long after Mina would have gone through. Love. She loved her. That was a thing she was capable of doing.

Whoever would have guessed?

"This was a mistake, I reckon." Jon told Rust. His friend looked at him in surprise.

"Absolutely not! This was just what you needed." He gave a gentle, awkward pat to Jon. Americans were always so squicky about touching each other. "Get your mind off her."

"When I said that, I had something else in mind. Something like—well, working our way through your Belgian beer collection. Frankly, I didn't think even *you* would come up with something like this. It's concerning to say the least, mate."

"Don't be such an old lady," Rust advised. "You gotta go into this with the right mindset."

"What mindset is that, pray tell? The one where I've given up on life? The one where I'm a total nutter?" It wasn't too late to back out, he thought. Not too late at all. Until the bouncer walked up to him, that was.

"Too late now, buddy," the giant said.

Oh, bollocks.

Too late, officially, then. And then Jon was buckled into his harness and shoved off the side of a building.

Here it was, his death. Here it was, the last moments.

Here it was—oh god. Here it was, the Skyjump off the top of a bloody building.

Why couldn't it have been a strip club? A brothel? A meth lab?

The shrieking noises were most certainly coming from his own mouth, but there was no way to stop them. It was the hippo feeding all over again.

The kitschy neon of his tomb raced alongside Jon's body as it hurtled through space atop the Strip. He supposed as ways to die went, this was a fairly rock-n-roll way in which to meet his maker. Then he remembered he was not, technically, a rock star and grew agitated all over again.

Stupid Rust. Although for almost thirty entire seconds, Jon had to admit, he hadn't thought about Greta, or the sorry state of his heart.

It was going to be a doozy, this heartbreak, he could already tell. With Leah, it was like, well, they would never ever be compatible. The blow to his ego was the worst part there. With various other girlfriends in the past, there had been something similar—a real reason it could never work.

But Greta? She was perfect for him. She was everything he'd ever wanted. There was no reason they couldn't be together, except for her own stubbornness. There would never be closure for that.

For a second, he closed his eyes, felt the rush of hot desert air slithering over his body, and remembered that falling for her was this same sense of freefall. And just like that, this could well end in disaster. His eyes popped back open, just in time for the ride to end.

If only someone could reassure Jon that the plummeting he still felt in his heart would end, too.

It was beyond weird to be sleeping alone in Jon's apartment, especially after the harsh reminder that it *was* Jon's apartment. Nothing about it was hers except for a few stray bottles of wine and the big splat of paint she'd carefully hidden beneath her suitcase until such time as she could find alone to sand it from the floor. Probably now would be a good time, but Greta didn't *wanna*.

In fact, she wished there was more. In fact, maybe she would just paint a bunch of stuff on his floor.

How dare he. Like a petulant child, Greta kicked all his blankets off in her irritation. He knew what a terrible time this was for her. He *knew* how much she was going through. He knew she was going to have to say goodbye to Mina and then basically die of her sadness.

All she wanted to do was marvel with him about the newfound depths to her feelings. This was even worse than not being able to celebrate the book. Because she'd done it all to herself. She may as well have sent him an engraved invitation to leave her. She'd worked so hard to push him away that he'd proved her right. They always leave.

Now she wondered how often they'd left through doors she'd opened for them.

The problem with kicking the blankets to the floor was that she had to retrieve them all by herself when her toes got chilly. Jon had never minded her chilly toes. She'd stuck them against the back of his knees, between his calves, once inside his armpit until he told her it was creepy . . . So weird to be in this bed without him.

Without knowing that he'd be home soon, that a gig or studio session had run over. Without the comfort of knowing Rust or Matt would drop him off soon enough, and he'd come warm into the bed, smelling of beer and sea-salt and leather, waking her from her doze into something better than a dream.

Something else that wasn't fair was how fast she'd grown accustomed to it, even enjoyed herself. That wasn't what was supposed to happen.

It was just too much, all at once. Every time she got her balance, a new rug got yanked out from beneath her feet.

Greta pulled the blankets over her head and screamed into them. She wished she'd never met the man who'd just cracked her open and left her feelings spilling out everywhere. If she'd never taken his jacket, none of this ever would have been a problem. She could have just left that stupid wedding with nothing more than a case of the shivers. Then right now, she'd be crying over Mina in a single small room with her roommates Amy and Summer.

She had told him this would happen. His own fault, for getting so hurt when what she'd said was nothing more than the truth. They were going to break up at some point, weren't they? Just because she loved Mina didn't necessarily mean she was going to fall for Jon.

Right? She wanted to ask Mina so badly that it hurt. Although, she supposed Angie would say that was an inappropriate place for a grown woman to be asking advice. She supposed it was also true. But who could she talk to? Who would back her up now?

She'd lost Mina, Summer, Amy, and of course she couldn't ask Jon. Angie had made it abundantly clear that she thought Greta needed to grow up. She kicked the blankets off again at just the thought. She had been an adult for too long today. She'd made the hard decision with Mina. She'd done the right thing.

She just thought there would be a little more satisfaction in knowing it. Instead, she just felt lonely.

It wasn't all that long ago she'd fervently wished on a coin for a private loft apartment, in which to enjoy nothing but alone time all the time. Here she was now, though, all alone in a gorgeous apartment. And all she could think about was the empty space next to her in bed.

It was too cold, too quiet here without him. Plus she kept running across funny things on the internet she wanted to show him because no one else giggled like a madman the way he did only he'd say, "I sound daft," because he was all British and cute.

Greta was never ever going to sleep at this rate. Her thoughts were just little gears, always turning but never going anywhere. How could she have been so cruel, Jon was a dick, she was a bad friend, Jon was stupid, where was Jon, why wasn't he here. As much as she kept trying to redirect her thoughts to making up with Amy and Summer, they just kept circling back to Jon.

His face, his laugh, his kiss, his bad jokes. How he always had a glass of wine, a hot bath, a long hug waiting. The way he was never afraid to stand up to her, to challenge her. She hated Jon, she lo—oh God.

She *did*.

She loved Jon.

"Son of a sea lion!" Greta said aloud, sitting bolt upright. "I *am* a stubborn idiot." She'd been thinking of falling for him as though it was a future event, as though it hadn't started the minute he grinned that crooked-toothed smile at her in a coatroom. How could she have missed it all along? The attraction and affection—it was there. But it was only one thread of the tapestry. And she'd managed to unravel the whole thing before she even saw the big picture.

Chapter 21

"I love him, Amy." Greta draped her arms around her friend.

"I know. I always knew." She wasn't even going to argue the point, to try and save face. That was something the old Greta would have done. Now she was an adult, and such maneuvers were far beneath her. Amy disentangled, and tossed a toothbrush on top of her duffel bag.

"I love him, Summer." Greta knew better than to drape herself on Summer, but she still wanted her friend to understand her sincerity, so she settled for meaningful eye contact.

"Stop staring at me. I'm still pissed at you." Sweet Summer. She was the most sensitive of the three of them, but sometimes Greta thought the three of them were the only ones in the world who knew that. That scowling face hid a heart that was bigger than her culinary ambitions. Clearly, Greta had really messed her up.

Well, she'd make it up. She'd fix it. What was it Summer had said when she and Amy had been fighting? That they were always going to be friends, so it didn't really matter if they stopped talking for a while. That meant she could spend the rest of her life being the best friend ever. Now that she was already going to be adult and be loving and even paying her own bills, she might as well toss some more lofty ambitions on the list.

"Not too pissed to drive to Vegas, though?" Greta needed the reassurance.

"Don't think too highly of yourself. My prospective boss owns a fusion place out there I want to try." Summer zipped her own overnight bag and raised a brow at the other two. "Shall we?"

"It's totally you," Amy whispered. "Took her hours to invent that excuse." Greta felt enormously better. All was well that ended well. Assuming, of course, that they could drive to Las Vegas before the festival closed. Otherwise, that really would be an embarrassing anticlimax.

"Do you need to pee?" Summer was asking Amy, who was shaking her head. "Do you want to at least try?"

"Stop it, *Mom*, I don't have to pee." She slung her duffel over her shoulder and opened the front door, leading the others out to Summer's SUV. "Bestie roadie!" she squealed.

"Bestie roadie!" Greta agreed.

"Bestie. Roadie." Summer reluctantly tossed her hat in the ring. She fired up the car, and they were off.

"Hey, Summer?" Amy said. "Can we stop? I have to pee."

Greta's heart grew even another size, if it was possible. Any more of this nonsense, and Greta would be completely out of Summer's doghouse. God bless Amy's predictably tiny bladder.

"Did you tell her yet?" Amy said, when she climbed back in a moment later.

"Tell me what?" Greta asked. She truly didn't think she could take any more paradigm-shifting news.

"My company got a big-ass grant! I'm an official employee again!" Greta couldn't honestly tell if the beam on Amy's face or Summer's was brighter. "I'm moving out!"

"That's great news, Amy." Greta meant it. The girl was only marginally employable, she really needed to stick with what was working. "When's the big day? I can . . . help . . ." It was the only downside to having friends that knew you that well—you really couldn't fake sick on moving day. Unless you started laying the groundwork a few days in advance.

"Stop fake-coughing, Greta, I'm not moving for a couple months. I have to find a whole new apartment, after all."

"And speaking of," Greta said conversationally. "I've recently come into a bit of money of my own."

"Explain," Summer sternly ordered, meeting her eyes in the rearview.

"Remember how you guys were the only ones who

bought my last book? And the one before that?" Amy was bouncing in her seat without even hearing the punchline. "Well the publishing industry as a whole was as impressed with this one as you two were with the last one. There was a big bidding war and everything. Anyways, I'm rich now. At least for the next two years."

She settled comfortably back into her seat, slurping a bit of soda through a straw, enjoying the countryside as the girls shrieked. It reminded her of Jon, another little twist in her chest. What if they got there and he refused to see her? What if the love that she had recently discovered wasn't enough? He had no reason to trust her, after all. The only thing she had to offer was her heart, and she'd just casually broken his.

"Hey, do you guys think there's any way I'll actually pull this off?" She was going for casual, but her voice was definitely wavering. There were just so many ways it could go wrong. And Jon was the biggest variable of all. The worst thing was, if he didn't take her back, she wouldn't blame him one single bit.

Things had gone quiet in the front seat, so she tuned back in, but the two of them were whispering without her.

Perhaps they were planning an appropriate congratulatory gift for the book. Perhaps she ought to get Amy one too. It would be polite, especially since the two of them were planning something for her. She practiced her surprised face a couple times until she realized Summer was staring at her in the mirror again.

"We need to talk. In fact, we may need to stop and

wine for this one." Well this was an interesting turn of events. Champagne to celebrate her success? What was the talk about, then? Undoubtedly Summer had some ideas about investment strategies. That was fine, Greta really didn't know much about that sort of thing except that she didn't want the sort of mess Bob had left.

"I saw a sign for a winery," Amy helpfully added. "Five miles back." Summer glared at her before getting off and then back on the highway. Terribly inefficient, and very un-Summer-like. Still, it was only a matter of minutes before the three of them were happily seated around a table made of a wine cask, sipping their pre-ferred styles of juice.

"Before you start protesting, hear me out," Summer said seriously. And then she proceeded to suggest something that shocked Greta to her very core. Again.

The worst part of all was that she was right. How come everyone else knew so damn much?

Some people were more creative when they were sad. That was just a fact of the artistic world. Heartbreak and heroin were the two quickest channels to a hit. That was the dirty little secret as to why agents and managers only suggested therapy or rehab when things were completely out of control. Because most of the time, it behooved them to keep their stars sad and stoned.

Jon was rapidly discovering that this did not apply to him. He was playing what had to have been the worst show of his career, in front of the biggest audience he'd ever been unfortunate enough to embarrass himself in front of.

CeAnna was only a minute away from coming out to perform their big single, but she'd already sent out several shots of Fireball ahead of her. So even she could tell he was sucking. And if he knew CeAnna, which he certainly did by this point, she was likely to be half-sloshed herself. If his set was bad enough to penetrate her pre-gaming . . .

Well, he was expecting DJ Force to be raked over the coals in tomorrow's press, and not booked for another festival this size for some time to come. If ever. Careers had ended over sillier things than this.

Great, not only had Greta broken his heart, she was ruining his entire life. *Boom*. But there was no pleasure left in a beat drop.

Wait—why was Nevaeh on the stage? His bodyguard was grinning like the cat that ate the canary. It was supposed to be time for CeAnna—was she going to turn this into some sort of performance? Jon was starting to sweat. The only thing worse than putting on a bad show was not having any idea what the show was at all.

Then someone else walked out, with a microphone. A tiny little someone in a vintage dress and sky-high heels. The crowd had no idea what was happening, but they cheered anyways. Jon had no idea what was happening either, but his heart leapt.

Why was Greta on his stage?

"Hello, Las Vegas!" She managed, before turning a violent shade of red. Next thing he knew, she was demonstrating a few of those peculiar dance moves that had caught his attention on the very first night. What *was* she doing? CeAnna came charging out and grabbed the mic.

"Yo, Vegas! My girl's a little shy, let's show her a good time, huh?" There was an answering roar from the crowd. As lost as Jon felt, he had to admit that it was the most responsive the audience had been in the entire hour he'd been spinning. "All right, this dancing queen right here's Greta, and she's got something to say to your favorite DJ and mine."

"I'm sorry," Greta muttered into the microphone CeAnna was waving in front of her face. She steadied it with one hand and said it again, louder. "*I'm sorry I was an asshole,*" and the feedback screeched. The crowd cheered again. They loved assholes, apparently.

"So will you marry me?" She asked into the microphone, as she stared him in the eyes behind his decks. At that, the crowd fell silent. So did the decks, as Jon did something he'd never done in his life—shut down in the middle of a gig. Full sonic train wreck.

"You're serious?" He asked into his mic. Which maybe came off a little asshole too, but—how was this really happening?

"I'm serious. I love you. I was just being stubborn before. And childish. And frankly, a little bit mean. Let's get married." Her voice was wavering again, but her eyes were steady.

"You were under a fair amount of stress, I suppose. Yes. Okay. Right, then." Jon was at an utter loss. This was not at all how he had seen this day going. Or his engagement, for that matter. He looked out at the audience, waiting for him. Then he looked back at the girl he'd been waiting for his whole life. "Let's get married!"

CeAnna had taken the mic back and was serenading them a cappella, but all Jon could hear was his own heartbeat in his ears as he climbed out from behind his equipment to get to his fiancée. His fiancée! Crikey, this set went from worst to best in a hurry.

Jon picked her up and held her, like he'd thought he would never do again. "What—why?" was all he could get out. How had she changed her mind? More importantly, how could he ensure she'd not change it back?

"First I realized I love Mina. Eventually I realized you too. Don't ruin this with I told you so's, Jon, or I'll sell your ring and buy wine." Wait, he hadn't bought her a ring. She held up her left hand and displayed an antique diamond. "If you had said no, this would have been beyond embarrassing."

"Just the buying-your-own-ring part? Not the turned-down-in-front-of-a-hundred-thousand-people part?" She was so damn cute, and she was all his, for always. She was still in his arms because he wasn't going to let her go.

"I think you're supposed to finish the show," she said into his ear as CeAnna ran out of things to sing at them while they enjoyed their moment.

"Not without you," Jon said, tugging her back. "I'm not doing anything without you ever again."

"Cool," Greta agreed. "You spin, I'll dance." *Oh dear God please no.* But yes. She was going for it.

Someday, someone was going to have to gently teach her some new moves. But here was CeAnna, that lovely, lovely, girl, using Greta's moves. He owed her so much Fireball for this.

Jon caught a glimpse of movement from the side of the stage. Rice was there, giving him excited thumbs-up and money signs. Of course that guy was interested in it from the business end. Nevaeh was towering above his diminutive agent, offering to kick him out. Jon grinned and shook his head at both of them.

This was the most intensely private moment of his life, but in a weird way it felt fitting to have shared it with the world. Because he wanted every single person in that audience to feel as good as he did right then. Jon dropped some new samples in, remixed the song live, felt the immediate positivity of the fans. This was the greatest show ever.

He wrapped things up with a dubstep wedding march. "I'm getting married!" He screamed at the sky. Greta crowd-surfed. CeAnna poured a bottle of Fireball over herself. Nevaeh and Jack danced out to lick it off. Greatest show ever.

A few hours later, Amy was sobbing already, and the Elvis impersonator hadn't even walked in yet. Summer smacked her. Greta smacked Summer for smacking someone in her wedding. Nevaeh made a threatening noise and everyone calmed down.

"Are you sure about this?" Jon whispered. Greta didn't blame him for asking. Even though he'd asked approximately every ten seconds since she'd proposed.

She realized it had been an abrupt turnaround. Only in her realization, though, because in retrospect it had always been coming to this.

From the first glance at Angie's wedding, there had been something so familiar about him. She realized now it was a premonition. All her efforts to keep him at arm's length were nothing more than a futile effort to keep herself from admitting how wrong she'd been. Of course love was a real thing. It's just that assholes like her father were a real thing too. The trick was not to fall for one.

Or be one. But she'd apologized. Publicly.

Elvis was now in the building, and Greta suddenly found herself blinking back tears, too. How had she never noticed how romantic Fat Elvis was? That white rhinestoned jumpsuit, like a wedding outfit of his own. A few tears spilled over. Jon smacked her.

Time simultaneously lasted forever and sped by as they repeated their vows. It was just like their first kiss all over again, and then suddenly it *was* their first kiss all over again, as Elvis pronounced them man and wife. This time, even Jon was teary.

Greta tilted her head up to him, and their lips met in a gentle promise that meant even more than the ones they'd spoken. After hopping from job to guest room to couch—Greta had finally found home.

They parted to uproarious applause from the gathered witnesses. Nevaeh was sobbing onto CeAnna, Amy was flirting with Jon's agent, Summer was casting dark looks at the provided cake while Rust cast longing looks at both her *and* the cake. All in all, Greta believed it was probably the best wedding she'd ever been to, and she'd been to more than she cared to admit. Everyone should elope! It was totally the best thing ever.

Greta sneaked off to the side to call her again-favorite sister Angie as Elvis cut the cake and poured sparkling wine that would have been right at home at one of Amy's fundraisers.

"Greta, where are you? Amy had texted you and Jon broke up so I came over to get you and I've been frantic!" Oh, Amy. Always quick to notify, not so good on the follow-up.

"I'm in Vegas."

"Oh my God, tell me you didn't gamble away all your new money. Damn it, Greta—"

"Angie, I didn't gamble away all my money. And Jon and I aren't broken up anymore," she was so excited to tell her, "We're married!"

There was a dead silence from the other end of the phone.

"You're what?"

"Okay, I realize it seems a little fast, but listen to me, Ang. No one is ever going to love me like Jon does. He sees exactly who I am and he likes all that stuff. Even the very super unadult stuff. We have so much in common, and the things we don't are still interesting. I knew all that already, but it wasn't until last night that I realized the missing piece of the puzzle. I'm never going to love anyone like I do him, either. And I really hope you can accept this, because it's not changing. Unlike our parents, I mate for life, I have decided. What?" Angie was laughing at her. "What?"

"I knew you loved him, I just think it's funny to hear you defending yourself. Everyone knew but you, of course."

"I'm getting a little sick of hearing that. Oy, save me some of that cake!" she called over to Summer, who thought she was being sneaky scooting the cake closer and closer to the trashcan, likely in some misguided attempt to salvage the wedding party from bad taste. Too late on that, she thought, as Elvis shimmied his way around topping up glasses.

"Well, you know you have to do the whole thing over again, right?" Wait—what? "After bridesmaiding for all of us, you know it's time to have all nine married ladies return the favor. Also, mom will be *pissed* if she can't be there. Was it even a Jewish ceremony? What about Jon's family?"

It was Greta's turn to be silent, then she hung up on her sister.

"Fuck!" she said. "We moved too fast!"

There was some small satisfaction in learning that Angie was on the hook for all the beers at her next reception, though it was slightly overshadowed by being the subject of yet another bet. Amy thought it was awfully funny she needed a do-over, and so did Summer, but Greta knew exactly how to put them in their place.

"Hand me some cocktail napkins, Jon," she said. "I have grooms to find for my bridesmaids."